AN ILL WIND

THE WITCHES OF CANYON ROAD: BOOK SIX

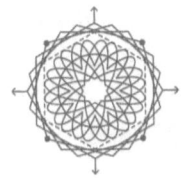

CHRISTINE POPE

Dark Valentine Press

AN ILL WIND

Copyright © 2019 by Christine Pope

ISBN: 978-1-946435-23-1

Published by Dark Valentine Press

Cover design by Lou Harper

Book formatting by Indie Author Services

1

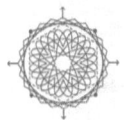

TRYING NOT TO SCOWL AND FAILING miserably, warlock Tony Castillo pulled into the parking garage at Albuquerque's Sunport—the city's whimsically named airport—took a ticket from the machine at the gate, and then went prospecting for a likely space. On a Tuesday morning, the garage wasn't quite as busy as it would have been on the weekend, but he still had to go up two levels before he found something near enough the elevator for his liking...just in case his unwelcome visitor brought some unexpected luggage with her.

The whole time, he tried his best to keep the irritation simmering in him from boiling over. It was so like his mother to use him as an errand boy. Sophia Castillo had acted as though he had nothing better to do with his time than to drive down to Albuquerque and pick up their visiting de la Paz witch. Point of fact, Tony really didn't have anything better to do, but still...it was the principle of the thing.

Sophia had called him the day before to let him know that a witch named Cassandra Sandoval would be coming from the de la Paz clan in Arizona to retrieve the books that Sophia had been hiding for almost a year now, magical tomes that the dark warlock Simon Escobar had stolen for his own nefarious purposes. Simon had gotten his ass kicked, thanks to the Castillo clan's new *prima*, Miranda—and also thanks to the demon lord that Tony's cousin Cat was now shacked up with—but Escobar had still left something of a mess behind, a mess that included those dangerous books.

It was still kind of crazy to think that the Castillos could now count a demon lord as part of the family, but when you were born into a witch clan, you had to learn to roll with the punches.

Tony's mother had been entrusted with the care of the grimoires, since her magical gift of being able to read any and all spell books no matter which language they were written in had made her sort of a natural for the job. Not many people in the Castillo clan even knew where the books were hidden, which was exactly how Miranda wanted it. Those books had already caused enough trouble as it was. However, Sophia had confided in Tony and his younger sister Ava, probably because she hadn't wanted to keep a secret of that magnitude from her own children.

Frankly, Tony would have preferred to be left out of the whole mess. The episode this past summer, when another dark warlock, this one based in New Orleans, had tried to get his slimy hands on the grimoires only seemed to prove how dangerous the damn things were. They belonged to the de la Paz clan and should have gone back to them as soon as they were discovered, although he supposed he could understand why his mother and his *prima* had wanted to keep them safely hidden until the de la Pazes were ready to take the books back.

Well, it looked like that day had finally come.

Why the Arizona clan had sent only one

witch to collect the grimoires, Tony had no idea. He supposed they had their reasons. Frankly, he didn't much care. All he wanted was to get this errand over with—pick up Cassandra Sandoval, whoever she was, drive her over to his mother's house so she could retrieve the books in question, and then bring her right back to Albuquerque. Apparently, the visiting witch wasn't even staying, had a return flight booked for seven-thirty this evening, giving her just enough time to make the round trip to Santa Fe with a little left over for a short visit with Sophia.

All business with this one, apparently.

He got out of his Fiat convertible, locked it, and headed over to the elevators. As usual, Albuquerque was a bit warmer than Santa Fe, so Tony unbuttoned his overcoat as he rode down to the ground level, although the early November day looked chilly here, too, gray but without any threat of rain. He had a feeling it was probably a lot more cheerful back in Tucson, which was where Cassandra Sandoval's flight had originated.

Lucky for her, she'd be going back to her sunshine once all this was over with, and he—well, he'd be back to the same old, same old. Probably a civilian—a person born to a non-witch family—would find it amusing that a warlock could be bored with his existence, but that was just about where Tony had found himself lately. He didn't have any great sense of purpose, didn't need to work or do anything except go from party to party, event to event, all in an attempt to keep himself from realizing there wasn't much of a point to anything he did.

His parents, both of whom had done a brilliant job of convincing their civilian neighbors that they were no more than they appeared…that is, a successful lawyer and his philanthropic wife…were less than thrilled with him. All right, he'd done his time at the University of New Mexico, mainly because they would never have let him live it down if he hadn't managed to get at least a bachelor's degree, but Tony had emerged with a degree in electrical engineering and no real need to do anything with that degree. His late and highly eccentric paternal grandfather had left him a large inheritance, supposedly because Tony was his namesake…but that largesse could have also been the result of a passing whim and nothing else. Ava hadn't been too thrilled with the situation, since she hadn't gotten anything at all except a few pieces of jewelry that had once belonged to their grandmother. To appease her, Tony bought his sister a new car for her twenty-first birthday, but that extravagant gesture had only served to annoy both their parents, who thought she should have gotten a part-time job and earned it herself.

Ah, family.

He moved through the crowds at the baggage claim in the Southwest terminal, then took an escalator to the second floor and yet another to bring him to the third level where the passenger greeting area was located. At least he didn't have to stand here and hold up a sign like an idiot—all witches and warlocks could sense when they were in the presence of another of their kind, so as soon as Cassandra got within a few yards of him, he should be able to tell who she was. The de la Pazes hadn't sent any kind of description, except that she'd be wearing a leather jacket. Considering that it was first week of November and almost every other woman he passed was wearing a leather jacket, that snippet wasn't much help.

Flight 303 on Southwest from Tucson

was right on time, and had already landed and was about to allow the passengers to deplane. That might have been cutting it a little close, but Tony hadn't been too worried. If he'd hit unexpected traffic, he would have just texted Cassandra to let her know, since he'd been given her phone number along with that vaguest of vague descriptions.

His eyes scanned the crowd as the passengers from Cassandra's flight began to filter through to the passenger greeting area, his gaze pausing on every woman wearing a leather jacket. None of them were witch-kind, however, and he began to frown. Was it possible that she'd missed her flight? No, that didn't seem right. She would have called or texted if something like that had happened.

Then Tony caught a flash of shimmering copper, long red hair gleaming against a sleek black leather jacket. Along with that glimpse of red hair, he felt the faint twinge he experienced whenever he met a witch or warlock for the first time.

Obviously, she'd felt it, too, because her eyes, an arresting hazel-green, immediately sought him out in the crowd. Their gazes met, and she gave the faintest of nods, possibly in greeting, or possibly to affirm to herself that she'd found the person she was looking for. She cut through the mass of humanity crowding the waiting area, then came up to him and paused a few feet away.

"Tony Castillo?" she asked. Her voice was a little lower than he'd expected, throaty.

Goddamn, he thought. *I wasn't expecting a goddess.*

Because…she was. Probably a few years younger than he, body slender with curves that the leather jacket accentuated rather than concealed. Then there was that gorgeous mane of red hair, and a full mouth with a wicked lift at the corners.

He realized he was staring, so he cleared his throat and replied, "That's me. You're Cassandra?"

"Yes." Despite the sexy huskiness of her voice, she was very brisk, all business. If she'd assessed his appearance the way he'd assessed hers, she didn't seem too impressed. "Thanks for coming to meet me. I could have taken a shuttle—"

"It's no problem," Tony cut in. "The Castillos don't leave people waiting at airports."

The lift at the corners of her mouth became a bit more pronounced. "You have a lot of visitors?"

"Well, no," he admitted. "I mean, sometimes we have cousins from down in Las Cruces fly directly into Santa Fe to avoid having to drive, but—"

"But mostly you don't get around too much," she finished for him. "I get it—it's the same way with us." Her gaze sharpened, and she added, "It's about an hour to Santa Fe, right?"

"Yes," he said, noting the change of subject. Clearly, it was going to be all business, all the time for her. Too bad—and too bad she wasn't going to stay in Santa Fe for any length of time. He thought he would have liked the chance to show her around. Then again, she didn't seem the type to be too easily impressed by local knowledge. "My car's in the garage across the way. Do you have any baggage you need to claim?"

One dark russet eyebrow lifted, and he got the impression she was inwardly laughing at him. "Um, no. I brought my big purse so I could have a few extras with me in case the flight got delayed or something, but I didn't see the point in packing much since I'm not staying over."

Of course. Tony wanted to smack himself for asking such a stupid question, but the damage was done. He didn't know what his problem was, because usually pretty women weren't quite enough of a distraction for him to develop a case of foot-in-mouth disease. In fact, his sister Ava had once accused him of being Santa Fe's biggest flirt, which he thought wasn't quite fair. Maybe the Castillo clan's biggest flirt, but all of Santa Fe? He didn't think so.

Maybe he was off balance because he'd been expecting the de la Paz clan's envoy to be older, a powerful witch who could guarantee the safe passage of those dangerous grimoires back to their territory. Cassandra, young and pretty as she was, seemed like an odd choice.

Well, the de la Pazes must know what they were doing. At least, Tony had to hope they did, although they'd proven to be almost criminally careless when it came to letting those valuable books out of their sight in the first place.

"This way, then," he told her, figuring it was probably safer to say as little as possible.

Cassandra followed him through the crowd and then out to the parking garage, where they rode the elevator up to the level where his car was waiting. Although she didn't say anything, Tony noticed the way her gaze traveled along the length of the low-slung black convertible. Had he impressed her with the car?

Judging by the way she got into the passenger seat and buckled the seatbelt without comment, probably not.

He held back a sigh as he got in as well, then engaged the self-driving mechanism to let the car back itself out of the space where it had been waiting. They moved down to the first level of the garage, where Tony fed the ticket into the machine and then waved his credit card in front of the reader to have the proper amount deducted from his checking account.

Too bad it was such a cold, gloomy day. He would have liked to put the top down so he could watch Cassandra's fiery red hair blow in the breeze. If he tried that now, he'd probably only succeed in freezing both their asses off, so he settled for asking, "Warm enough? I can turn on the heater."

"Thanks," Cassandra replied. "That would probably help. I guess I wasn't expecting Albuquerque to be so chilly."

If she thought this was chilly, she was

going to be in for a shock when they got to Santa Fe. Tony figured it was probably better not to comment, especially since she wasn't going to be spending enough time in his hometown for her to get too frozen. He pushed the button to set the heater at a low but comfortable level, then asked, "Better?"

"Yes, thank you."

She turned her head then, apparently intent on taking in the scenery outside the car window. There wasn't really much to look at, just the freeway on-ramp they were approaching, but Tony took it as a sign that she didn't want to talk.

All right, she was gorgeous, but she sure as hell wasn't very friendly. Or maybe what he'd interpreted as frostiness was simply discomfort at having to be here at all. No matter how you looked at it, her clan had screwed up pretty spectacularly, first by allowing books as dangerous as the ones Simon Escobar had stolen to be taken at all, and then by acting as though nothing was wrong once the thefts had been discovered. Sure, it had to be embarrassing as hell to admit that you'd been robbed by a dark warlock, but the de la Pazes should have at least reached out to the other Arizona clans to let them know what was going on. At least that way his *prima* Miranda's parents —who were the *prima* and *primus* of the McAllister and Wilcox clans, respectively— could have let their daughter know that Simon Escobar was even more dangerous than everyone had first thought.

But that was none of his business. The books would soon be gone, and since they were still safely hidden at his mother's house, Tony supposed he could say things might have been a lot worse. However, even though it was pretty obvious that Cassandra really didn't want to talk, he couldn't help asking the one question that wouldn't leave him alone.

"So…why did your clan send you?"

Now she turned toward him just the slightest bit, a tight smile touching her lush mouth. "You mean, instead of someone older and more experienced?"

Oh, hell. He could tell he'd already put his foot in it, but he decided to plow ahead. "Well, yeah."

"It's because of my talent," she said. One hand played with the strap of her over-sized purse, which currently rested in her lap.

Asking about a witch's talent was considered rude, but Tony figured she'd already halfway volunteered the information. "Which is…?"

A small hitch of her shoulders before she replied, "It's…I can cast a shield, but not around myself. Instead, I can make the shield appear around anything I want—other people, buildings, cars, and so on. I guess it's kind of the inverse of a talent one of my cousins has. He can cast a shield that will protect him and anyone else inside it. That shield keeps him safe from anything—magical attacks, falling rocks, raindrops, whatever. It's impervious. What I do…well, it's basically the same, except that it protects objects."

"Including magical books," Tony suggested, and now the glance she gave him was almost impressed.

Or maybe he was just fooling himself.

"Right. If I cast the shield around the books, they're protected. No one can touch them, which means they're safe from theft or damage. I have a couple of small carry-on bags folded up inside my purse, and I'll put the grimoires in the bags, cast the spell, and stick them in the overhead compartment for the trip home. Easy."

She made it sound easy, and Tony hoped it would be. He had to admit that an airplane would probably be safer than taking the books back overland in a car, where there would be far more opportunities for someone to interfere and try to steal them, magical shield or no. This way, she'd have them nearby for the short flight, and then he guessed a large contingent of de la Paz witches and warlocks would be waiting for her at the airport to make sure the grimoires made it safely the rest of the way to the home of their clan's *prima,* who apparently had built a library addition onto her home in order to make sure nothing like this ever happened again. Even the most dedicated book thief would think twice about trespassing on a *prima's* property.

"That's an interesting talent," he said, making sure his tone sounded casual. It wasn't his business to second-guess the de la Pazes' plans. All he had to do was ferry Cassandra to his mother's house and back to the airport, and then they'd be done with all this. "I don't think I've ever heard of it before."

"I guess it is pretty rare," she admitted. "My cousin's is rare, too. I'm just glad I didn't get his wife's talent. She's a seer."

Yes, being a seer could be pretty rough. A witch with that talent—seers were almost always witches, not warlocks, although no one had ever been able to explain why— owed her gifts to the clan even more than the rank and file. A seer often consulted with the *prima,* and had a position of importance in a clan. But that wasn't usually enough of a trade-off to compensate for having your life interrupted every time a vision of the future decided to take up space in your brain.

He nodded, not sure how to respond.

"Besides, it would have been too much of a joke for me to be a seer, considering my name," Cassandra remarked.

"Because of the Trojan princess." Thank God that bit of Greek mythology had managed to stick to his gray matter. He'd already made enough of an ass of himself by asking about her luggage; compounding it with another spectacular display of stupidity would have only been the cherry on the cake of his day.

"Right." Cassandra's lips pursed, but Tony couldn't tell whether she was impressed or just glad he wasn't quite as stupid as she'd first thought. "Anyway, my gift seemed the natural one to use in this particular situation. My cousin Zoe—our *prima*—decided it was better to send only me rather than a large delegation. Having so many witches and warlocks leave our territory at the same time might attract outside attention, but a single witch should be able to fly under the radar, so to speak."

"Who do you think would be watching for that kind of thing?" Tony asked, genuinely curious.

"I don't know for sure, but considering that a dark warlock in New Orleans knew about the books and tried to go after them, it seems pretty obvious that there are more watching eyes in the world than we thought."

He couldn't really refute that remark because it was only the truth. How Nicholas Toulouse had found out about the stolen grimoires, no one really knew, but somehow he'd discovered they'd been taken from the de la Paz clan...and that Simon Escobar had brought them to Santa Fe. And if Toulouse could dig up that information, then conceivably someone else could as well. These days, you couldn't be too careful.

"Makes sense," he responded, and left it at that.

By that point, they were out of the center of Albuquerque and headed toward the open highway, so Tony figured it was safe to disengage the self-driving mechanism and take control of the vehicle. While he understood why it was better to have the car's AI handle things in-town, he'd bought the Spider so he could enjoy the act of driving, and he might as well enjoy the sensation of freedom while he could.

The sidelong glance Cassandra sent toward him as he activated the manual controls told him she'd noticed what he'd done, but at least she didn't say anything, only looked back out the window. "How far is it to Santa Fe?" she asked. "I looked on a map, but…."

"It's about forty-five minutes from where we are now to my mother's house," he said. The change of subject had been fairly abrupt, but he knew better than to comment on it. "The drive back should take about the same, or maybe even less, since in the afternoon there are more people heading home to Santa Fe—or to Bernalillo or Rio Rancho, which are on the way—from Albuquerque than vice versa."

"Got it."

Her expression seemed to indicate she wasn't overly ecstatic about being stuck in a car with him for that long. Well, there wasn't much he could do about that, except speed, which wasn't an option. Cassandra already seemed disapproving enough; he'd hate to see her expression if he managed to get pulled over by the police.

However, Tony chose not to engage the cruise control, deciding that handling their speed manually would help to keep him occupied. Further conversation didn't seem like a very good idea, and he had to wonder what it was that made Cassandra so prickly. He didn't think he'd said anything that could possibly have offended her. Then again, she probably wasn't thrilled about being sent on this expedition, and probably even less thrilled that her presence was due entirely to sloppiness on her clan members' part. He had to wonder whether she'd ever made a mistake in her life.

Eventually, though, they reached Santa Fe's city limits. He held back a sigh of relief as he got off at Old Pecos Highway, then headed into town along that old, old road. They cut north, skirting the edges of downtown and its throngs of tourists, before he turned onto the street that took them toward the ski area.

Cassandra must have noticed the signs

for the ski resort, because she shifted in her seat and asked, "Your mother lives up on the mountain?"

"Partway," Tony replied, wondering if she'd asked the question because she was worried about it being even colder at that elevation. "There are some neighborhoods up in the hills here. That's where her house is located."

"But not your house."

Did she really think he was that much of a loser? Like he would have been caught dead still living in his parents' house. He was twenty-five years old, for God's sake.

Or had she been probing because she was wondering why a warlock his age wasn't married yet? Witch-kind tended to marry young, so it wasn't so strange a question to cross someone's mind.

Not that he would flatter himself that Cassandra Sandoval gave a damn about his marital status.

"No, I live down the hill, on the edge of downtown. My parents bought this house when I was in high school."

"Oh."

She settled back in her seat, watching as the road rose and the land on either side grew thick with pine trees as well as the ubiquitous junipers. Tony turned off into his parents' development, pausing to wave a casual hand at the heavy steel gate that guarded the entrance to the upscale neighborhood. It opened at once, thanks to the witchy power that allowed all of his kind to view door locks and electric gates as temporary delays rather than barriers.

A few more twists and turns, and then they were at the big two-story house at the end of the cul-de-sac that had been his parents' home for the past fifteen years. It had never felt exactly like home to him, since he'd only lived here for a few years before heading off to college and then a house of his own, but at least it was familiar enough.

He pulled into the driveway and parked. Since it wasn't quite four-thirty, Tony doubted his father would be home yet, which was just as well. With only his mother there—his sister Ava was down in Albuquerque working on her own degree at the university—this should be a quick trip, a fast in-and-out. He knew his mother had planned to offer Cassandra some snacks before the two of them turned around and headed right back down to the airport, but even that shouldn't delay things by too much.

With her following a step or two behind him, he went up to the front door and let himself in, then paused in the foyer so he could call down the hallway.

"Mom, we're here!"

It felt strange to be saying "Mom" with Cassandra's cool green eyes watching him, but it wasn't as though he could call his mother by her given name. He didn't want to think what her expression would be if he strolled in and casually referred to her as "Sophia."

No reply to his announcement, and he frowned. Well, it was a big house. Maybe she was in the kitchen, working on getting the refreshments ready. His mother tended to get more elaborate than she really needed to when it came to having company over.

"Come on back," he told Cassandra. "She's probably in the kitchen."

A brief nod was her only reply, but she followed him as he went past the spotless living room, so formal that he still wondered whether anyone actually set foot in there, and the equally elegant and tidy dining room, and on into the family room, which had always felt like the heart of the house to him. The books had been kept all this time in a closet in that room, one whose door had been concealed by a spell of protection that Miranda, the *prima*, had put on it.

Except now the door yawned open, showing a dark rectangle in the pale beige wall. Tony barely had a chance to register that alarming detail before he realized there was something else out of place about the room. His mother was lying on the rug, a silver tray still clutched in one hand and the sandwiches that had been arranged on top of it scattered all around her limp form. Her eyes were wide open, staring in terror, although at what, he didn't know.

Even as Cassandra made a shocked sound, he hurried forward and knelt next to his mother's limp form, then reached for her wrist. It took a couple of tries—maybe because his fingers were shaking so badly— but then he found a pulse. Faint, yes, but at least it was there.

"Is she…?" Cassandra asked.

"She's alive," Tony replied. He couldn't exactly allow himself to be too relieved, though, because the pulse he'd found was thready and weak, arrhythmic. With his free hand, he reached into his back pocket to retrieve his phone. He needed to call Yesenia, the Castillo clan's healer, and then his father.

As he pushed the entry for Yesenia's phone, Cassandra moved past him to the open closet door. She looked inside, her full mouth set and grim. "The books were stored in this safe?"

"Yes." The phrasing of the question struck home, and he sent the de la Paz witch a sharp glance. "They're gone?"

"Yes. All of them. This isn't good."

No, it wasn't. Right then, however, he had to focus on his mother's condition. Whoever'd done this was long gone—they hadn't passed any cars coming out of the gated neighborhood, and there hadn't been that many people driving down from the mountain, either. That seemed to indicate the theft had to have occurred at least fifteen minutes earlier, plenty of time for the perpetrators to disappear.

"Tony?" Yesenia's voice came through the phone. "Is something wrong?"

"Yes," he said, his voice tight. The sight of his mother lying on the floor like that had unnerved him even more than the theft of the books. She was always so put together, so in control of everything around her, that it didn't seem possible for her to be slumped there with her hair partly in her face and her blouse coming untucked from her wool slacks. "There's—there's been an attack at the house. My mother's alive, but she's in a coma or something."

"I'll be right over. Fifteen minutes at the most. Hang on."

The healer ended the call there, but that was okay. They didn't need to waste time in chitchat, and Yesenia knew how to get moving when the situation called for it.

Cassandra still lingered by the open closet door, fingers moving along the frame without touching it.

"Do you feel something?" Tony asked. She hadn't mentioned possessing that sort of ability, but sometimes witches and warlocks had a secondary talent to complement their primary gift. Maybe she could sense who had come that way, what kind of magic they'd used.

"A little." She stopped there and pulled her hand away, crossing her arms over her chest. "I'm not that good at it, but sometimes I can feel it when magic has been used, get a little sense of what sort of talent or spell was in play."

"And?" With some reluctance, he got to his feet. Maybe he should have remained kneeling by his mother, but she sure wasn't going anywhere, and he couldn't really do anything to help her except be here and keep an eye on her in case something about her condition changed.

Cassandra's full lips pressed together, and she looked away from him. Tony couldn't be absolutely sure, but it seemed almost as though she was a shade or two paler than she'd been when they first entered the house. "Something dark. The residue is…." She pulled in a breath, nostrils flaring in distaste. "It's like a slime trail left behind by a snail or a slug or something. Whoever came here, they were definitely up to no good."

"Well, that's obvious enough," Tony returned. After the words left his mouth, he realized he probably should have been a little more diplomatic…right before he decided he really didn't care. His mother had just been attacked, for God's sake. Being polite was the least of his worries.

To his surprise, Cassandra didn't snap back at him, but only looked thoughtful. "I know. I'm sorry. It's not my primary talent, so it's not going to give me all the information I want or need. I'm just...." The words trailed off, and he saw the way her hands clenched as she uncrossed her arms. "I wish I could do something else, but I can't."

Neither could he. Since any words of reassurance seemed to have fled him, about all he could do was shrug.

The books were gone. And what they were supposed to do next, he had no idea.

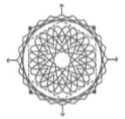

2

THE CASTILLO CLAN'S HEALER WAS A SLIM woman in her late forties or her early fifties, her sleek dark hair pulled into a low pony-tail at the back of her neck. She murmured a greeting to Tony and spared the barest of glances for Cassandra, who stood awkwardly to one side, not exactly sure what to do with herself, before she knelt on the thick Persian rug in subtle hues of brick and blue and cream. The healer took Tony's mother's wrist in her hand, then laid her palm against the unconscious woman's forehead.

Through all this, Tony stood off to one side, arms crossed, handsome features impassive. His dark brows were pulled together, but he remained silent, obviously waiting for the healer's verdict before he said anything.

Honestly, Cassandra didn't know what she would have done if she'd come home to find her mother unconscious and her house burglarized. She'd like to think that she'd stay calm the way Tony had, would know the right people to call and the right order in which to call them, but she had no idea if she could hold it together under that kind of pressure.

This wasn't supposed to happen. When Cassandra had been called to talk to her cousin Zoe, the de la Paz *prima*, about traveling here to Santa Fe to reclaim the clan's grimoires, it had all been described as a very cut-and-dried sort of endeavor, one that shouldn't have presented any particular problems. The books had been safely hidden for almost a year now, and everyone seemed to agree that Miranda's powers were pretty staggering, and definitely up to the task of keeping the books safe until they could be handed over to Cassandra.

Now it seemed clear that those powers weren't quite as impressive as everyone had thought...or, worse, that whoever had come here to take the grimoires and incapacitate Tony's mother was so powerful that even Miranda Castillo's insanely strong spells had been broken under their assault.

Not good. Not good at all.

"I don't think we need to take her to the hospital," the healer said as she rose from where she'd been kneeling by Sophia Castillo's side.

"She's going to be okay?" Tony asked, a hint of relief showing on his face.

"That's not what I said." The healer's tone was gentle, but firm. Cassandra had no idea what the woman's name was; she hadn't introduced herself, and Tony hadn't said her name when he made his phone call. "Right now, I don't know one way or the other. Her pulse isn't strong, but it seems to be normalizing, and I don't think a hospital could do much for her, either. In a way, her condition reminds me of what happened to Malena and Louisa."

"Who are Malena and Louisa?" The question slipped out before Cassandra could stop herself. Possibly it would have been better for her to stand by and remain quiet, since she was a stranger here, but at the same time, she didn't want to ignore any clues that might possibly lead them to the person or persons who'd stolen the grimoires.

Tony glanced over at her, and something about his taut expression softened just a hint. When she'd first caught sight of him at the airport, she'd allowed herself to acknowledge that he was good-looking, then pushed the thought aside. She wasn't here to meet eligible warlocks, but was on a mission given her by her clan's *prima*. Now, though, Cassandra couldn't help being struck by his appearance once again, mostly because he seemed completely oblivious to it.

"They're my cousins," he said. "Daughters of Genoveva, the former *prima*. They were attacked by Simon Escobar's dark magic and were in comas for a while."

Right. Cassandra had been told about the unorthodox way Miranda had become the current *prima* even though that title had first gone to one of her husband Rafe's older sisters. All the goings-on in Santa Fe had been a topic of several discussions in the Sandoval household, not least of all because Cassandra and Miranda were very distant cousins by marriage. Anyway, the whole thing had sounded kind of crazy to Cassandra—since when could a new *prima* voluntarily pass on her powers to someone else?—but she'd accepted it because that really was what had happened.

She looked over at the Castillo healer. "You think whoever did this used the same kind of magic? But Simon Escobar is dead." A horrible thought came to her, and she added, "Isn't he?"

"In the ground dead," Tony said, and a sudden glint entered his eyes, as if he was all too glad to be able to inform her of that fact. "I was there."

"You were there when he was buried?" Cassandra asked, surprised.

"It was his right," the healer said. "He was there during the final confrontation with the Escobar warlock, so no one was surprised that Tony would want to make sure the man really was dead and buried."

Now he looked almost embarrassed. Maybe he hadn't wanted that unexpected bit of heroism exposed. To be honest, Cassandra was a little surprised by the revelation; Tony's off-hand manner didn't exactly make a person think that he was the type to run headlong into a battle with an insanely strong warlock.

"Anyway, he's dead," Tony said, trying to sound casual and not quite succeeding.

"I know that for a fact, so whoever did this, it's not Escobar risen from the grave."

Small comfort. At least Simon Escobar was something of a known quantity. But it was a mystery as to who could have managed to tear aside Miranda Castillo's illusion spells and take the prize with no one even being able to detect that a stranger with those sorts of powers had come to Santa Fe.

Before anyone could respond, the front door slammed, and they all jumped. A moment later, a tall man with gray-frosted dark hair rushed into the room, a man so like Tony in appearance, Cassandra guessed the stranger had to be his father.

He ignored all of them and went at once to kneel by his wife. Only after touching her hand and apparently reassuring himself that she was still alive did he look up at Tony. "You found her like this?"

"Yes. But Yesenia says she should be okay here."

The man's dark gaze immediately flicked up toward the healer. "Is that true?"

"For now," the woman—Yesenia—said gently. "And now that you're here, we can move her to her bed."

"Of course." He glanced over at his son. "Tony?"

Without speaking, Tony came forward and knelt as well, and then the two men lifted Sophia from the rug and carried her out of the room. Yesenia began to follow them, then paused, her dark eyes taking in Cassandra as if really noticing her for the first time.

"You were here when he found her?"

"Yes," Cassandra replied. She hesitated, wondering how much the healer knew about the books, if anything. Zoe had made it sound as though their presence here in Santa Fe was a secret shared by only a few, so she guessed it was probably better to say as little as possible. "I'm—my name is Cassandra Sandoval. I'm here from the de la Paz clan on the *prima's* business."

"I assume that 'business' has something to do with what happened to Sophia?"

About all Cassandra could do was nod and pray that Yesenia wouldn't try to probe any further.

But part of being a healer was knowing how to keep secrets, and so the older woman didn't say anything else, only gave her another considering look before she excused herself and hurried out of the family room. Since she didn't know what else to do, Cassandra trailed along in her wake, following her to the sweeping staircase that led to the house's second floor.

As soon as they got to the upstairs landing, Yesenia hurried through a pair of double doors to their right. This was clearly the master bedroom; Tony and his father had laid Sophia down on the bed and removed her shoes, then pulled the white comforter over her.

It seemed better to wait near the door, so Cassandra stayed there, watching as Yesenia went over to Tony's father and murmured something to him. The older man's face was bleak, calm, as if he'd already resigned himself to the worst, but Tony stood on the other side of the bed, hands shoved into the pockets of his jeans, the shocked expression he wore now appearing to shift to one of anger.

Well, Cassandra could understand that. She knew she'd be on a rampage if someone had attacked her own mother in such a way. A flicker of fear went through her, but she told herself that there was no reason for anyone to go after her parents. They were safe in the heart of de la Paz territory. Anyway, this attacker was clearly after the books, and since all of her clan's pilfered grimoires were now in this strange witch or warlock's possession, there probably wasn't much left in Phoenix or Tucson to even tempt them.

Tony went over to his father and said something in an undertone, and the older man nodded, then placed a hand on his son's shoulder for a moment before he turned back to the unconscious woman in the bed. After that exchange, Tony came over to where Cassandra was waiting.

"We should go," he said, his tone quiet, as if he was somehow worried that his comatose mother might be able to hear him.

"All right," she replied, glad of an excuse to slip away. She felt far too much like an interloper here, an unwilling spectator to an unexpected tragedy. As soon as they were headed back down the stairs, she added, "We should really go talk to Miranda and let her know what happened."

Tony looked a little startled at the familiar way she'd referred to his clan's *prima*, but then he seemed to brush the matter aside, maybe reminding himself that Miranda and Cassandra were distant cousins. "I can call and talk to her," he said.

"But she's not really receiving visitors right now."

"Why not?" Cassandra demanded. "This isn't exactly dropping in to have tea and cookies. She needs to know what happened."

"And we'll tell her," Tony replied, his tone equally brusque. "But her baby's due in seven weeks, and she's been confined to bed because she fell last week and had a few issues, and Yesenia doesn't want her to exert herself."

Oh, hell. Talk about putting your foot in it. She hadn't heard anything about Miranda's unfortunate mishap and wondered if even Zoe knew. The two *primas* talked to one another fairly frequently, but it seemed there were some matters Miranda didn't wish to share. "Sorry," Cassandra said. "I didn't know."

"Well, it's not exactly the sort of thing we're advertising to the other clans. I mean, obviously Miranda has talked to her parents, but I doubt they're spreading the story all over the place, either."

No, probably not. Still, this was an unsettling and unwelcome turn of events. At the back of her mind, Cassandra had been thinking they could call Miranda in to offer assistance if necessary, but it sounded as though she was sidelined until the baby was here. "So what do we do now?" she asked, wishing her voice didn't sound quite so plaintive.

"We can go to my place and regroup." Expression somber, he went on, "And you'll probably need to call the airline and cancel your ticket."

Right. She hadn't even thought about that, but it seemed obvious now that she wouldn't be heading back to Tucson any time soon. Maybe it was pointless for her to stay here, since her whole job had been to protect the books while she ferried them into de la Paz territory. Something inside her told her that she needed to stay, though, to help the Castillos figure out who was behind this attack. If they could discover who had stolen the books, then maybe they'd also be able to find out where they had been taken.

"Okay," Cassandra said. "Let's go to your house."

~

Tony's place wasn't what she'd been expecting. It looked as though it had been built sometime in the late 1800s, and the furniture was just as old, matching the architecture of the house. Not exactly the home of a bachelor warlock, although he explained a little of the decor as he ushered her into the kitchen.

"The house is haunted," he said cheerfully, going to the refrigerator so he could extract a couple of bottles of a local microbrew, then pop the caps using the bottle opener bolted into the cabinet next to it. "Her name is Victoria."

"Really?" Cassandra took the bottle he offered her, fought a losing battle with her conscience, and said the hell with it. Obviously, she wasn't going anywhere soon, and a beer might help to relax her jangly nerves. "Did she introduce herself?"

"Not in so many words, but she let my uncle—he owned the house before I bought it—know that she wasn't a fan of his foosball table or any of the other 'improvements' he tried to make."

After a swallow of beer, Cassandra asked, "Is that why the place looks like a museum?"

Despite everything that had happened during the course of the afternoon, Tony appeared remarkably cheerful. Maybe the beer was already helping. "What, you don't like my decorating style?"

"It doesn't feel much like you," she said frankly. "Not that I know you very well, but—"

He grinned. "No, the downstairs is pure Victoria. Well, except the kitchen. She didn't make too much of a fuss about me modernizing that space. And she let me do what I wanted with my bedroom."

"Oh." Cassandra wasn't sure how to reply to that remark—something felt weird about discussing bedrooms with a guy she'd just met—and so she only said, "I guess that's not so bad, then."

For a moment, they were both silent, sipping their beers. She did take a few surreptitious glances around, confirming that the appliances were new and shiny, the countertops a pale grayish granite to match the whitewashed cabinetry.

"You actually cook in here?" she asked. The kitchen seemed spotlessly clean, and visits to the abodes of several of her male cousins had provided the knowledge that the kitchens of most men in their middle twenties didn't look quite so much like something out of a magazine.

Another grin. Yes, he was really good-looking, with that devilish lift on one side of his mouth and the way the eyebrow on that same side would cock at precisely the correct rakish angle. "Does making coffee count?"

"No."

"Then I don't."

She'd thought as much. Another sip of beer, and then she said, "So...what do we do next?"

"I don't know." The grin disappeared, and Cassandra found herself wishing that she'd stayed on a lighter topic, if only for a few more minutes. She liked how Tony looked when he smiled, but now the somber expression had returned. "I can call Rafe and Miranda, but, like I said, there's not a lot Miranda can do right now."

"Is there anyone in your clan with the gift of detecting magic...you know, what I was doing, except hopefully stronger, more accurate?" Cassandra asked the question without any real hope that Tony would reply in the affirmative, and was surprised when he nodded.

"Actually, Louisa is really good at that."

"She's the one who was supposed to be your *prima*, right?"

Now his dark eyes were sharp, focusing

on her face like a laser beam. "You know about that?"

"Well, yes," Cassandra admitted. "Don't worry—it's not like it was an open topic of conversation in the de la Paz clan. But my father is my *prima's* uncle, and they talked, so we talked. I don't know all the details, though."

Some of the tension seemed to go out of Tony's shoulders. "I guess that's not so bad. But yeah, Louisa is Genoveva's oldest daughter, and should have been our *prima,* only once she went up against Escobar, she realized she really didn't have what it took to win against him. So she handed her powers over to Miranda. Luckily, though, her own individual powers—the ones she had before she became *prima* when Genoveva died—are still in place. And that means she's probably the best person to help us."

"Maybe you should call her first, then."

"No, I'll call Rafe and Miranda. They're the heads of the clan, so they should be the first to know what's happened." Tony's shoulders lifted slightly, and he took another sip of beer. "I'm sure they'll come to the same conclusion about having Louisa look into it. In the meantime…." He stopped there. "I hope your plane ticket is refundable."

"It is," Cassandra assured him. Even as she spoke, though, she found herself reluctant, as if calling the airline to cancel her ticket would put her on an irrevocable course, one that would force her to see this through to the end. But wasn't that what she'd already determined to do? Zoe had entrusted her with this mission, and she needed to stay with it, no matter what happened. She hated knowing that it was the negligence of her fellow clan members that had led to the books being stolen in the first place, and even though Cassandra realized she'd had nothing to do with their failings, she wanted to do whatever she could to restore the de la Paz clan's honor. "I'll call now."

She pulled her phone out of the purse and brought up the app that contained her electronic ticketing information. A swipe of her finger, and then she was on hold, waiting for the pablum music to go away so she could talk to a real person. Why this part of the operation wasn't automated, she didn't know, except that maybe the airline didn't want to be liable for people fat-fingering something and canceling a ticket when they really didn't mean to.

As she waited, she saw that Tony had gotten out his own phone and was talking to someone in a low voice. Rafe, or possibly Miranda? Probably. They needed to be brought into the loop, even if there wasn't a whole lot they could do to help, except maybe allocate any necessary clan resources to assist in the search for Sophia Castillo's attacker. For all Cassandra knew, they'd decide her unique magical gift wasn't going to be of much use, given what had just happened, and they'd send her home anyway. Which meant that making this phone call might turn out to be sort of pointless.

However, the operator picked up just then, and Cassandra took a breath and told the woman that her stay in Santa Fe had been extended indefinitely, and so she had to cancel her ticket. A few minutes later, she was off the phone, feeling oddly at loose ends.

Well, that's not so strange, she thought. *You're here in Santa Fe with the clothes on your back and a travel-size tube of toothpaste and a travel toothbrush in your purse and not much else. Didn't really stop to think that everything might not go exactly to plan, did you?*

Maybe not. But it wasn't as though she was marooned in the middle of nowhere. Once they'd decided on their next step, she could take a break to go and buy a few changes of clothes and some toiletries. There was a mall here in Santa Fe, and plenty of other shopping. She could get whatever she needed if it turned out her stay was going to be extended for an indefinite amount of time.

Tony was still on the phone, his back turned slightly toward her, so Cassandra couldn't hear what he was saying. Since she knew she'd have to make the call anyway, she lifted her phone and said, "Call Zoe."

It had been a toss-up whether she should call her clan's *prima* or her parents, but Cassandra guessed it was probably better to contact Zoe first. She needed to know what had happened here. And her parents, well, they hadn't been thrilled about her being sent to Santa Fe on her own, but they hadn't argued with Zoe's decision. Cassandra was a grown woman with her own condo and a job at a local advertising agency. True, the agency was owned by a de la Paz cousin, and she knew she probably wouldn't have her graphic design position if it weren't for that family connection, but still. She didn't live at home anymore, could make her own decisions about what to do and where to go.

Apparently, Zoe had been expecting her to call, because she answered right away. "Hi, Cass. Are you on your way back to Phoenix?"

"Well, no," Cassandra replied. "There's been a complication."

"'Complication'?" Zoe repeated, her tone sharpening.

No point in trying to make this sound any better than it was. "Someone attacked the witch who was guarding the books and managed to steal them."

"Seriously?" Zoe demanded, sounding aghast.

"Seriously. She survived, but she's in some kind of coma. And right now we don't have any clues as to who could have taken the books, or where they are now. I guess Tony has a cousin who might be able to help, but—"

"Who's Tony?"

"The warlock who picked me up at the airport. It's his mother who was attacked."

"Oh." A pause, as if Zoe was trying to

figure out what she should say next. But really, what was there to say? At the moment, it seemed as if they were all pretty royally screwed.

"I'm going to stay and help with the search," Cassandra continued.

"I don't see how that's going to help."

Well, thanks. Cassandra made herself take a breath and count to five. All right, her cousin had a point—Cassandra's talent wasn't the kind that, on the surface, seemed as if it would be of much use, given the current situation. But that didn't mean she was entirely without resources. "My dad's a cop, remember? He's taught me a lot about investigating crime scenes. There are other ways I can help besides just using my talent."

Silence for a moment. All right, maybe it had been a stretch to say that Jack Sandoval was a cop, since he'd quit the Scottsdale P.D. before Cassandra was even born, but once a cop, always a cop, at least when it came to a certain type of mindset. And he had taught her a good deal of what he knew, as well as making sure she was a crack shot with a pistol and a rifle, and also knew how to defend herself against an armed assailant.

All of which might or might not stand her in good stead when it came to open conflict with a powerful witch or warlock, but it was probably better than nothing.

Another pause, and then Zoe said, "Maybe you're right. I don't know." She let out a small sigh of a breath, then added, "I suppose I could order you to come back to Arizona."

"And I could ignore your order," Cassandra said cheerfully. She wasn't too bothered by the threat, mostly because she knew that Zoe wasn't the type to throw her weight as *prima* around. Although she'd held that title since the time when she was around the same age that Cassandra was now, she still didn't always seem comfortable with the position, as if even now, more than twenty years later, she expected someone to come along and tell her that it had all been a mistake and she wasn't really supposed to be *prima*.

"Yes, you could...and Jack would probably back you up. All right. Go ahead and stay, but make sure you keep me posted if you find out anything."

"I will," Cassandra replied. "I'll talk to you again soon."

She ended the call there and turned

slightly to find Tony leaning against the kitchen counter, phone idle in one hand. "That was your *prima?*"

Cassandra nodded. "I needed to let her know what was going on. What did Miranda say?"

"Actually, she was resting. I talked to Rafe." Tony ran a hand through his thick dark hair, pushing it back from his forehead.

"And?"

"Well, he wasn't happy to hear what had happened, but I guess none of us are." Tony set down his phone and picked up the half-drunk bottle of beer waiting for him on the countertop. After taking a swallow, he went on, "But he said he'd get in contact with Louisa and have her come up to the house, take a look around."

"Good," Cassandra told him. "Because I should have done the same thing. I guess I was so shocked by what had happened that I forgot my training."

"Your training?" Tony asked, now looking almost amused. "Are you a cop or something?"

"No," she replied. "But my father was. He taught me a few things. It never hurts to look at things methodically, even if you're not performing a formal investigation."

This response only made Tony lift an eyebrow, but at least he otherwise looked as though he was willing to take her words at face value. "Well, then, finish your beer and we'll head back out."

She did just that, not exactly chugging the remainder of what was in the bottle, but drinking it faster than she normally would have. When she was done, she put the bottle down on the counter next to Tony's.

He didn't comment, only led her out the back door to the detached garage. As she followed him, Cassandra found herself oddly satisfied. He hadn't laughed at her, or told her the Castillo clan didn't need some amateur playing cop when the situation was so dire. No, he seemed as though he was disposed to give her a chance, let her see what she could do.

Now she would just have to prove that it made sense for her to stay here in Santa Fe and offer what help she could.

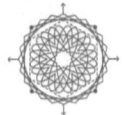

3

THERE HADN'T BEEN MUCH CHANGE IN HIS mother's condition, but Yesenia had had to excuse herself and leave, since she'd gotten a call from a Castillo cousin on the city's south side that her son had fallen out of a tree and broken his arm. And since Tony's father seemed unwilling to leave his wife's side, it meant Tony could stay downstairs with Cassandra and Louisa, and keep watch over what they were doing.

Louisa stood by the closet door that had once concealed the de la Paz grimoires. Her fingers began to trace the outline of the frame, and Cassandra made a small sound of protest.

"What's the matter?" Louisa asked, looking somewhat exasperated. When she'd arrived on the scene, she'd seemed less than happy to see a witch from another clan here, even though Tony had explained the reason behind Cassandra's presence. Now he could tell his cousin didn't think much of the younger witch's interference.

"I was hoping I could check for fingerprints," Cassandra explained. "I don't have a real kit with me, but cornstarch or talcum powder should work. Oh, and some tape."

Even as Louisa began to shoot her a disbelieving glare, Tony hurried to say, "Cassandra's father is a police officer. That's why she knows about this stuff."

"Homicide detective, actually," Cassandra put in, which didn't seem to mollify Louisa in the slightest.

"I doubt whoever did this was foolish enough to leave fingerprints behind," she said. "And right now, I need to focus."

She closed her eyes and laid her fingers against the doorframe once again. Cassandra's mouth tightened in annoyance, but she didn't say anything, possibly realizing that it wouldn't take much to overstep her boundaries here.

Tony felt a rush of sympathy for her, although he also remained silent. Louisa might not be quite as imperious as her late mother, the *prima*, but she still could be plenty bitchy if someone rubbed her the wrong way. And with his own mother lying in bed upstairs in a magically induced coma, he really didn't feel like trying to play peacemaker.

At least it seemed as if Cassandra had gotten the message. She moved away from Louisa and went to crouch down next to the spot where they'd found Sophia, outstretched hand moving over the thick pile of the Persian carpet. There were no obvious indentations, no real sign that a woman had been lying there unconscious less than an hour before, but maybe Cassandra could sense something despite that.

Louisa spoke then. "Yes, this was dark magic." The forefinger of her right hand rested on the doorframe, and a tremor went through her. "It feels almost familiar, as though I've encountered this kind of magic before." Her well-arched brows drew together, and her nostrils flared in distaste. While objectively Tony realized most people would think his cousin an attractive woman, there was still something off-putting about the elegance of her features. "In fact, it feels very like

Simon Escobar's magic, but that's impossible."

A chill shivered its way down Tony's spine. It had to be impossible. As he'd told Cassandra earlier, he'd been there when they put Escobar's lifeless body in the ground. He now rested in an unmarked grave in a corner of Rosario Cemetery on the north side of town, and good riddance.

And while zombies might have been good fodder for movies and TV shows, there was no such thing in real life, no chance that an undead Simon Escobar had risen from his grave to seek vengeance almost a year after he'd died. This had to be something else.

Cassandra pushed herself up from the rug and briefly dusted the palms of her hands on the thighs of her jeans. "We don't know very much about where Simon's father came from. Central America is what I heard, but even that's just based on what Simon's half-sister Olivia has said. Since she came to Southern California to live with the Santiago clan when she was very small, she really didn't remember much of her life before then."

"What about Simon's mother?" Louisa

asked. "She's the *prima* of the Santiago clan —she must know something."

Something in Cassandra's expression darkened. Obviously, that hadn't been a very tactful question. "Simon's father forced her," she said in a voice that was almost too calm. "Controlled her mind. I doubt he was revealing any secrets about his past during the time she was under his spell."

Louisa's mouth tightened, and she looked away without responding. In a way, it was almost amusing to watch how Cassandra had managed to get her to back off, especially when you considered that she had to be the other woman's junior by more than a decade. Even though Tony guessed Cassandra was no more than twenty-one or twenty-two at the very most, she had the kind of self-possession of a much older woman.

Because her father was a former cop? Maybe. Or maybe she would have been like that no matter who her parents were.

Either way, Tony guessed it was probably time for him to step in. "None of us know very much about the magic practiced in other parts of the world, because all our clans tend to stick to their own territories.

What if Simon's father came from a place where they all use that kind of dark magic? That would explain why the magic you sensed here felt familiar, Louisa."

She nodded, although she didn't seem very happy with this particular piece of deduction. "Maybe. Although the last thing any of us need is an entire region filled with witches and warlocks as strong as Joaquin Escobar and his children."

True enough. Tony really didn't want to think what the consequences of such a population suddenly setting their sights on the Castillos might be.

"I'm not sure that's it, though," Cassandra said, her tone musing. "For one thing, if they were all so powerful, you'd think we would have heard something about it by now. That kind of power is hard to keep secret, if for no other reason than they'd probably already have attacked other witch clans. We keep to ourselves, but we also communicate with one another if the threat is big enough."

Which was also true. It was because the *prima* of the McAllisters and the *primus* of the Wilcoxes had come to Castillo territory to get help from Louisa's grandmother Isabel to fight Joaquin Escobar that the New

Mexico clan and the Arizona clans had become involved at all. Before that, they'd had very little contact.

"Maybe," Louisa allowed in grudging tones. "We're certainly not going to solve the mystery today, though. I can sense what kind of magic was used here, but I don't know anything about the person who used it, or where they might have gone."

"But it's a start," Tony told her. "It's more than we had an hour ago."

She seemed somewhat mollified by the praise, which had been his intention. The last thing he'd wanted was for her and Cassandra to start bickering, comparing theories that didn't have much in the way of fact to back them up.

"And we'll keep picking away at it," Cassandra said. "At least now we have a direction for where to start looking."

Right then, Tony's father came to the arched opening that connected the family room to the hallway that split the bottom floor of the house. "She's doing a little better," he said, his expression not quite as strained as it had been an hour ago. "She has more color in her cheeks, and when I squeezed her hand, she pressed down on my fingers."

Relief flooded through Tony. Maybe his mother wasn't sitting up and talking, but if she could respond to a stimulus like that, seemed to be somewhat aware of her surroundings, then she wasn't in as bad shape as Tony had thought. "That's great news, Dad," he said.

"I hope so." He looked over at Louisa. "Did you find anything?"

"Just that whoever did this is dabbling in some very dark magic," she replied. "But I suppose that's sort of a given, because no one who wasn't traveling the left-hand path would even want those books in the first place."

As she spoke, she sent a pointed glance at Cassandra, as if accusing the de la Paz clan of dabbling in black magic, since otherwise there was no reason for them to have collected the grimoires. To be honest, Tony wasn't really sure why they'd had them, either, except that it sounded as though they'd been collecting books of magic, both dark and light, for centuries, and so it was more of a tradition than anything else.

Cassandra's jaw tightened, but she said politely, "I'm very glad to hear that your wife is doing better, Mr. Castillo."

"Henry," he said, but his tone was

absent, as though he'd made the response automatically, his thoughts far away.

Which they should be. Tony knew that in a way he'd been distracting himself from his mother's condition by focusing on the investigative side of things, but what else was he supposed to do? He wasn't a healer, or someone with the kind of gift that could reverse another witch or warlock's magic. That talent had existed once, but no one in the Castillo clan had possessed it for longer than he or his parents had been alive.

"Do you need us to do anything?" Tony asked. "Get you some takeout, maybe?"

"No, I'm fine," Henry said. "There's plenty of food in the fridge, and I'm not hungry anyway."

"But maybe you should stay, Tony," Louisa put in. "There's always the chance that whoever did this might return."

Now Tony's father sent her a sharp look, the sort of laser-like glance he used to good effect in the courtroom. "Why would they come back? They've already gotten what they wanted. There wouldn't be much point in returning to the scene of the crime, especially if they know we're waiting for them."

Louisa drew in a breath, then seemed to

think better of what she was about to say
and shook her head. "You're probably right.
But I don't like the thought of you being
here alone with Sophia."

"I won't be alone for too long," he said.
"I called Ava to tell her what happened,
and she's already on her way here. She said
she can afford to miss a few days of school
and wants to be here to help out."

How very selfless of her, Tony thought,
then wanted to shake his head at himself.
He and his sister had never gotten along all
that well, possibly because he didn't tend to
take things all that seriously, and she was
pretty much the opposite. Far too earnest
and serious for him to really understand
what was going on in her head half the
time. After all, who the hell went away to
college and didn't have time for at least a
little partying?

"Oh, well, then," Louisa said. "I
suppose that should be fine. Such a steady
girl, Ava."

This seemed to be Tony's cue, so he put
in, "Then I guess Cassandra and I can go."

"Do you have someplace to stay?"
Louisa asked.

"Oh, I'm crashing at Tony's place,"

Cassandra said without batting an eye. "Right, Tony?"

"Right," he replied, also without missing a beat. "She's going to stay in the spare room upstairs."

"Sounds like you're all settled," Henry said. If he thought there was anything strange about Cassandra staying with someone she'd just met, rather than at one of the numerous hotels that dotted Santa Fe's downtown, he didn't show it. Or maybe he was so preoccupied with his worry about his wife that all these minor details were barely registering with him.

"We are," Tony said. "Call if anything changes, though." He looked over at Cassandra. "Ready?"

"Sure." She shifted toward Louisa and added, "It was very nice to meet you, Ms. Castillo."

Something in her tone seemed to indicate just the opposite, and Tony had to quell a smile. More than once, he'd wished he could come up with a way to knock Louisa off her high horse, and Cassandra seemed to have managed that feat within five minutes of meeting the former *prima*.

I think I like this girl, he thought, even as

Louisa's lips thinned and she murmured something empty and polite.

He made his goodbyes, and the two of them went outside. Now there was a dark gray Volvo next to his Fiat in the driveway, parked close enough that Cassandra, even as slender as she was, had to angle herself to climb into the passenger seat to avoid banging the car door into Louisa's vehicle. Had Louisa done that on purpose just to be bitchy, or was she in such a hurry when she arrived that she simply hadn't been paying attention?

Probably better not to answer that question.

Neither he nor Cassandra said anything as he backed the car out, then engaged the self-driving mechanism. Once they were back on Hyde Park Road and heading down into the city, though, she blew out a breath and shook her head.

"Well, *she* was lovely."

Tony laughed out loud. "Louisa is kind of prickly."

"Kind of?"

"All right, prickly as a patch of cholla cactus."

Now Cassandra was the one who chuckled. He liked her laugh, warm and throaty, just like her voice. "Honestly, I didn't mean to step on her toes. But when you see someone contaminating a crime scene like that—"

"Do you really think you could have found something?" he asked, genuinely curious.

Her shoulders lifted. "I don't know. Maybe. It's harder to pull prints than the TV shows want you to think. And when magic is involved…." The words trailed off, and she frowned. "It's not like there was any sign of forced entry, so the thief probably got into the closet with the safe the same way he got into the house, using some kind of spell that got him past the wards. Or maybe he didn't even have to do that much, and just went straight there."

"You mean he might have teleported, like Miranda can?"

Surprise was clear on his companion's features. It didn't seem as though she'd heard about that particular talent. "Really, Miranda can teleport?"

"Yes. I guess her parents can, too."

"Right. I suppose I should have thought of that." Cassandra played with the ring on her right hand, an intricate piece of silver set with a clear pale blue stone. Aquamarine, maybe. "I forget how many things Angela and Connor can do, since they're so low-key about their talents. And I guess Miranda is like that, too?"

"Sort of, I guess. To be honest, she and Rafe don't talk about it that much. But as far as I can tell, she can do almost anything, magically at least."

Although even the crazy powers she possessed hadn't been enough to prevent her from slipping on that bit of icy side-walk. Tony knew Rafe blamed himself for his *prima* wife's accidental fall, although it hadn't been anyone's fault, just some bad luck.

"Must be nice," Cassandra remarked. "I wish I had the talent to be able to touch something and see what happened in a room. Then I'd know exactly who did this, maybe where they went."

"Whoever it is, they must have a lot of Simon Escobar's same tricks."

"What makes you say that?"

"Because he had the ability to mask what he was. Usually, a *prima* can sense it when a strange witch or warlock enters her territory. But I could tell Rafe was totally surprised when I called him to let him know about the break-in, so Miranda must not have known that there was an intruder in Santa Fe."

"Right. I'd forgotten about that." Cassandra twisted the ring on her finger again, and Tony wondered suddenly who'd given it to her. A boyfriend, maybe?

Somehow, though, he got the feeling she was unattached. Definitely not married or in a serious relationship at least, or she probably would have found a way to mention the guy, if for no other reason than to make it very clear what her boundaries were. Anyway, Tony knew if he were with a girl as impressive as Cassandra, he wouldn't be too thrilled about her going alone to another clan's territory to ferry a bunch of dangerous grimoires back to her *prima's* house. Not that he would have tried to stop her. He didn't know the de la Paz witch well at all, but he could already tell she wasn't the type who'd put up with an over-protective boyfriend for very long.

"Are you hungry?" he asked, and she looked over at him, obviously surprised.

"I don't know," she responded. "Maybe a little, but it's still early. I was actually hoping you could take me someplace to get a few odds and ends. No luggage, remember?"

Right. She'd gotten off the plane with the oversized bag she had tucked into the footwell now, and nothing else. Obviously, she'd expected to perform her errand and head straight back, but fate had intervened.

"I'll take you to the mall," he said. "Then some food. Sound good?"

"Sounds perfect. Thank you."

No, thank you, he thought. Right then, he was just glad of the chance to spend a little more time with her, no matter how that time was spent.

Even…*groan*…shopping.

To his relief, though, Cassandra was just as efficient about procuring herself enough clothes to get by as she seemed to be about everything else. She told him there was no reason for him to come in the store with her, and sure enough, she was gone for fifteen minutes at the most while she disappeared into Macy's. When she emerged, she was carrying two large bags, and Tony obligingly popped the trunk so she could stow them right away and climb back into the passenger seat.

"Drugstore?" she asked as she closed the door.

"There's a Walgreens up on Cerrillos. I'll take you there, since it's on the way back downtown." Tony sent her a quick glance from under his eyelashes. "That was some pretty impressive shopping."

Cassandra shrugged. "I shop at Macy's enough that I know where things are, which brands and which sizes to get. No biggie."

Maybe not, but after getting dragged along on more than one shopping expedition with his mother and sister back when he was younger, he could still appreciate a woman who went in, got what she needed, and got out, rather than aimlessly wandering from rack to rack, searching for God only knew what.

Rather than reply, he pointed the car north on Cerrillos, doing his best not to get too frustrated with the inevitable rush-hour traffic. More than once, the city had tried to recalibrate the lights to improve traffic flow, but it seemed that no matter what the planners did, Santa Fe's main artery turned into a cloggy, sluggish mess every morning and afternoon—and wasn't that much better during the hours in between.

Eventually, though, they reached the Walgreens in question, and Cassandra hopped out to purchase the items she couldn't get at Macy's. Once again, she was in and out with surprising alacrity, especially impressive considering how crowded the parking lot was, probably thanks to people picking up prescriptions and other odds and ends on their way home from work.

"Hungry yet?" he asked as he eased the Fiat back into northbound traffic. "It's going to take another fifteen minutes or so to get where we're going, so it'll be after six by the time we get there."

"I could eat something." She tilted her head to look over at him. "Where are we going?"

"One of my favorite places downtown," Tony replied. "It's mellow, mostly locals. Sandwiches and stuff."

"Sounds good."

She didn't say anything after that, but seemed content to watch the streets outside the car window as they passed by various local landmarks, although with the sun now fully down, it wasn't as easy to see any detail as it had been a few hours earlier. Still, he altered his route slightly so they could pass by the Loretto Chapel and the bulk of the La Fonda hotel, just so Cassandra could catch a glimpse of those impressive buildings on the way to their destination.

They got lucky, because as they turned down Lincoln Street, someone pulled out from the curb, and Tony was able to snag the spot before anyone else could get it. "We're here," he announced.

She looked around. Shops lined the streets, but there wasn't much else to see. "Where is here?"

"You'll see."

A brow lifted, but she seemed to shrug and got out of the car, being careful not to scrape the bottom of the door on the overly high curb. Tony came around the back and led her into the shop on the corner, which specialized in local gourmet items.

"We're buying stuff to take back to your place?" she asked, clearly mystified by her surroundings.

"No," he said. "Follow me."

At the back of the shop was a set of stairs that went down into the basement, and he headed over there, Cassandra right behind him. As soon as they paused at the base of the steps, she glanced around and nodded in approval at the dark wood tables and booths, the nicely lit local art on the exposed brick walls, the large bar off to one side.

"I like it."

"The food's good, too."

He took her over to a corner booth, and they both sat down. Paper menus were provided at each table, so Tony plucked two from their resting place behind the condiments and handed one to Cassandra. "It's mostly sandwiches, but they have some good soups, too."

"A sandwich sounds great. I haven't eaten since breakfast." Her smoky green eyes scanned the menu. "And another beer. What were we drinking at your place?"

"Santa Fe Brewing Company nut brown ale," he replied, inwardly pleased that she'd liked the beer and wanted more. "They have it on tap here."

"Some of that, then."

The waiter on duty was Ellis, a guy Tony liked to hang out at the bar and shoot the shit with when The Cellar wasn't too busy. He came up to the table now to take their order, and, judging by the way Ellis glanced at Cassandra, then over at Tony, it was pretty obvious that he'd expect more details the next time Tony came into the restaurant by himself.

Problem was, he knew he'd need some time to figure out an explanation for her that didn't involve exposing the whole Castillo clan for the witches and warlocks they were.

Luckily, Ellis was on his best behavior and took their drink orders without comment, despite the look he'd given Tony a minute earlier. He said he'd be back with their beers in a minute, then headed over to the bar.

And of course Cassandra knew better than to say anything too sensitive in public, because all she did was remark, "This is a cool place. I can see why you like coming here—and why the tourists have a hard time finding it."

"Do you have to do a lot of tourist-dodging in Tucson, too?"

"Tubac, actually," she corrected him. "It's an artsy little town about forty minutes south of Tucson. But yeah, we get a lot of tourists, especially in the winter. I doubt it's anything like Santa Fe, though."

Probably not. Like any other destination city, Santa Fe had its slow times, but they were few and far between. "I've never heard of Tubac."

Her eyes glinted at him from across the table. "Most people probably haven't."

Ellis came by with their beers then, and asked if they were ready to order. Cassandra nodded and ordered a French dip, while Tony got his favorite Reuben. Belatedly, he realized that dripping sauerkraut all over the place while trying to look suave in front of his guest probably wasn't the best idea in the world, but it was too late to change his mind.

Anyway, this wasn't about impressing Cassandra. It was about trying to figure out who the hell had attacked his mother and stolen those damn books.

"That was good news about your mother," she murmured, after stealing a quick glance to make sure Ellis was out of earshot.

Tony nodded. "Kind of the same thing happened with Louisa and Malena when Si —when he attacked them. They were both in comas for a few days, but their condition was never bad enough that Yesenia thought they needed to go to the hospital. And then they just sort of woke up on their own."

"I was wondering if that was why you didn't seem too worried."

Was that a sideways rebuke? He allowed himself to study Cassandra's expression for a moment before he picked up his beer, but all he saw in her pretty features was a certain thoughtfulness, as if she'd been trying to figure out why he'd reacted to the situation the way he had.

"I like to hope for the best," he said, his tone neutral, then took a sip of brown ale.

"As long as you prepare for the worst," she remarked before also sipping at her beer.

"Is that what you do?"

Her reply was guarded. "I suppose."

About all he could do was chuckle. "I'm surprised you didn't become a cop like your father."

"I thought about it," she said, expression serious. "But he sort of talked me out of it. He said that when you're—well, when you're like us, then you have to hide a big part of who and what you are from your partner, and that makes it difficult when you're faced with life-and-death sorts of decisions. It's a strain. It makes a tough job that much harder. So I decided not to pursue it."

"What do you do now?"

"Graphic design, a little web stuff."

"That's a switch."

"I guess so. I always liked design, though, so it seemed like the natural thing to pursue." She drank some more of her beer, then asked, "What about you?"

"I'm not much of anything," he replied, and she looked at him in some surprise.

"That's kind of a crazy thing to say about yourself."

"It's the truth," he said, and wished he could tell her he was a neurosurgeon or an astrophysicist or a guy who built houses for Habitat for Humanity. Something impressive, something that would make her think of him as something more than a guy who'd inherited a lot of money and therefore didn't have to do much of anything with himself except go from party to party in an attempt to keep himself amused. "I don't work."

"Really?" Her fingers tapped against the side of her beer glass. "I mean, I know we all have some family money, but in my clan, pretty much everyone has a job so we don't attract attention."

"That's how it is with the Castillos, too. But my grandfather left me a big chunk of money, so it seemed even more pointless than usual to get a job for protective camouflage." He flashed a grin at her and added, "It drives my parents crazy."

Most women would have reacted to that smile by returning it, or maybe blushing and looking away. That had been his prior experience, anyway. But Cassandra looked back at him, her gaze level, expression thoughtful. "Don't you get bored?"

"No," he told her, but even as the word left his lips, he knew he was lying. It wasn't a huge lie, because there were large chunks of his existence where he was perfectly content, happy to sort of roll along and occupy his time with whatever seemed amusing at the moment. However, he also knew that there were other instances where he thought if he had to go to the movies by himself one more time, or listen to the excuses of his much busier friends as to why they couldn't go to a party or a concert or even a gallery opening, he might just have to bash his head against a wall.

Something about those hazel-green eyes seemed far too piercing. Cassandra regarded him for just a second or two longer, mouth slightly pursed, and then lifted her beer and sipped again. "Well, if it works for you."

Tony wasn't sure if it was working as well as it used to. Then again, his parents' nagging him to find a suitably distant cousin and settle down didn't help much, either. It wasn't as if the world was exactly lacking in Castillo witches and warlocks; he didn't see much point in contributing to the clan's population just because he was expected to.

But maybe that was because he'd never met anyone sufficiently interesting before now.

To his relief, Ellis came up with their sandwiches then, and that provided enough distraction for Tony to turn his thoughts to far less fraught topics. Cassandra seemed to guess at his mood, or at least she'd decided it wasn't worth it to push the issue, because she ate quietly, only pausing here and there to ask questions about the restaurant or Santa Fe itself, acting as though she was just a friend visiting from out of town and nothing more.

And when they were done, and waiting for Ellis to come back with the bill, Tony had to reflect that there was something to be said for a girl who seemed to understand you and was okay with being quiet. If asked, he would have once said he was all for the lively, party-girl types, but now he wasn't so sure. Cassandra had a quiet steadiness to her that made him think vivacity was highly overrated.

Was it crazy for him to be thinking these sorts of things about a girl he'd just met, especially one who'd come here to Santa Fe on secret and dangerous business?

Probably. It would be smart for him to suggest that she'd really be more comfortable checking into a hotel, that he'd help her find a place to stay.

Tony knew he wouldn't do that, though. Whatever happened, he wanted to make sure he spent as much time as he could with Cassandra…for as long as he could.

4

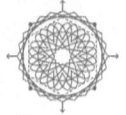

IT WAS A LITTLE STRANGE TO BE CRASHING here at Tony's house, but Cassandra told herself that it was a big place, and the room he occupied was all the way at the end of the upstairs hallway, with two other bedrooms—one used as a sort of office, and the other a workout space, from what she could tell—sandwiched in between. He shouldn't be able to hear her coming and going from the bathroom across the hall, and she doubted she'd be able to hear anything he was doing, either, unless he turned out to be the world's biggest snorer.

This was definitely not how she'd planned to end her day. By now, she should have been back in Phoenix, and the books should have been safely stored in the library Zoe had built onto the back of her big hacienda-style house in Scottsdale. That task done, Cassandra would have gone home to Tucson and gone back to work, glad that she'd been able to be of service to her clan.

Instead, she was in a bedroom that definitely had more of the ghostly Victoria's influence in the decorating, from the dark green paint on the wall to the mahogany antiques that furnished the room. The bed was narrow but had a very tall headboard; Cassandra hoped she'd be able to sleep there without worrying about whether it was going to fall over on her.

After dinner, they'd come back and watched TV for a while, neither of them really sure what they should do next. Tony's father had called and the two of them had talked for a bit—Sophia seemed to be all right, more in a very deep sleep than a medical coma, although she showed no signs of waking up. And Cassandra had called her parents as well, even though she knew Zoe must have already been in touch to let them know what was going on. Her mother wanted her to come back to Arizona as soon as she could, but Cassandra's father was a bit more measured.

"If you're determined to see this through, then we can't do much to stop you," he said. "But you need to be careful, Cass, especially if we're dealing with a branch of the Escobars here, or at least someone who practices the same kind of magic."

"I'll be careful," she promised him, right before she ended the call. "Honestly, I don't even know what my next step is right now. But I'm the best person to secure the books, because of my talent, so the Castillos need me." Or at least, that was what she'd told herself. It felt better to think of herself as indispensable, rather than a very minor cousin in the huge de la Paz family.

A half-civilian one at that.

Cassandra realized she'd forgotten to mention to Tony that her mother wasn't a witch. He didn't seem like the sort of person who'd really care one way or another, but then, she'd heard that the Castillos tended to be snooty about that kind of thing, and that the former *prima* really frowned on mixed marriages. Miranda wasn't anything like that, of course, but who knew what sorts of prejudices lingered among the rest of the family?

She told herself that it shouldn't matter,

that she was just here to do a job and leave, but….

But nothing. Tony was friendly and attractive and one of the more easy-going guys she'd ever met, and in the end, that didn't mean anything. Cassandra had never been one to lie to herself, so she wasn't going to start now. It had been a while since she'd felt this comfortable with a member of the opposite sex. She thought she might like him, or at least, she liked spending time with him, despite the circumstances that had brought her to Santa Fe. Even though she'd started out being her usual prickly self—probably part of the reason she'd sparred with Louisa was that their person-alities were maybe a little too similar—Tony had still been nothing but friendly and easygoing. She'd already started to relax around him, which was a bad idea. This wasn't the reason why she'd come here.

She had a job to do.

Despite the tall headboard, the bed itself was very comfortable, the mattress new and obviously barely used. But why would it be? In a town where you were surrounded by family, it wasn't often that you had overnight guests…and any other "guests" Tony might have brought home would have slept in his room down the hall. She wondered what the ghostly Victoria had thought about that kind of activity.

No, better not to dwell on that too much.

Okay, then focus on the problem at hand. Her father had always told her to go back to the bare facts of a case, and that was what Cassandra needed to do now. The fact was that someone had been able to get past the defenses Miranda had set up and take what they wanted. Louisa's impressions were of someone using magic similar to that practiced by the Escobars. Those impressions might or might not be correct, but they were pretty much all Cassandra had to work with. Whoever it was, they'd taken the books and left Sophia Castillo lying there in a magically induced coma.

Why didn't they kill her?

The thought had crossed Cassandra's mind earlier, although she hadn't voiced it aloud, knowing that kind of speculation would only upset Tony. But still, if they were talking about some type of Escobar involvement here—or even someone who was using an analogue of the Escobars' magic—then why had they left the only witness to the crime alive? From the way Sophia had been lying there, it seemed clear that she must have heard something, must have come to try to stop the intruder. Otherwise, she would have remained in the kitchen, putting together a snack for her son and their visitor, oblivious to what was going on in the next room.

Which begged the question...had Sophia seen the thieves?

If she had, then it was strange that they'd left her alive. It was kind of terrible to think such a thing about the mother of a man she liked, but Cassandra knew she needed to be coldblooded and logical about all this. After all, it wasn't as though the Escobars had ever scrupled at killing people before now. More than twenty years ago, they'd left a trail of bodies through California and Arizona, and the late *prima's* powers were probably the only reason they hadn't done the same thing here in New Mexico.

Except....

Maybe the thief had planned to kill Sophia, but had heard Cassandra and Tony arriving and had fled the scene before he could get caught. It was frightening to think they might have been that close to the perpetrator, and yet the theory made sense. Better to get away with the precious books than risk running up against two more witnesses and possible adversaries.

Tony had said his mother seemed to be getting better, at least according to his father's report. With any luck, she'd wake up soon, and then maybe she'd have a description of the person who'd assaulted her. Armed with that information, she and Tony could try to track him down.

Lying there in bed, Cassandra had to shake her head at herself. Even if Sophia woke up and provided a description, there was little to no chance that she and Tony would be tasked with such a dangerous undertaking. The Castillo clan must have people whose talents were better suited to that sort of thing, although she had to admit she didn't even know what Tony's magical talent was. He hadn't mentioned it, even though he probably could have slipped the subject into their conversation on the drive to Santa Fe, when she'd told him about her peculiar "shield" gift. Maybe his talent was something awesome and powerful, and that was why he'd been the one to pick her up at the airport. A more likely scenario, though, was that he'd been given that task because it was his mother who'd been watching over the books all this time, and her house they were going to, and he was one of the few people who'd been let in on the secret.

Besides, based on what he'd told her, it didn't sound as if he had much else to do with his time.

Lacking any further information, it seemed the most logical thing to do would be to talk to the Santiagos. After all, Joaquin Escobar had controlled their clan for months, and it was among the Santiagos that his two oldest children had lived since the time they were very young—basically a babe in arms, in Matías Escobar's case. Someone had to know something. Even the smallest lead might be the very thing they needed to follow the trail to the thief who'd stolen the books.

Never mind that she and Tony didn't have permission to enter Santiago territory, or that they might be following a dead end. Cassandra knew they had to try...or at least, she had to try.

Somehow, though, she had a feeling Tony would be up for it as well.

～

"Road trip!" he said enthusiastically as soon as she mentioned the idea over coffee the next morning. "Sounds like a great idea to me."

"We aren't exactly going sightseeing," she reminded him, although there wasn't much bite in those words. After all, this had been her idea.

"I know that," he told her. "But I've never been to Southern California. It's gotta be a lot warmer than here."

"Well, I suppose so," Cassandra said. "I've never been there, either. But it was in the low seventies back in Tucson, so I have a feeling it's probably a little cooler than that in Pasadena."

"It still sounds great." He was quiet for a minute, though, clearly pondering the plan. "We're not going to say anything to anyone about this, right?"

She knew they should. Protocol among clans demanded that Miranda, as *prima*, should call Marisol, the *prima* of the Santiago clan, to ask permission for Tony to come see her in California, just as Cassandra's cousin Zoe should do the same for her. But if they did that, then they ran the very real risk of having Marisol say no, and since Marisol's clan was vital to Cassandra's fact-finding mission, she knew they didn't have much of a choice, not if they wanted any real chance at finding the stolen grimoires.

Summoning a shaky smile, she said, "Better to ask for forgiveness than for permission."

Tony grinned, teeth almost blinding in the bright sunlight that came in through the dining room window. The kitchen wasn't big enough to have a breakfast area, so they sat at the dining table, an enormous cherry-wood piece that looked as if it should be used for state visits rather than a casual cup of coffee. "I like the way you think, Cassandra."

"'Cass,'" she said. "That's what my friends call me."

If possible, the smile broadened. "Cass, then. This sounds like a great plan."

"I don't know how great it is. I'm probably going to get us both in a lot of trouble." She wasn't just saying that; she knew they would be taking a big risk merely by going to Southern California without getting permission first. At the very least, they would strain relations between the de la Pazes and the Santiagos. Probably with the Castillos as well, although since their territories didn't border the Santiago lands, the situation there wasn't quite as problematic.

"It's kind of a stupid tradition, though," Tony remarked after taking a swallow of coffee. "I mean, it's a free country. We should be able to travel where we want, when we want."

Privately, Cassandra agreed, but now she only shrugged. "Preaching to the choir. I guess I can see some of the reasons behind the rule—it's always good to know who's coming and going in your territory—but in a lot of ways, I think it's hurt the witching world more than it's helped. I mean, we all come and go pretty freely among the three Arizona clans now, and the world hasn't ended."

"No, it hasn't." He tapped his fingers against the side of his coffee mug, expression thoughtful. "Although it's not really the same thing here in New Mexico, since it's only Castillos here."

He sounded almost wistful, as if he wished that his state was home to more than just the one witch clan. Cassandra could see why he might feel that way— she was glad of the way the de la Paz and McAllister and Wilcox families all moved here and there within Arizona's borders without anyone having to stop and ask for permission. There had been a lot more intermarriages, too, which she supposed the purity police might have issues with. On the other hand, it was an obvious solution to the ongoing problem of a witch clan getting too inbred.

However, she didn't feel quite comfortable mentioning such a side benefit to Tony. The last thing she wanted was for him to think she was making any kind of a hint about such a possibility existing between the two of them. This trip was all business, nothing more.

And if she liked his smile, or the way he had of making her feel as if she was instantly at home, that they'd had been friends for years...well, she could admit those things to herself without agreeing that they meant much. Besides, she had the impression that Tony was like that with pretty much everyone. She certainly shouldn't ascribe much importance to the way she felt so comfortable with him, except to be glad that he was going to be easy to work with.

Then he leaned forward slightly, his

manner becoming more brisk. "Do you know much about Marisol Santiago?"

"Marisol Valdez," Cassandra corrected him. "But no, not a lot. I mean, I know that Joaquin Escobar was able to control her after he killed the previous *prima* and her husband, and killed Marisol's husband, too. Among all Escobar's talents, that one was probably the worst—the way he was able to control people's minds. I guess his son Matías had the same gift."

"So did Simon," Tony said. "Or at least, he could control some people. Miranda doesn't like to talk about it, but I know he played some serious head games on my cousin Rafe...and on Miranda, too."

So much power, so much talent...and all of it used for ill. Had Joaquin been born bad, too? Was there a strain of evil that had somehow been passed down through generations of the Escobar clan? Cassandra really didn't want to think that, didn't want to believe a witch family was somehow inherently evil—after all, even the Wilcoxes had proved themselves to be much better than their reputation might have indicated —but the evidence against the Escobars did seem to be pretty damning.

However, she couldn't really say one

way or another, since they knew so very little about Joaquin. Which was why they needed to go talk to Marisol, and hopefully Olivia, Matías' older sister, as well.

"Right," Cassandra said. "Marisol never remarried, never had any other children. Her *prima*-in-waiting is the granddaughter of the former *prima*, I think. Things have been very quiet for them for the past twenty years."

"Except for letting Simon run amok," Tony remarked with a curl of his lip.

"Well, that. Although they really didn't have any idea what he was up to, so I'm not sure how much you can blame them for his actions."

For the first time, Cassandra saw a flash of true anger in Tony's dark eyes. "Based on a few things Miranda has said, I can blame them for a lot. If he hadn't been treated like a castoff, maybe he wouldn't have grown up into such a goddamn psychopath."

Well, he had a point there. Marisol had given Simon to his half-sister Olivia to raise, and he hadn't even known the Santiago *prima* was his true mother until he was in his teens. By then, his powers were already out of control, and he'd ended up living with Marisol for a while, until at last they reached a breaking point and he walked out and disappeared. Who knows what would have happened if he'd been able to have a fairly normal childhood, if his mother had tried to love him on his own terms, rather than only seeing him as the result of her rape by Joaquin Escobar?

Problem was, they couldn't go back and change the past. All they could do was deal with the problem they faced now.

Voice gentler than she'd intended, she said, "Yeah, they screwed up, and your clan had to deal with the consequences. But as much as you might like to say those things to Marisol Valdez's face, it's probably better if you don't."

Surprisingly, Tony smiled again. "I wasn't planning to. I know when I need to spread the old charm around."

I'll bet you do, Cassandra thought. *One of those smiles, and maybe Marisol will be willing to tell us whatever we need to know.*

Or maybe not. The questions they needed to ask couldn't help but dig up old, buried pain. Obviously, Marisol wasn't too good at dealing with the trauma in her past, or she wouldn't have handed Simon off to his half-sister to raise. But again, that was a painful topic they'd do better to avoid.

"Good to know," she said lightly. "Now, is anyone going to notice right away if you sort of just…disappear?"

Tony rubbed the dark scruff on his chin, appearing to ponder her question. Clearly, he hadn't shaved yet this morning. "Normally, I'd say no," he replied after a moment. "I mean, I'm usually running around town doing something, but it's not like I go and have dinner at my parents' house every Thursday or something. But with my mother the way she is, my father and sister are probably going to wonder why I've suddenly made myself scarce."

"Well, maybe you should go visit this morning sometime," Cassandra suggested. "Then we can slip away after that."

"Good idea. Except…."

"Except what?"

"Except if Ava is there, she's going to figure out something is up."

"Why?"

"Because her talent is reading minds."

Oof. That could be a problem. "Really?"

"Really. I mean, she has to consciously do it. She doesn't just pick up thoughts randomly. But if I'm acting at all suspicious, then she might dip in and take a look around…so to speak."

No, that really wasn't good. "You're sure she'll be at your parents' house?"

"If she said she was coming to Santa Fe to help out with Mom, then she's here. Ava does what she says and says what she does. Probably because of her talent, but that doesn't make it any easier for the rest of us."

As usual, Tony's words sounded off-hand, almost amused, but Cassandra had to think it would have been pretty hard to grow up with a little sister who could pull every exaggeration or lie out of your brain without breaking a sweat. No wonder he'd moved into his own house after graduation rather than going back to his childhood home, which was what a lot of witch-kind did before settling down and getting married.

"Can she tell what you're thinking when you're on the phone with her?"

Tony shook his head, a certain light dawning in his dark eyes. "No, she has to be in the same room with you."

Well, that was something. An idea was forming in Cassandra's mind. Maybe it was wrong to pull Tony away when his mother was still in a coma, but she knew if they hesitated, waited to get permission, they ran the risk of never being able to track down who had attacked Sophia and stolen the grimoires. "Then tell them I decided to go home, since there wasn't anything I could do here. Say you're driving me down to the airport. That'll give us a little lead time."

To her relief, he didn't argue. "Okay. But that's still only going to buy us a couple of hours, tops. Sooner or later, they're going to figure out I'm not coming back to Santa Fe any time soon."

"It's okay," Cassandra replied, even as she hoped it actually would turn out to be okay. "We just need to make sure we're far enough away by the time they figure out what's going on that they can't try to stop us."

His dark eyes glinted, and he grinned again. "Sounds like we've got a plan." However, his expression sobered almost immediately. "Um…do you actually know where we're going?"

She'd been wondering when he was going to ask. "Yes, I do. I mean, Marisol's address isn't exactly common knowledge, but I was able to figure it out."

"How?"

"A lot of time poring over Google street-view maps." As Tony shot her a disbelieving look, she went on, trying not to sound defensive, "It wasn't that hard. I knew her house was in an older, upscale part of Pasadena, and I knew it was Spanish style with a turret in front."

"And how did you know all that?"

"I listened when people were talking." That sounded simplistic, but it was only the truth. All right, maybe it was easier to pick up that kind of privileged information when your cousin was the clan's *prima* and your father a former detective who just happened to be the *prima's* uncle, but really, people dropped all sorts of interesting tidbits when talking around children. Cassandra had always liked listening to the adults talk at family parties, mostly because she never really knew what she might overhear. She'd filed the info about the Santiago *prima's* house away for future reference, thinking it might come in handy one day. "Anyway, I had an idea about the neighborhood and the architecture of the house, and so I just started poking around online. Eventually, I was able to figure it out, so I looked up the parcel information on the L.A. County assessor's website and saw that it had been in the Santiago family since the 1940s. Easy."

Tony shook his head, expression bemused. "Sounds to me like you should have gone into police work after all. Or maybe been a private detective."

Maybe she should have, despite her father's warnings. Now wasn't the time to worry about her career choices, though. They had a job they needed to do. "No, this was just a little pastime of mine. And it seems like it's finally going to pay off. Anyway, you don't need to worry about us running off with no clear destination. I know exactly where we're going."

"Good," Tony said, now looking rather grim. "I guess that makes one of us."

Cassandra didn't bother to offer him any reassurances…even if she'd had any to give. They were taking a huge risk without any idea of whether it would pay off or not. About all they could do was go ahead with their plan and hope for the best…

…and, like she'd told him the day before, plan for the worst.

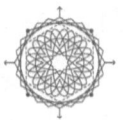

5

LUCKILY, IT WAS HIS FATHER WHO ANSWERED the phone, not Ava. Even though Tony had told Cassandra that his sister couldn't read the thoughts of anyone who wasn't in the same room with her, he still didn't like lying to Ava, as if all the years of knowing she could pick out the truth from his mind had made him gun-shy no matter what the situation.

"I can understand why Cassandra would decide to go home," Henry said. He sounded more relaxed this morning, possibly because Ava was there to trade shifts keeping an eye on Sophia. "There isn't much she can do here, unfortunately. But it was nice of her to stay over, just in case the situation changed, rather than turn around and go straight back to Arizona."

"Yeah, she wanted to be sure," Tony replied. "But she talked to her *prima,* and they decided there wasn't any point in her staying."

"Was Zoe very angry?"

"Um, no," Tony said, thinking fast. That last lie had slipped out before he'd stopped to think about the ramifications of dragging the de la Paz *prima* into all this. "I mean, she was worried, and upset, but I don't think she thought any of this was at all our fault. I guess they're going to try to figure out what they should do next."

"Just as we are over here," Henry said. "At least your mom seems to be improving. She squeezed my hand again, and I could have sworn I saw her eyelids flutter. So I really think it's just a matter of time."

"That's great news, Dad," Tony replied. And it was. He hadn't been quite able to free himself from a sense of nagging guilt at the thought of disappearing with Cassandra while his mother was in such a state, but if she was going to emerge from her coma at any moment, it meant the situation wasn't as dire as it could have been, and therefore he didn't have any real reason to stay here in Santa Fe.

Rationalization was a wonderful thing, wasn't it?

"Thanks for letting me know about Cassandra," his father went on. "Have a safe drive down to Albuquerque."

"I will. Gotta go—I don't want her to miss her flight."

They said their goodbyes, and Tony ended the call and allowed himself a small sigh of relief. It hadn't been a complete lie, anyway—he and Cassandra would sort of pass by the Sunport as they headed west on I-40.

"Are we good to go?" she asked. She'd been standing by the kitchen door as he made his call, one of the nylon overnight bags she'd had folded up in her purse sitting on the floor by her feet. The stuff she'd bought yesterday had somehow magically all fit in there, although he wasn't sure how she'd managed it.

"Sounds like it," he replied, then bent down to pick up his own bag. He'd packed enough for about three or four days, give or take. It was sort of hard to know what you'd need when heading off into the unknown, but he figured he could always buy more underwear and socks in California if necessary. "My mother seems to be doing even better, so they really don't need me here."

Cassandra looked a little relieved at that statement. "That's good news. I was starting to think whether we were doing the right thing, but…."

"We are," Tony said firmly. He didn't pretend to be psychic or anything like that, but something told him that he and Cass had made the right decision. Maybe Miranda was consulting with Louisa, trying to figure out what they should do next. However, if that were the case, he sure as hell hadn't heard anything about it. He supposed it was possible they didn't need to keep him in the loop, because although it was his mother who'd been attacked, he really didn't have the right skill set to help out in this particular situation.

Which begged the question of why he was running off into the blue with Cassandra. She'd convinced him that they could do this, but deep down, he knew he had agreed to this expedition more because he wanted to spend time with her than because he had any particular hope for a good outcome. In the back of his mind, he considered those damn books well and truly gone. About all they could hope for was that whoever had stolen them would be using the grimoires to make life miserable for those immediately around them, and not any of the Arizona or New Mexico witch clans.

Looking over at Cassandra's lovely, expectant face, he thought he knew exactly why he was doing this. He wanted to be around her, be with her. And if that meant heading to California so they could question the Santiago *prima* about the Escobar warlock who'd made her life a living hell, so be it.

"Let's go," he said.

It was a twelve-hour drive from Santa Fe to Pasadena, but Cassandra said it would be better if they went straight through and didn't stop. "We can take turns if we have to," she said, and Tony reluctantly agreed. There was less chance of any interference by either the Castillos or the de la Pazes if the two of them only stopped for food and bathroom breaks, rather than finding someplace to crash at the midway point of the journey. And while almost all cars were self-driving now, the law required that someone still be behind the wheel in case of system failure. It wasn't as though he and Cassandra could get cozy in the back seat while the car did all the work.

When they passed the border between New Mexico and Arizona, and he spotted the big sign with the striking blue and yellow sun-rays of the Arizona state flag, Tony felt a strange twinge. Maybe it was only knowing that he was now out of Castillo territory for the first time in his life, but he couldn't help wondering if he'd somehow set off an invisible alarm somewhere, and whether members of the Wilcox clan, who claimed this section of northern Arizona as part of their territory, would come out of nowhere and surround his car, demanding to know why he was there.

Of course, they didn't.

They stopped at an In 'N' Out burger on the outskirts of Phoenix for dinner, since Cassandra said the burgers were awesome and he'd been deprived his whole life, since there weren't any In 'N' Outs in New Mexico. He agreed that the food was good, but he refrained from commenting that he thought Five Guys was equally good. Actually, he was just glad of the busy anonymity of the fast food restaurant, of the sense that no de la Paz witches and warlocks had ever set foot in the place.

The meal passed without incident, and he got back behind the wheel.

"I told you I could drive," Cassandra protested, although she went ahead and dutifully fastened her own seat belt.

"I know," he said, unruffled, "and maybe we'll trade places at some point. But I'm not tired yet, and all the caffeine in that iced tea I just drank should keep me going for a few hundred more miles."

"Okay. But let me know."

Smiling a little—and wondering if she secretly just wanted a chance to drive the Spider—Tony replied, "I will. Now, let's get out of here."

They drove west, toward a horizon that was little more than a sullen smudge of deep orange. Night fell, and the brilliant desert stars came out. Although Cassandra had said she would drive, he noticed the way her head started to droop as they crossed the California border, then lolled over on her shoulder the farther they went into the state.

Which was fine. Even though they'd

been on the road for more than ten hours, he didn't feel at all sleepy. It could have been the caffeine buzzing through his veins, or maybe just the sense of being someplace utterly foreign to him. He wished it wasn't dark out so he could see more of the landscape, but that was all right. The glow from the highway and the stars overhead helped to give an impression of a sere, empty landscape, a desert utterly unlike the scrubby high desert of New Mexico, blank and harsh.

They drove through Palm Springs, then dropped down into what his nav system told him was a town called Redlands, followed by San Bernardino. The suburban sprawl surprised him, even though he knew California was far more populous than New Mexico, that the entire population of his home state was less than that of Los Angeles alone. Rather than be overwhelmed by it, he found himself impressed by its size, by all the possibilities such a place might offer. Too bad he and Cassandra were here on such a serious mission, because otherwise he'd love to go exploring with her, to search out the interesting restaurants, the best clubs.

Did she even dance? It wasn't the sort of

thing that had come up in their conversations so far. He'd like to go dancing with her, but a slow dance, so he might hold her in his arms.

Somehow, he doubted she would allow him to do that. She'd been friendly but almost deliberately casual the whole day, as though doing her best to fight the sort of forced intimacy that this kind of road trip might invite. And though they would share a hotel room at journey's end—he'd booked one at the Hilton while they were stopped in Phoenix for their fast food dinner—he'd gotten a room with two queen beds. Anything else would have been completely out of the question.

The nav told him to get off at Lake Avenue, and he wearily pulled over to the right, noting that it was almost eleven-thirty. He'd done his best to not look at the clock on the dashboard, because obsessing over the time wasn't going to make the car move any faster, but as the hours had worn on, doing so had gotten harder and harder.

Now he was just glad to cut over to Los Robles and point the car south, following the nav system's directions. At this hour, Santa Fe would have been quiet, only a few vehicles still out and about, but Pasadena's streets were busier than he'd expected them to be. He was glad to let the nav take over and guide them the rest of the way to the hotel, and then into the parking garage. A minute later, he pulled into an open space not too far from the elevators and turned off the ignition.

"We're here," he said, and in the passenger seat, Cass stirred and looked around her with dazed, sleepy eyes.

"Where?"

"At the hotel."

Voice accusing, she said, "I told you to let me drive part of the way."

"It's fine," he replied. "You were sleepy, and I wasn't."

Her lips pushed together in disapproval, but then she seemed to let it go, saying, "Sorry I conked out. I guess I was more tired than I thought."

"I'm glad you were able to sleep. We're probably going to have a big day tomorrow."

That comment earned him a nod, even as she reached down to undo her seatbelt. "You're probably right."

They both got out and retrieved their bags, then headed toward the elevators. When they emerged into the lobby, Tony halfway expected to see a delegation of Santiago witches and warlocks waiting there so they could demand what these interlopers were doing in their territory.

All he saw, though, was a tired-looking woman around his age standing behind the front desk, and a couple in their thirties sitting in a sort of conversation pit off to one side, half-drunk martinis on the table in front of them. They looked a little worse for wear, but at least they didn't seem to be paying attention to anyone except themselves.

Check-in went smoothly enough, and within a few minutes, Tony and Cassandra were in another elevator, this one taking them up to the eighth floor. No one was out and about in the hallway, so they were able to slip into their room unobserved. To his Santa Fe–bred eyes, the room looked very sterile and modern, but at least it was clean, and the beds were probably comfortable enough.

Not quite meeting his eyes, Cassandra said, "I'll just be a few minutes in the bathroom. Take whichever bed you want."

Still holding her bag, she disappeared into the bathroom. He went ahead and set his own suitcase on the bench at the foot of the bed closest to the window, then pulled out the T-shirt and sweat pants he'd brought to sleep in. Usually he went to bed in just his underwear, but he had a feeling Cassandra wouldn't be too thrilled if she came out of the bathroom to find him lounging there in only his boxer briefs.

Since the bathroom door remained closed, he hurriedly got out of his jacket, jeans, and long-sleeved shirt, and into the sleep things he'd brought along. He was just running a hand through his disheveled hair to straighten it a bit when Cass emerged, wearing an outfit almost identical to his, except the T-shirt had long sleeves.

"All yours," she said, still not quite looking at him.

Awkward. Well, there wasn't much he could do about the sleeping arrangements, except to act as matter-of-fact as possible. "Thanks," he replied, and took his toiletry case with him into the bathroom, where he took care of business, then splashed some warm water on his face and brushed his teeth.

When he came back out, Cassandra had already slid under the covers in the second bed, and had them pulled up almost to her chin. What she was trying to hide, he wasn't sure, since her sleepwear wasn't exactly what you could call revealing. Still, he didn't comment, only went over to the bed he'd claimed for his own and got in as well, then reached over and pushed the button to turn off the lamp on the table between the two beds.

"Good night, Cass," he said, although he wondered whether it actually would be a good night. Would it be hard to sleep, knowing she was only a few feet away?

"Good night, Tony," she responded. In the darkness, her voice sounded brisk and no-nonsense, not at all sleepy. However, neither did it invite confidences or further conversation, so he knew there wasn't much point in doing anything except rolling over and trying to go to sleep.

And so that's what he did.

He woke up to the sound of the shower in the bathroom. After turning over, he did his best to focus on the clock radio on the bedside table. Eight-thirty. That was actually kind of early for him, since he didn't have a job to go to each day and his nighttime activities often kept him awake well past midnight.

Clearly, Cassandra didn't have the same sleeping patterns. Her bed was already made, her overnight bag sitting open at its foot, indicating that she'd probably rummaged through it to find the things she needed to take with her into the bathroom.

In a way, it was kind of disappointing to have missed seeing her with morning-mussed hair and no makeup. She might have seemed more vulnerable that way, a little less tough. It was hard for him to realize that she had to be four or five years younger than he was, because in a lot of ways, she seemed far more grown-up, far more prepared to deal with the unpleasant-ness of adult life.

Since he couldn't do much until she was out of the bathroom, Tony picked up the remote and turned on the TV. A local news-cast was on, with a slick-looking meteorolo-gist predicting that temperatures would range from the mid-sixties at the coast to the low seventies inland.

Low seventies in early November? He thought he could probably get used to that.

The water in the bathroom shut off. A minute or so later, a hair dryer was turned on. So much for getting in the bathroom any time soon.

However, there was a coffeemaker on the desk across the room, along with a basket of premixed coffee in a variety of flavors. He got out of bed, selected mocha java, and put the cup in the machine. In less than a minute, he had a cup of coffee in hand and wandered over to the window so he could pull the curtains aside and take a look at their surroundings.

This felt like the big city, even though he knew Pasadena was nowhere near the size of Los Angeles. Even so, he could see a number of tall buildings flanking the wide boulevard in front of the Hilton, as well as on all the surrounding streets. The sky overhead was bright blue, unbroken by a single cloud, and far off to his right he caught a glimpse of tall, purple-hued mountains.

Tony felt obscurely comforted by their presence. He'd spent his whole life in places where mountains were part of the landscape, and it would have felt completely alien here if he hadn't been able to see their comforting bulk filling in some portion of the horizon.

"I'm out," Cassandra said, and he turned

to see her moving toward her overnight bag so she could put some of her supplies away. Today she was wearing the same tall boots and a pair of slim-fitting jeans, along with a plain black long-sleeved T-shirt. He supposed she was wearing some makeup, but she just looked glowing and gorgeous and natural.

Damn.

"Thanks," he replied, trying to sound casual. It wasn't really fair for someone to look that good so early in the morning. "There's coffee, if you want some."

"I do." She came over and studied the offerings in the basket, then selected the one remaining mocha java cup. Tony felt oddly pleased by her choice, as if them both having the same taste in coffee made it seem as if they would be compatible in other things as well.

He took a swallow of his coffee and did his best to ignore the sweet scent of her freshly washed hair. It was probably stupid for him to be so focused on her presence when she hadn't shown any signs of interest in him. In fact, she'd barely glanced in his direction before she started making her coffee.

"I'll get in the shower now," Tony said,

then put down his cup. There was still about a third of it left, but he figured they might as well get things moving, especially since Cassandra obviously wasn't the type to dawdle in the morning.

"Okay," she replied, gaze still fixed on the coffeemaker as she slid the cup into place.

He decided to take his entire overnight bag into the bathroom rather than stand there and rummage for clean underwear right in front of her. The air still felt steamy from her shower and a faint fog obscured the outer edges of the mirror, although she'd left the fan running. He also thought he could catch a soft floral scent on the damp air, probably from her shampoo or body wash.

Since he knew he'd only get himself in trouble if he thought about Cassandra showering in here, he pushed the mental image aside and went ahead and brushed his teeth, then got into the stall and turned on the hot water. The heat was immediate, which he appreciated; the hot water heater at his house was balky and needed to be replaced, although that was only one in a long list of issues with the house that he'd promised himself he'd get to eventually and still hadn't fixed.

Over the years, he'd gotten fairly good at not thinking about anything when he needed to, and so that was what he did now—let himself go on autopilot and get cleaned up, the whole time doing his best not to think about Cassandra, or the reason why they were here in Pasadena...or the coming confrontation with Marisol Valdez. Somehow, he had a feeling she wasn't going to be very happy about a couple of out-of-state witches showing up on her doorstep unannounced.

Or maybe she already knew they were here. He still hadn't quite figured out whether all *primas* shared that particular sixth sense, or whether only the very strong ones were able to know when outsider witches and warlocks crossed over into their territory.

After his shower, he wiped the steam off the mirror, inspected the scruff on his chin, and decided it could go another day or so before he had to shave again. With any luck, by then he'd be back home with the books in hand, proving that he could actually accomplish something worthwhile from time to time.

But no, his imaginary little scenario wouldn't play out like that, mostly because he assumed that if they were somehow lucky enough to recover the grimoires, then Cassandra would take them back to her own clan for safekeeping. Then, he supposed, he would go his way and she would go hers, and that would be the end of things.

He didn't want that to happen. In fact, he found himself hoping they wouldn't be immediately successful, because right then he wanted this road trip of theirs to continue, for them to keep searching for the thief and the books he'd taken for days and days.

Weeks, maybe.

Right. Tony doubted he and Cass would be allowed free rein for quite that long. Sooner or later, both their *primas* would reel them back in, or at least, someone in his clan would step in and say enough was enough. Miranda might not be in good enough shape to do such a thing right now, but he had no doubt that Louisa would be more than happy to play bad cop if need be.

He emerged from the bathroom to see Cassandra sitting at the foot of her bed, coffee cup in one hand as she scrolled through the messages on her phone with the other. Judging by the faint frown she wore, she didn't much like what she was looking at.

"Is something wrong?" he asked as he went over to retrieve his shoes from the spot where he'd left them next to his own bed.

"Not really," she replied. "At least, not yet. I just had to send another vague text to Zoe to the tune of 'we're working on it' and hope she doesn't start asking any hard questions."

"But she doesn't know you're here."

"No, of course not, and I'll do what I can to keep it that way. She thinks I'm still in Santa Fe, working with you Castillos to find out where our stolen books were taken." She set the phone down on the bed and slanted a glance up at him. "What about you?"

"I haven't even looked at my phone," he said honestly. "But I didn't hear anything from my father or sister last night as we were driving, so I guess that means there aren't any changes to report."

"They wouldn't drop by your house without asking, would they?"

"I doubt it. I'm in and out a lot, and

they're both probably occupied with looking after my mother."

Cassandra's hazel-green eyes suddenly seemed very keen. "And you're sure it doesn't bother you?"

"That I skipped out and left them to keep watch over her?" Put that way, it did sound pretty bad. But he knew there really wasn't anything he could have done for his mother, and it still felt better for him to be tracking down her assailant than staying in Santa Fe and hanging around in an attempt to look useful.

The remark didn't even earn him a blink. "Yeah, that."

"Not really. I'm helping, just in a different way." He went to his coat, which he'd draped over the back of a chair the night before, and dug his cell phone out of the inside pocket. To his relief, it didn't look as though he'd missed anything too important—there was a text from Ava around nine o'clock the night before, telling him that their mother seemed stable, and then another text from his cousin José about a party coming up on Saturday night. Tony wanted to think he'd be back in Santa Fe in time for that party, but he couldn't know that for sure. He held up the phone and went on, "It looks like everyone thinks I'm still in town, so I think we're safe for a while longer."

"Good. That's something, I guess." Cass glanced over at the clock radio. "It's probably a little early to drop in at Marisol's house. Do you want to get some breakfast first?"

"Definitely." Their quickie meal at In 'N' Out had been almost fourteen hours ago, and Tony realized he was hungry. Really hungry. "Ready when you are."

"I'm ready now." She went and retrieved her jacket from the closet, although she draped it on her arm rather than putting it on. The phone went in her oversized purse, which she slung across her shoulder. "Let's go."

They took the elevator down to the lobby, then went to the separate parking garage elevator to ride the rest of the way to the level where they'd left his Fiat convertible. As soon as he pushed the button to unlock the vehicle, however, a group of tall men, all in their twenties or thirties, converged on Tony and Cassandra.

Warlocks, he thought at once, feeling the distinctive twinge at the back of his neck that told him he was in the presence of witch-kind.

Next to him, Cassandra shot him a worried glance, but she was otherwise very still, as if bracing herself for what was about to come next.

One of the warlocks stepped forward. He wore a black leather jacket and had a barely visible tattoo encircling his neck, although the parking garage was dimly lit and Tony couldn't tell exactly what the tattoo was of.

"You'll have to come with us," the strange warlock said. "Our *prima* would like a word with you."

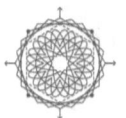

6

CASSANDRA SAT NEXT TO TONY ON A CREAM-colored leather sofa, hands clasped in her lap. The room they were in was objectively beautiful, with its tall windows and expensive furniture and even more expensive art, but at the moment, she could think of many places she would much rather be. This was definitely not how she'd envisioned their meeting with Marisol Valdez, the *prima* of the Santiago clan.

The other woman looked to be in her forties, slim and pretty, with heavy dark hair she wore pinned up in an artfully casual manner and dangly silver earrings—Mexican work, by the look of them. She sat in a leather wing chair opposite the couch, arms crossed, a frown tugging at her elegantly arched brows.

"We were on our way to see you—" Cassandra began, but Marisol held up a hand.

"Maybe you were, but you know you should have reached out to me before coming into my territory at night and with no warning, no permission. The only reason I waited until this morning to speak with you was that it was so late when you got into town. Since I knew where you were staying, I decided to hold off until a decent hour."

"And thanks for that," Tony said. He'd deployed one of his winning smiles, but it seemed a little shaky, possibly because the *prima* seemed singularly unimpressed by his looks or his charm. "It's just that our business was urgent—and my own *prima* isn't feeling well—"

"Yes, you're very good at offering excuses," Marisol cut in, this time staring at Cassandra. "From what I've heard, your de la Paz relatives were also fairly good at it back in the day."

That was a low blow. All right, from what Cassandra had heard, Angela McAllister and Connor Wilcox hadn't bothered to ask for permission when they came to California years ago, and neither had Cassandra's own cousin Alex. Still, they'd all had very good reasons for dropping in without an invitation. It wasn't as though they'd all gotten a wild hair about going to Disneyland or something.

"This couldn't wait," Cassandra said. Although she'd gotten a fairly decent night's sleep, she still felt tired from the long car ride of the day before, and she knew she didn't have a lot of patience. Besides, it was pretty obvious that Tony's charming act wasn't working, so she might as well cut to the chase. "We needed to talk to you about Joaquin Escobar."

At once, Marisol went rigid, her dark eyes glittering. "Do not say that name in my presence."

"We're sorry," Tony broke in, shooting Cassandra a quick warning glance. "But we're worried that an Escobar witch or warlock has committed a crime in Castillo territory, and we really need to know what you know."

"I know nothing," Marisol shot back. Her hands gripped the knees of her dark jeans; her hands were bare of rings, and Cassandra recalled how the *prima* had never married again after Joaquin Escobar murdered her husband, never had any children after Simon...a child born of rape. "You are young and possibly don't know the whole story, but my mind was not my own when Joaquin Escobar took over this clan. There is nothing for me to remember because he did not allow me to remember anything. In a way, I suppose that was a mercy."

Cassandra and Tony exchanged a glance. From the strained set of his mouth, she could tell that he was rethinking this plan, thinking that they'd come a long way for nothing.

But she wasn't about to give up so easily.

"What about Matías, then?" she asked. "I mean, he grew up in your clan, didn't he? You were probably around the same age, right?"

Once again, Marisol's mouth tightened. Very likely, she didn't like remembering that the man who had forced her, who had given her an unwanted child, was old enough to be her own father. "Matías was a year or two older than I," she said, although the words came out tight, controlled, as if she had to force herself to push each syllable out between her lips. "The Santiagos are a large clan. I didn't associate with him very much."

Probably because you were the prima-in-waiting *and they didn't want you hanging out with an orphan boy from nowhere,* Cassandra thought, although she only nodded and hoped her expression wouldn't give away anything of what she was thinking. "You never spent any time with him at all?"

"I said I didn't," Marisol snapped, and Tony shifted uneasily.

"That's fine," he said. "We understand. But what about his sister...Olivia, right?"

"Much the same. She's about four years older than I am, and they lived in a different part of our territory, down in Orange County. There was no reason for us to be around each other, although I remember she came here a few times when her mother—she was a healer—came to check on my aunt, the former *prima*."

Cassandra remembered hearing that the Santiago *prima* had been confined to a wheelchair for years, thanks to a very bad fall and the Santiagos' lack of a healer. No wonder they had taken in Matías' and Olivia's mother. They'd been hoping for a miracle, that the woman who had turned up on the clan's figurative doorstep might be able to do what the civilian doctors couldn't.

Unfortunately, even her skills weren't up to the task of healing a spine that had been broken years before. The Escobars had remained in Santiago territory, since the clan had been in dire need of a healer, but that was definitely a case of no good deed going unpunished, considering what Matías had turned into.

"Maybe Olivia knows something," Tony suggested.

At once, Marisol's expression brightened, as if she was glad of an easy way to get rid of them and their questions. "Possibly. She was a very young child when she came to California, but there's a chance she remembers something of her life before her mother left Central America."

"Would you mind if we talked to her?" Cassandra asked. This had been part of their plan all along, although they would have to rely on the Santiago *prima* to provide the other woman's contact information.

"No, if you think it might help. Let me get you her address and phone number." Marisol lifted a hand, and one of the burly men who'd escorted Tony and Cassandra from the Hilton's parking garage appeared out of nowhere. Or at least, it seemed that way, although Cassandra had noticed how he'd been lurking in the foyer the whole time she and Tony had been talking to Marisol.

He handed a slim, gunmetal-gray phone to the *prima*, and she entered her passcode and navigated to her address book. "Here it is—Olivia Gutierrez. She's in Temecula—that's about an hour drive from here." Marisol rattled off the phone number and address, and Cassandra hurriedly entered them on her own phone.

"Thank you," she said once she was done. "We're sorry we bothered you, but we were just hoping to get some information that might lead us to the Escobars."

"What makes you think they were involved in the crime in your territory?" the *prima* asked, looking over at Tony.

"Just an educated guess," he said. "One of our witches said the residue of the magic they used felt very similar to the sort of magic Simon Escobar dabbled in. Not the world's biggest lead, but it's the only one we have."

Marisol's jaw tightened, and Tony

glanced down at the floor in obvious embarrassment, clearly realizing that the name he'd uttered so lightly had belonged to her wayward unacknowledged son.

When she spoke, however, her voice was soft, sad. "I am sorry that he caused such havoc in your clan. I suppose I thought—I hoped—that he would find his own way to be a better person, that his father's blood would not come out in him as strongly as it did."

Well, maybe if you hadn't neglected him and tried to hide the fact that you were his biological mother, he wouldn't have been such a sociopath. Cassandra drew in a breath, willing those thoughts words away. Marisol had probably beaten herself up mercilessly over the way she'd treated her unwanted son, so there wasn't much point in berating her about it now.

"It's all right," Tony said, and Cassandra felt an inward sigh of relief, glad that he had been the one to reply to the *prima*. It was his clan that had borne the brunt of Simon's dark powers, so she supposed it was better for Tony to do the talking now. "Luckily, we had Miranda McAllister fighting on our side. She kept us from suffering too much harm."

"Yes, I've heard that she's grown up into quite a remarkable witch," Marisol said, although her tone was absent, as if she didn't much care one way or another. Maybe it had been tough for her to see the daughter of another *prima* do so well when she had no children of her own to carry on her magic. That had to have been from choice, though; Cassandra had never heard anything about Marisol not being able to have more children after Simon. More likely, she'd simply never recovered from what Joaquin Escobar did to her.

"She is," Tony said, but he stopped there, possibly guessing that it was better not to wax too rhapsodic about Miranda's gifts. "And thanks for Olivia's information. Like you said, since she was there from the beginning, she's probably the best person to talk to."

"I hope she can help," Marisol replied, then stood up. That seemed to indicate the audience was over, so Cassandra rose as well, quickly followed by Tony. "I'll let it be known that you two are free to travel within Santiago territory for the next few days. That should give you ample time to find what you're looking for. If not...."

The words trailed off, but it was pretty

obvious what she meant. If they didn't have any success—if Olivia couldn't offer any information of substance—then they needed to head back to their own territories and not linger here, poking around for random clues.

"That's fine," Cassandra said hastily. "We'll drive down to Temecula now, and we shouldn't have to stay more than a day anyway."

"Good. Then best of luck to you two."

Those words were clearly a dismissal, so Cassandra told her goodbye, a farewell that Tony echoed. Within the space of a minute, they were back out in Tony's car, which one of the goon squad had driven here while the two of them rode in the back seat of Marisol's big white Suburban.

On the ride back to the hotel, they were both quiet. It wasn't until Tony pulled into the parking garage that he finally spoke. "I guess we'd better get our stuff together and check out."

Cassandra nodded. She didn't see the point in hanging around Pasadena, not when it was painfully clear that Marisol had no intention of providing any useful information. "I guess we can look for some hotels in the Temecula area. There's got to be something—I've heard it's kind of popular with wine tourists."

Tony shot her a relieved smile. "Sounds like a plan. I don't think I ever even heard of Temecula before today, so I'll let you do the research on that one."

They went up to their room and gathered their few belongings, and then Cassandra sat down with her phone and searched for anything in the general Temecula area that had a room available. Apparently, early November was a popular time to vacation there, but she was able to snag one of the last two rooms at the Best Western right in the heart of town, and allowed herself a quick sigh of relief.

"Okay, we're set," she told Tony, who had just put away his own phone. "Everything still quiet on your end?"

"Looks that way," he replied. "At least, I haven't missed any important texts or phone calls, so I guess my mother is maintaining for now."

That was a relief. If Sophia took a turn for the worse, would Tony be willing to stay here in California and continue the search? Cassandra hoped so, but she knew that was a choice he'd have to make for himself—she wouldn't try to put any pressure on him to remain here. That wouldn't be fair.

Luckily, it seemed as though he wouldn't have to make that decision. About all she could do was hope that Sophia continued to improve and that her health wouldn't be a determining factor in whether or not to continue looking for their thief.

Since the room at the Hilton had been booked on Tony's credit card, they didn't have to do anything to check out except follow the prompts on the TV to close out the room and then leave their key cards on the dresser where they'd be plainly visible. After loading up the car, they headed to the freeway.

"You know, we never stopped for breakfast," Tony remarked as he eased onto the eastbound 210 Freeway.

He was right. During their interview with Marisol, Cassandra had been too keyed up and tense to think about her empty stomach, but now it asserted itself, growling loudly.

Tony chuckled. "I guess that means you want to get something to eat."

"I guess so," she said. "But maybe drive

through? I don't want to waste time in a sit-down place."

"Well, see if you can find something on your phone."

She pulled it out of her purse and did a quick scan on Yelp. "It looks like there's something called a Farmer Boys right off the freeway in Irwindale. That's about five minutes from here. They're still serving breakfast."

"Sounds good. You can guide me in."

It wasn't that hard, because the place really was right off the freeway. It was late for breakfast and a little early for lunch, so there was only one car ahead of them in the drive-through. A lot of the breakfast options weren't really portable, but they were still able to order a burrito for Tony and a sandwich for Cassandra, along with a couple of iced teas for the road. In less than five minutes, they were back on the freeway, with Tony pausing to read Olivia's address to the Fiat's nav system so the self-driving function could take over.

"About an hour and a half," he announced before beginning to unwrap his burrito.

"That's not so bad," Cassandra said, glad that Marisol's estimate for the drive had been correct and that she hadn't made it seem closer than it really was in order to quickly get rid of her unwanted guests. "Now we just have to hope that Olivia will be home."

Tony took a bite of his food, chewed for a minute, then sort of nodded to himself, as if reassured that someone outside New Mexico could make a decent burrito. The gesture reminded Cass that she should eat her own breakfast sandwich before it got cold, so she allowed herself a few bites as Tony spoke.

"Do you think she won't be there?" he asked.

"Well, it's a weekday. I have no idea whether she has a job or not. I don't know much about her, except she's a *nunca* and is married to a civilian. Or at least, she was." Unfortunately, there hadn't been a lot of contact between the de la Pazes and the Santiagos after the whole Escobar debacle, and Cassandra knew a lot of her intel was woefully out of date.

"A *nunca*, huh?" Tony said, then drank some of his iced tea. "That had to be rough with a brother like Matías."

She hadn't thought of it that way, but she supposed he was right. A *nunca* was someone born to witch parents who never developed any powers of their own. Everyone had thought Miranda McAllister was one, too, but her witchy talents had come out full force after she moved to Santa Fe to be Rafe Castillo's bride.

However, Olivia hadn't enjoyed that kind of fairy-tale ending. Apparently, she was the next thing to a civilian, which was probably why she'd married one. That seemed to happen a lot in those instances, partly because of worry that a *nunca* might pass on their lack of any magical talents to their offspring. Whether or not that was true, Cassandra had no idea. As far as she knew, there weren't any *nuncas* in the de la Paz clan. People with a wide range of talents and powers, but no one who had absolutely no magic at all.

"Probably," she said. "Matías sounded like a real winner, so I'm sure he did whatever he could to make his sister's life miserable."

Tony's mouth twisted, but he didn't reply, only ate a few more bites of his burrito. Maybe he was thinking about his own sister, or maybe just pondering the dark strain that seemed to run through all the Escobars. You couldn't even say it was only the men who committed such terrible acts, because Joaquin Escobar's daughter had caused plenty of havoc before Cassandra's own parents took her down.

Not before the Escobar witch's dark magic had touched their family, though.

She must have frowned, because Tony shot her a quick proving glance. "You okay?"

"I'm fine," she said.

"You didn't look fine."

"I was just thinking."

"About?"

Cassandra opened her mouth to tell him it wasn't any of his business, but that would have been rude. Besides, it was sort of his business now. He needed to understand exactly what they were up against.

"About the Escobars. About how Joaquin Escobar's daughter killed my grandfather."

Behind his sunglasses, Tony's eyes widened. "Jesus. I hadn't heard that."

"I don't know why you would have. I mean, none of that really touched the Castillos until the end, when Angela and Connor asked for your *prima's* help." She hesitated, not sure of the best way to explain. "It's kind of complicated. No one even knew Escobar had a daughter, but he sent her to Arizona to create what mayhem she could. She struck at my mother's ex-husband, mostly because my uncle Colin was married to a McAllister witch and the Escobars wanted revenge for what Angela and Connor did to Matías."

"Which was…?"

"His punishment for using McAllister and Wilcox witches to power his dark magic was to have his own magic taken away."

"Wait." Tony rested his half-eaten burrito on his leg and shifted in his seat so he could look her straight in the eye. "You're saying that Angela and Connor stripped Matías of his magic? They can do that?"

"I guess so. This all happened before I was born, though." And in a strange way, if it hadn't been for the Escobar witch's intervention, Cassandra's parents might never have met at all. "My father was working for the Scottsdale P.D. at the time. He was assigned to the murder case and quickly realized my mother wasn't a suspect, that something much darker was going on. The trail eventually led to Matías' sister, but since my mother shot her and she died at the scene, they never were able to get any real information on where she'd come from or anything about the rest of the Escobar clan."

Tony was looking a little dazed. Cassandra supposed she could forgive him for that, since it was kind of a crazy story when the facts were stated so baldly. When he spoke, however, his comment surprised her. "So…you're related to *both* the McAllisters and the de la Pazes?"

"The McAllisters only by marriage, but yeah." Her sandwich was starting to get cold, so she took another bite before continuing. "My uncle Colin is married to Jenny McAllister. Her mother is one of the clan elders. When I was a kid, we'd usually go up to Jerome to visit at least once a year so I could hang out with my cousins for a few days." With a pang, Cassandra realized they hadn't made one of those visits for more than three years now, not since her first year in college. She'd always enjoyed going to Jerome.

Maybe she could again…once this was all over.

"And I thought my family history was convoluted," Tony commented with a shake of his head.

"Your parents met during a murder investigation?"

He chuckled, then picked up his burrito and helped himself to a large bite. "No, nothing like that. It was the typical 'we're distant enough cousins that it's okay to get married' thing, as far as I can tell. I guess I just meant all these branches of the family looping in and around each other. I'm glad I'm not the one who has to keep track of it all and make sure it's safe for the various people involved to be married."

After making that comment, he suddenly looked a little embarrassed, as if he'd realized that talking about marriage might be kind of awkward. It shouldn't be, Cassandra thought, but she knew she was just kidding herself if there wasn't a bit of sexual tension sparking between the two of them. Nothing neither of them would act on, mostly because they had far more important things to occupy themselves at the moment, but still. She'd caught a couple of admiring glances, had noticed the way their gazes would lock for a moment before they both realized what they were doing.

"Well," she said, doing her best to keep her tone light, "if Miranda is anything like her mother, then she's probably going to encourage your clan to be a bit more open. Maybe it won't be so hard to keep track of consanguinity when you get a little McAllister or Wilcox blood mixed in with Castillo."

"Genoveva would probably roll over in her grave," he remarked, but that dancing light was back in his dark eyes, and the corners of his mouth quirked into a smile, so Cassandra guessed she didn't have to take his comment too seriously.

"Was she a member of the purity police?" she asked. "We have a few of them in the de la Paz clan, too. I know my parents tried to keep me sheltered from that sort of thing, but I know there were some in the old guard who weren't happy that my father married someone who was both a *gringa* and a civilian."

To her relief, Tony's smile only broadened, telling her that he sure didn't care whether she was of mixed blood or not. "'Purity police'? I like that. And yeah, Genoveva was definitely old school. She understood why we had to add a little civilian blood here and there, but she sure as hell didn't like it."

"It's kind of silly when you think about it," Cassandra said. "I mean, there's no proof that being part civilian dilutes your magic. My talent is a rare one, and pretty strong, despite having a civilian mother."

"And my talent is just kind of there," Tony said, "even though both my parents are Castillo through and through."

"What is your talent?" Cassandra inquired, then quickly added, "If you don't mind my asking."

Obviously, he didn't, because he replied right away. "Wind."

"'Wind'?" she repeated.

"I can summon wind from anywhere," he told her. "Everything from a little breeze to a full-blown gale. I'll admit that it did help a little when we were fighting Simon Escobar, but as witchy talents go, I'd say it's sort of underwhelming."

"I don't know," she countered. "You could do a lot with that."

"Not really," he said. "I mean, it does make sort of a cool weapon, but I can count the number of magic duels I've been in on the thumbs of one hand, so it's not as useful as you seem to think."

Since he seemed determined to disparage his talent, Cassandra decided to let it go. She lifted her shoulders, then picked up her now very lukewarm breakfast sandwich and ate the last few bites. Tony did the same with his burrito, his gaze now seeming to avoid hers. Was he embarrassed by what he'd said, or was he simply trying to give her the signal that it was time to move on to other topics of conversation?

It was hard to tell. Now that she'd finished her sandwich, she rolled up the wrapper and stuffed it in the paper bag their food had come in. Tony handed her his burrito wrapper as well, and for a while they both focused on the scenery passing by outside the car windows, which now seemed to be more agricultural than the endless suburban sprawl. In a way, she was glad to see the neatly plowed fields, the huge dairy farms with their herds of cows, just because she'd begun to wonder if this part of California was nothing more than endless housing tracts punctuated by strip malls.

Once they crossed over the 91 Freeway, the landscape became even more open, rolling hills dotted with low trees that might have been some kind of oaks. The sky was blue and mild, traffic lighter than she would have expected for a weekday. Then again, it was only a little after twelve.

She was sure this freeway would tell a very different story a few hours from now.

They passed through a few smallish towns, then turned off on Winchester Road and headed east before turning again into a tract of nicely maintained houses, most of them two stories tall. For all its neatness, though, Cassandra wasn't sure she could ever live in a neighborhood like this, with all the houses smashed in together on tiny lots. She thought of her parents' house in Tubac, of the wild country that surrounded it on every side. The only way to reach it was by a dirt road, and the nearest neighbors were half a mile away. She'd been glad to assert her independence and move to her condo in Tucson, but she had to admit that having people on every side had taken some getting used to, even though the condo complex backed up to open land and the neighborhood wasn't nearly as built up as this one.

"There it is," Tony said, pointing to a two-story house on a corner lot, its garage and the shutters on the two picture windows on the front of the house painted a cheerful red. He took control of the car then, slowing down so he could park on the side of the house, rather than right out in front.

Cassandra was glad he'd done that. This way, it wouldn't be quite so obvious to anyone inside the house that they were about to get a pair of visitors. She lifted her purse from where it had been sitting in the footwell. "Ready?"

"I suppose so." He glanced past her at the house, and didn't look quite so at ease as he usually did. "Maybe we should have called first."

The thought had crossed Cassandra's mind, but she decided that it was probably better for them to have the element of surprise on their side. If she'd called to make an appointment, so to speak, there was always the chance that Olivia would make sure she wasn't at home when they showed up. Some of the matters they needed to discuss had to be awkward, or even painful for the other woman to relive. But they also couldn't be avoided.

"Too late for that," Cassandra said lightly, then touched the button to open the door and got out.

Tony climbed out of the driver's seat, and together they walked around the corner and began to head up the front walk.

The air here was mild, a cool breeze sending the leaves on the trees dancing.

Just as they reached the stoop, the red-painted door opened, and a dark-haired woman wearing jeans and a floral-print blouse looked out at them.

"Hello," she said. "I've been expecting you."

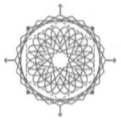

7

"Marisol decided to call and warn me that you were coming," Olivia explained as she ushered Tony and Cassandra into the family room. It was a bright and cheerful space, the walls painted a warm yellow, the furniture beige linen with blue and yellow pillows. A pitcher of iced tea and several glasses sat on the pale wood coffee table. Tony sat down on the couch and Cassandra took a seat next to him, a little closer than he'd been expecting. It was nice to have her there, to catch the faint drift of sweet shampoo scent from her hair, even though he knew that was probably the last thing he should be focusing on.

"I'm sorry about just dropping in like

this—" Cassandra began, but Olivia only shook her head.

"It's all right. To be honest, I'm surprised no one from either of your clans came to talk to me before now." She paused there, and although her expression remained serene enough, Tony thought he could catch a glimpse of sadness in her big dark eyes. "That is, word filtered through eventually about what happened to Simon, but...."

"I guess someone in my clan should have reached out directly," Tony said. "But we were all a little traumatized by what happened."

"I can imagine." Olivia gave the two of them a tired smile. He guessed she had to be somewhere in her middle forties, but even though she was a pretty woman, she looked somehow older than that, as if the terrible things her brother had done had left an indelible mark on her soul, one that also showed in her features.

Cassandra reached for one of the glasses and poured herself some iced tea. Voice brisk, she said, "There's been another attack in Castillo territory. Tony's cousin said the magic felt like the magic your brother used."

That remark made Olivia's eyes widen, and some of the color seemed to go out of her cheeks. "Oh, no. How is that possible? There are no other—I mean, Simon was the only Escobar remaining here in the United States."

"We think whoever it was teleported in and out," Tony said. "At least, there didn't seem to be any other way for them to get inside my mother's house. So it's really hard to say where they were teleporting from."

"You said 'attack.' Was anyone hurt?"

"My mother," he replied. As Olivia appeared to turn even paler, he hurriedly added, "She's okay. I mean, she's in some kind of coma, but my father says she's improving, so I think she'll be fine." Why he felt the need to reassure this woman, when it was probably someone from her former clan who had assaulted his mother in the first place, Tony wasn't quite sure. He supposed it was that she seemed so fragile, so worried. And really, she might have been born an Escobar, but she'd been raised by the Santiagos and couldn't really be held accountable for the things her blood kin might or might not have done.

"I am so sorry," Olivia said. She'd been

hovering this whole time, but now she sat down in the armchair opposite the couch. "I suppose it is possible an Escobar could have been involved, but I'm not sure what I can do to help you find the person responsible. My mother took my brother and me away from the Escobars when we were very young."

"We know that," Cassandra responded. Her voice was a little gentler now, as if, now that she'd seen Olivia for herself, she could see that she needed to be handled carefully. "But really, anything you could tell us might help. Do you remember anything of the time before you were brought to California?"

Olivia's lips pressed together, and she glanced away from the two of them, gaze moving to the carefully groomed pocket lawn just outside the family room's sliding glass doors. "I was very young. Barely three. It's difficult to remember much from so long ago."

"Please try," Tony said. He didn't want to push her too hard, but he also knew that she was their only hope in tracking the Escobar witch or warlock—if that truly was who'd stolen the grimoires—back to their

lair. "You were from Central America origi-
nally, right?"

A sigh escaped Olivia's lips, and she
nodded. "Yes, El Salvador. I remember the
heat, so much more intense than here in
Southern California. Tropical heat, moist.
You know?"

Both Tony and Cassandra nodded,
although he had to reflect with grim amusement that neither of them really *could* know.
Desert dwellers both, but he supposed
Cassandra at least had more exposure to
extreme heat down in the Tucson area than
he ever had in Santa Fe. As for humidity...
well, you might get a little right after a
monsoon storm, but otherwise it really
wasn't something you had to worry about
in northern New Mexico.

"Did you live in a city or a town?"
Cassandra asked.

"A small town, not much more than a
village...I think." Olivia's eyes shut for a
moment, as if she could visualize the scene
better when not distracted by her current
surroundings. "The streets were muddy, full
of ruts. And I remember a spire on a church,
but I don't know for sure if it was part of the
village or not." Still with her eyes closed,

she went on, "I remember my mother crying. It was nighttime. She came and got me out of my bed, and took Matías from his cradle. She took us away from the house and walked with us to another village. Someone there drove us into the city."

"Which city?" Tony asked. "San Salvador?" To be honest, that was the only city in El Salvador he even knew of, but he figured it was worth a try.

Olivia's eyes opened, and she shook her head. "I don't know. I know we got on a bus and traveled all night. We came to another town, and then there was a train. I'm not sure how long that part of the journey took, but it seemed like we were on trains for a long time. Then there was another bus, or maybe two. By then it had been several days since we left the village. The whole time, my mother was afraid— she didn't speak to anyone unless she had to, and she kept looking over her shoulder."

"Worried that Joaquin was going to come after her?" Cassandra said.

"I would guess so. At last we came to a place that was bright and hot, and where I heard people speaking English and Span- ish. I didn't understand the English, but I knew we must be far from home if that many people on the streets were speaking another language. There were many cars, some of them new and expensive. Now I know we were in Tijuana, although my mother never said the name of the place to me."

Tony looked over at Cassandra, whose shoulders lifted a fraction. This was interesting, but he didn't know how the information could help them if Olivia couldn't remember any place names.

"There is something else, though," Olivia said then, eyebrows lifting as though something had just occurred to her. "Let me see if I can find it."

She got up from her chair and left the family room. A minute later, Tony could hear her light footsteps on the stairs.

Cassandra murmured, "What do you think she's going to get?"

"I have no idea," he replied. "What do you think of her story?"

"It sounds about like what I've heard through the family grapevine," Cassandra said. "That must have taken some guts, though—to run away from a warlock like Joaquin Escobar and go through miles of jungle on foot." She paused there, frowning slightly. "I wonder why he wasn't able to catch up with them. It doesn't sound as though it would have been all that difficult."

"Maybe Olivia's mother had some kind of gift that made it hard for her to be tracked," Tony suggested.

"I thought she was a healer, though."

Oh, right. He'd forgotten about that. While it was possible for a witch to have a secondary talent in addition to her main magical gift—just as Cassandra did— usually that secondary talent wasn't nearly as strong. Even if Olivia's mother had the skill to hide her presence, he doubted that particular magical power would have been enough to keep Escobar off her trail.

They both fell silent then as Olivia came back down the stairs, something clutched in her right hand. She resumed her seat in her chair and put something down on the table in front of them. Leaning forward, Tony saw that it was a small religious medal of some gold-colored metal, probably bronze.

"*El corazon de María?*" he read aloud in questioning tones, and Olivia nodded.

"Yes, that was the convent associated with the halfway house that took us in. Of course, I didn't realize it at the time—I only knew we were someplace safe, with real beds to sleep in and warm food. We stayed there for several days, and then a man came to take us away."

"A man?" Cassandra asked. "Do you know who he was?"

"He was Simón Santiago, the consort of the *prima* here in Southern California."

That piece of information made both Tony and Cassandra sit up a little straighter.

"He came to you in Tijuana?" she asked, clearly surprised by this revelation. "I thought—or at least, I'd heard that your mother went to him and asked for refuge."

"No," Olivia replied. "That is, I know my mother asked for the Santiagos to take us in, but he came to us. My mother told me later that one of the sisters at the convent was a witch, and so she immediately recognized my mother for who she was. Because it was well known that the Santiago *prima* had become crippled from a fall, the sister passed on word that a powerful *curandera*— a healer—had come to them. That was why Simón came to take us away."

And possibly why Joaquin Escobar hadn't tried to take his runaway family back to El Salvador, even if he finally had figured out where they'd ended up. Yes, he'd made his move years later, but that was after his children's mother was dead and Matías had had his powers stripped from him by Angela and Connor Wilcox. By that point, thoughts of revenge had probably been tempting enough that he'd decided to make his move, regardless of the risks involved.

Or maybe he'd had completely different motivations for what he'd done. It was hard to guess at the reasons behind the actions of a dead man, especially one as cruel and relentless as Escobar. Tony really didn't want to put his brain into that kind of head space.

"Anyway," Olivia continued. "The convent's halfway house is where we were given a place to stay. It was a very long time ago now, but possibly the nun who helped my mother is still there. She is the only person I can think of who might know something of where we came from. I remember them talking together in low voices, but I don't remember anything of what they were saying. It's possible, though, that my mother confided in her."

Talk about your slim leads. That had to have been more than what, forty years ago?

Tony supposed the nun might still be there, as long as she'd been fairly young when the little refugee family turned up on the convent's doorstep. But still, that was pinning a lot of hopes on a very nebulous connection.

"Do you know the nun's name?" he asked, and Olivia shook her head.

"No. I suppose my mother did, but she never told me what it was."

This reply made Tony think their chances of success had to be even lower than he'd previously guessed, but Cassandra didn't look at all fazed by the odds stacked against them. "The convent is still there?" she asked.

"Oh, yes," Olivia replied. "They do a lot for the poor people of Tijuana. I try to send them donation checks when I'm able. I can get you the address."

"Wait a second," Tony said, giving Cassandra a sharp look. "Are you suggesting we go to Tijuana next?"

"Well, yeah," she replied. "Like Olivia just said, the nun at that convent is probably the only person who would have the information we're looking for."

Maybe he was belaboring the obvious, but Tony couldn't help pointing out, "Um, you know Tijuana is in a foreign country, right?"

"So?" Cassandra responded. "I have my passport with me."

"You have a passport?" he asked, incredulous. "What does a witch need with a passport? We don't travel, remember?"

"Speak for yourself," she retorted, although she looked more amused than angry. "Tubac's only twenty miles or so from the Mexican border. I've been down into Nogales lots of times."

"And the local clan in that part of Mexico doesn't have a problem with it?"

"No, because we're distantly related to them. The de la Paz clan came north from there about three hundred years ago."

Tony supposed he should have thought of that. All of the witch clans in the United States had obviously come from somewhere else, as the magic they practiced was very different from the magic used by the continent's indigenous peoples. But although the Castillos had arrived in Santa Fe nearly five hundred years earlier, coming there with the earliest Spanish settlers eager to exploit their new land grants, they had had no contact with those who'd remained behind in Spain. It was a little unsettling to think that the de la Pazes were still friendly with the Mexican clan they'd split from so long ago.

"I assume you don't have a passport?" Olivia asked, a tinge of amusement entering her voice.

"No," Tony said. "To be honest, this is the first time I've even been out of New Mexico."

Olivia nodded, apparently not all that surprised by this revelation. "I think I can help you. My husband works in construction, and he hires a lot of Mexican workers. Sometimes it's easier to get them fake papers than to wait for the government to process their visas. I have a feeling the people who produce the false green cards could also get a passport for you, although we've never asked for something like this before."

Tony assumed that obtaining a false passport was highly illegal, but did that matter so much? He wasn't a terrorist or someone looking to cause a little holiday mayhem in one of Baja California's seaside resorts. However, since even an expedited passport would take weeks through normal channels, he knew they didn't have much of a choice. He'd never broken the law like this before, but if Cassandra had a passport and so could travel where she wanted, then he wasn't about to be the one who threw a monkey wrench into things by preventing them from getting out of the country.

Assuming, of course, they went ahead with this crazy plan.

"How much?" he asked, glad that his voice sounded steady. Not that the cost was really an issue, but he might as well know what he was getting himself into.

"I'm not sure," Olivia said. "Probably around a thousand dollars."

Oh, was that all? Of course, he'd have to add that thousand bucks to the cost of traveling to Tijuana, and then whatever plane tickets to El Salvador were going for these days.

After that thought passed through his head, Tony wondered if he'd gone crazy and just hadn't noticed until that moment. He couldn't seriously be considering a trip to El Salvador, could he?

If the determined set of Cassandra's chin was any indication, probably.

First things first, though. "Can you call your people and find out?"

"Well, I'll have to call my husband Will,

and then he'll get in contact with them. Just a minute."

Once again, she got up from her chair and went upstairs, probably so she could make the phone call in private without them listening in. Tony took advantage of her absence to turn toward Cassandra. "Is getting a fake passport a felony?"

She tilted her head slightly, thumb rubbing against her chin. "I don't know. I doubt it, though. Anyway, we're not going to get caught. It's just a formality for crossing the border. Half the time when I went down to Nogales, they barely even looked at it."

He hoped she was right. It made sense that in busy border-crossing spots like Tijuana, the authorities probably wouldn't pay a lot of attention to American citizens returning to U.S. soil. And while his family background was Hispanic, his woeful lack of proficiency in Spanish would probably prove to any inquisitive border agent that he was definitely not a Mexican national.

However, these musings only pointed out another flaw in their plan. "I don't speak Spanish, you know."

Now Cassandra grinned at him. "I love that someone with a last name of Castillo can't speak Spanish. *No te preocupes — tomé español en la escuela secundaria y la universidad.*"

Tony supposed he shouldn't have been surprised. He was starting to wonder whether there was anything Cassandra couldn't do. "What was that in English?"

"I've got about seven years of Spanish in high school and college under my belt," she told him. "Not to mention a lot of practice with the de la Pazes who feel more comfortable speaking it. We'll be fine."

Olivia came back downstairs then, looking much happier than she had when they'd first arrived on the scene. "Will says he'll talk to his guy, but we'll need some pictures. There's a place near downtown that'll take them and email them for you. Here's the address."

She rattled it off, and Tony hurriedly entered it on his phone. Conveniently, the photo place wasn't very far from their hotel, so they could probably get the pictures taken and then go check in afterward.

"Thanks, Olivia," Cassandra said, her gratitude obvious in the earnest expression she wore.

But Olivia only shook her head. "I'm

glad I could give you the help you were looking for. Only...." She stopped herself there, dark eyes worried.

"Only what?" Tony asked.

"Only I'm not sure you understand what you could be walking into if you try to follow the trail all the way to El Salvador. It's not nearly as dangerous a place as it once was, but...."

Tony wasn't all that thrilled about the idea, either, but he tried to sound unconcerned as he said, "Well, up until now, the Escobars have been pretty quiet. If that's even who we're dealing with."

"If the magic felt like theirs, then they are probably the ones you seek." She was silent for a moment before continuing. "My father might have been defeated twenty years ago, but simply because we haven't heard anything from his clan, it doesn't mean that they aren't just as dangerous in their own way. He wouldn't have come here to Santiago territory if he hadn't left someone behind to manage things for him, and that person might be just as bad as he ever was."

"Or maybe that's not the story at all," Cassandra said, although Tony could tell from her thoughtful tone that she wasn't trying to be combative, only exploring other possibilities. "Maybe Joaquin was driven out because the Escobars didn't want to deal with him anymore, and that's why he tried to take over the Santiago clan."

The corners of Olivia's mouth lifted slightly, but there wasn't much humor in her expression. "Possibly. I'm not sure whether that would be worse. After all, would you want to face a warlock who's even more powerful than my father?"

And for once, Cassandra didn't seem to have an answer.

They said their goodbyes to Olivia, then went out to the car and programmed the address for the photo place into the Fiat's nav system. After they pulled away from the curb, Tony made himself ask, "Do you think she was right? About there possibly being witches and warlocks down there in El Salvador who are even stronger than Joaquin Escobar was?"

For a moment, Cassandra was silent, her fingers playing with the strap of her purse. At last she said, "Maybe. I mean, anything is possible. Whether it's *probable* or not is an entirely different matter. The problem is that we really don't know what's been going on down there all these years. If the Escobars committed the theft, then what changed to have them make such a targeted strike after so much time has passed?"

Good question. Tony had no real idea, but he ventured, "They must have heard about the grimoires somehow. For all we know, that warlock over in New Orleans—Nicholas Toulouse—was blabbing about it in some chat room or something."

That remarked earned him a rueful little smile. "I somehow doubt he'd be that careless, but you're right. Or maybe someone in my clan said the wrong thing to someone, and they put two and two together. I don't know. It's not like we're working for some secret government installation. We all know we're not supposed to talk about clan business to outsiders, but it's impossible to completely police everyone."

And in the end, Tony supposed it really didn't matter one way or another. If the information was already out there, they couldn't exactly take it back. About all they could do was make sure nobody else got sucked into this mess.

The car took them to Temecula's downtown area, which was comprised of several streets with shops and restaurants and a bunch of wine tasting rooms. Most of the architecture had a vaguely frontier, Wild West theme to it, although Temecula wasn't exactly the kind of place Tony tended to think of when someone mentioned the old west and cowboys and all that.

But he wasn't here to comment on the architecture, only to get some business handled. The two of them got out of the convertible and went to a two-story structure that had shops on both levels, most of them clothing or jewelry stores. However, one of the stores on the ground floor sold postcards and trinkets and sunglasses and phone batteries...and also advertised its passport photo business.

They went inside, and the burly man behind the counter—who looked like he might have been a nightclub bouncer in a former life—called out, "Help you with something?"

"A friend recommended you for passport photos," Tony replied.

"Right." The man paused, giving Tony a searching look with his pale blue eyes. "You need them emailed?"

"Yes, sir."

"Gotcha. Come over here."

Tony followed him to a little alcove toward the back of the shop that had been fitted as a photo backdrop, the walls a blank white.

"Stand there," the man instructed him.

He did as he was asked, and stood in the designated spot with his toes touching the piece of blue masking tape on the floor. A few flashes from the camera, and it appeared they were done. Hopefully, he wouldn't have a goofy expression on his face, but it probably didn't matter all that much. This wasn't for a real passport, after all.

"How much?" he asked when they were done, reaching for the wallet in his pocket.

"Forty bucks. Write down the email address where you need them sent." The man pushed a pad of paper and a pen across the counter toward him, then took the two twenty-dollar bills Tony handed over.

After pulling up the information on his phone, Tony wrote the email down on the paper and gave it back. The man didn't even look down at the notepad; Tony had a feeling the guy already knew the email address where the photos needed to be sent.

That seemed to be that. They went to the car and drove it over to the hotel, even though it was an easy walk. But since it made much more sense to leave the vehicle in the parking lot and roam around on foot, Tony left it parked in a convenient space while he and Cassandra headed into the lobby. It wasn't quite two o'clock yet, a little early to be checking in, but he hoped they might still be able to slip in anyway.

Luck was with them, because the room turned out to be ready. They dropped off their luggage, and Cassandra turned toward him, hands on her hips. "So...what now? Olivia made it sound like the passport won't be ready until tomorrow sometime."

"Not a problem," Tony said with a grin. He'd scoped out the downtown area while they were conducting their business, and so he already had a game plan in place. "I think we should go wine tasting."

8

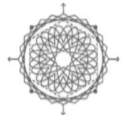

She'd never been much of a wine drinker, had always preferred beer or the occasional hard cider. And Cassandra knew how silly that sounded, considering she'd just turned twenty-one eight months ago and didn't exactly have years of drinking under her belt. So even though the place where they'd ended up—a cute bistro that offered food along with its drinks—served beer in addition to wine, she decided to go with the flow and have a glass of something called Black Dog from one of the local wineries.

It was actually really good. So were the truffle fries they'd ordered to go along with their wine, since by that time they were both feeling a little hungry.

"This is great," Tony remarked after

taking another sip of his petite sirah. "I guess it's not exactly wine tasting, but I'm okay with that."

They'd walked into the bistro because they'd both decided that an actual wine tasting would require more mental energy than either one of them had to spare right then. Even though the meeting with Olivia had gone well, at the same time, it had opened up a possibility both tantalizing and troubling.

Maybe, just maybe, they really would be able to find their way to the Escobars' hidden territory in El Salvador.

Which in itself was crazy, as Tony had pointed out. Cassandra's power was a strong and unusual one, but it wasn't the sort of thing you could exactly use to mount an all-out attack. The winds that Tony commanded might be able to do something along those lines, true, and yet she knew that probably wouldn't be enough when push came to shove. After all, they were quite possibly going to be taking on an entire village of Escobars, not a single warlock.

The smartest thing to do would be to go to Tijuana, see if the nun who had helped Olivia's family all those years ago was still ministering to the poor at her convent and had any recollection of where the refugees had come from, and then take that information back to their clans. Unfortunately, Miranda was out of commission until her baby came, but there had to be other Castillos who could offer their assistance. And if not, well, there were plenty of de la Paz witches and warlocks who would be invested in reclaiming their stolen property.

But...what if they all decided such a mission was too dangerous? What if her *prima* Zoe expressly forbade her to pursue the books?

That would be terrible. The Escobars were powerful enough on their own; the last thing they needed was a bunch of grimoires filled with dark and deadly magic. God only knew what they were doing with the books now that they had them in their possession.

Well, as she'd remarked to Tony the day before, it was usually easier to get forgiveness than permission.

"Hey, Earth to Cassandra," he said, and she blinked.

"Sorry. I guess I was pondering worst-case scenarios."

"Don't." They'd sat at a bar-height table

near the window, rather than at the bar itself, just because they'd both figured they would have more privacy that way. "I know we're already starting to go off the rails, but for right now, can't we just pretend we're on vacation and enjoying a drink?"

That would be nice. Sitting here by the window did sort of feel like being on vacation, since they were both someplace they'd never been before, and this little downtown area was clearly a tourist destination. A large group of four who didn't look that much older than her and Tony occupied the conversation area in the center of the room, and they were all chatting and laughing as they drank their wine. Cassandra couldn't help feeling a small stab of jealousy as she glanced over at them. It would be great to enjoy herself like that, to look as if she didn't have a care in the world. Unfortunately, it was rarely that easy when you were a member of a witch clan.

"I'll try," she allowed, then took a truffle fry from the pile in the bowl between them and munched it down.

"I suppose that's about all I can ask for," he said. "At least it seems everything is still quiet on the home front—Ava texted me to say that my mother seemed about the same, but that's all I've heard."

"Same here," Cassandra said. "But then, the last my family heard from me, I was going to be staying in Santa Fe for the foreseeable future. I'll probably need to check in at some point, but for now, it feels like I'm off the leash."

Which she should be. Her parents weren't exactly the overprotective type—thank God—but she also knew they hadn't been happy about her being sent off to New Mexico on her own. She had the feeling they'd both had to bite their lips and remind themselves that she was a grown-up of almost twenty-two, and so there wasn't a whole hell of a lot they could do to stop her from going on this mission.

Going to Santa Fe was one thing, however. She had a feeling they'd have a whole host of choice words on the subject of her tearing off to El Salvador with Tony Castillo in tow.

"Do you have a plan?" he asked then. "I mean, a *real* plan, if this whole side trip to Tijuana pans out and we get the information we need?"

"No," she said frankly. "Because it's kind of hard to make a plan for something when you don't even know exactly where you're going or what to expect once you get there. But I'm good at thinking on my feet."

For a few seconds, he didn't say anything, only looked across the table at her. She could feel color rise in her cheeks and wished she'd inherited her father's darker complexion. Well, there wasn't much she could do about that.

"Thanks for being honest," Tony said. "I mean, it doesn't make me feel that much better about tackling a bunch of Escobars, but at least you're not blowing sunshine up my ass."

"I would never do that," Cassandra replied, doing her best to look at him directly, even though it was harder than she'd thought it would be. "I'll always tell you the truth."

His warm brown eyes caught hers, and held. "I'm glad to hear that," he said softly.

Oh, hell. While one part of her was all too happy to have Tony Castillo looking at her like that, the more rational side of her brain told her she really didn't need these sorts of complications in her life.

Especially not when they were sharing a hotel room.

To cover up something of the awkwardness she felt, she reached for another fry and ate it, then washed it down with some wine. "There's not much point in lying, is there?" she asked. "I mean, we both know we're going in cold here."

For a few seconds, he was silent, his gaze still fixed on her face. However, it wasn't a flirtatious kind of stare, but almost a measuring one, as if he was trying to get a feeling for what she would be like in a crisis situation.

She wanted to think that she would be calm and cool, like her father. Or both her parents, really; neither of them was the type to easily get flustered or overreact.

When Tony spoke, however, it was with a question that surprised her. "But you'll lie to your parents, won't you? About where you're going, if it turns out that we will be going to El Salvador after all?"

"I'm hoping the topic won't come up," she replied honestly. "Like I said, it's not as if they're checking in on me every five minutes. I'm not some kid who still lives at home and has to do what her parents tell her to do."

As soon as the words had left her mouth, Cassandra wondered if Tony might think she was indulging in some false bravado. If he did, there wasn't much she could do about his opinion. However, she'd only told him the truth. She'd made it clear to her parents that she was taking on the mission to Santa Fe because her talent was the one best suited for recovering the grimoires. No babysitters, no one tagging along. Luckily, Zoe had sided with her on that one, because none of them wanted to attract attention, and a big de la Paz delegation to Castillo territory might have done exactly that.

"I never said you were," Tony replied, his tone oddly gentle. "It's just...I know how it can be with our families. Most of the time, they don't seem that big on independence for their kids. We're supposed to go straight from the house we grew up in to starting our own families, with not a lot of opportunity to strike out on our own."

Well, that much was true, partly because witches and warlocks tended to meet their soul mates—for lack of a better term—when they were fairly young and settle down right away. She was kind of surprised that someone like Tony would still be unattached at twenty-five or twenty-six, even though it wasn't unusual at all in the civilian population, where the average age for a first marriage hovered just below thirty.

Why had he held out? Just hadn't met the right person, or some kind of innate stubbornness that kept him from getting married and starting a family, doing all the things his clan expected him to do? She didn't think it was because he was gay; she might be flattering herself, but she was pretty sure a gay man would never have given her the sorts of admiring glances that Tony had sent her way.

"Luckily, my parents aren't old-fashioned," she said, thinking that was probably the safest way to reply. It was hard enough being around someone she knew she should treat as a partner on this quest and nothing more, even when she was realizing more and more how much she liked him, how well they seemed to get along together. The last thing she wanted to do was stumble into the awkward territory of marriage and family. "They always told me I could do what I wanted."

"You're lucky," Tony replied. He picked up his glass of wine and drank from it—a large swallow, probably bigger than Cassandra herself would have risked. Well, they'd walked here from their hotel;

besides, Tony seemed like the kind of guy who had plenty of practice at holding his liquor. "Is it because your mother's a civilian?"

"Maybe," she allowed, stealing a quick glance at the group of people drinking and sharing appetizers on the sofas just a few feet away. Good thing that they were laughing and talking, and apparently not paying any attention to anyone else in the restaurant. "I mean, she didn't grow up with our culture, so she's a little less likely to expect me to do something just because it's what everyone else in the clan has always done. But my father's pretty mellow, too—he was in his late thirties when he married my mother, so obviously he didn't care too much about doing what was expected, either."

This piece of information made Tony nod in an approving way, as if he was glad to hear that people in the de la Paz clan weren't quite as lockstep as the Castillos seemed to be. Although to hear her father tell it, he'd been under plenty of pressure to get married; he'd just ignored the subtle digs and gone on with his life, which Cassandra thought was a pretty good way to handle the situation. Whether all those people pressuring him to settle down had been exactly thrilled when he'd finally gotten married to a civilian was a matter for debate. She'd never felt like an outsider, despite being both mixed race and mixed witch/civilian, but that was probably more due to her father's determined efforts to keep her from being exposed to that kind of prejudice than because it didn't actually exist.

"Anyway," she went on, trying to steer the conversation away from the thorny topic of matrimony, "it's not that I'm going to keep completely quiet if it really comes down to us going to Central America. My parents deserve to know where I'm going. But they also have no right to stop me."

"Except that whole part about not meddling with other clans unless your *prima* expressly commands you to do so," Tony said dryly after swallowing the last bit of wine in his glass. He looked at it ruefully, then reached for the untouched glass of water by his plate.

"Well, you could say that Zoe already told me to do this," Cassandra pointed out, although she had a feeling she was stretching the definition of "permission" in this particular context to almost the breaking point. "She told me to bring back the grimoires. That's exactly what I plan to do—it just may require me to travel a lot farther than I'd planned."

He shook his head in amusement, but didn't reply right away because he was busy flagging down the waitress so he could order another glass of wine. "You want one?" he asked as the waitress paused at their table.

"No, I'm good," Cassandra said. She'd only drunk about half her wine so far, and besides, she thought it was probably a good idea to take it easy. If she'd known Tony better, she might have told him to slow down a bit. He didn't seem like the kind of guy who got aggressive if he drank too much, but….

Pushing those misgivings aside, she ate a few more fries and drank some water. Tony did the same, and remained quiet until the waitress dropped off his replacement glass of wine. Once she was gone, he spoke.

"I'm not trying to get drunk," he said quietly. "I can handle it."

"I'm sure you can," she said, her voice carefully neutral. "But it's only three in the afternoon."

"And I'll stop after this one, and then we can wander around and look at the shops. I swear, I won't touch another drop until dinner."

Despite herself, Cassandra felt her lips twitch. He'd looked so earnest, like a little kid promising he would behave so he wouldn't be sent to bed without supper. But no, that wasn't exactly right. Tony might have a perpetual boyish gleam in his eyes, but his features were strong and defined, not boyish at all. Rugged, leading-man kind of looks. It was kind of a shame that witches and warlocks had to stay away from the entertainment industry, due to the overwhelming need of their kind to remain hidden, because she thought he would have looked pretty damn good up on a movie screen.

"It's cool," she said, adding, "I'm not your mother."

He grinned. "No, you're definitely not." A sip of his wine, and he went on, "You know, you don't look very much like a de la Paz."

"That's because my mom is a *gringa*."

His grin broadened. "Does she know you talk about her like that?"

"Yes," Cassandra replied, smiling in

return. "Because I think the first time I heard the word, she was using it to refer to herself. Even she's not sure where the red hair came from, though—hers is light brown."

"I like it," Tony said. "I always was a sucker for a redhead."

Once again, his eyes were fixed on hers, now with a dancing light in them, as if daring her to give him crap for trying to flirt. And while part of her sort of did want to rebuke him for being so openly flirtatious when they were on an important mission— even if they were kind of hanging fire until they got his fake passport—the other part of her wanted to flirt right back. This would all have been a lot easier if he weren't so damn good-looking...so easy to get along with.

"I didn't know there were that many redheads in Santa Fe," she replied lightly.

"There aren't," he said. "But we get a lot of tourists."

Was that how he handled his love life? Casual relationships were frowned on in witch clans; you were supposed to find your "one" and settle down as soon as possible. But Cassandra supposed Tony could have gotten around that conundrum by dating civilians. It would be easy, and maybe a little thrilling, to hook up with pretty women as they came to Santa Fe to visit and then were just as quickly out of his life. No muss, no fuss.

Then again, she wasn't sure she liked the idea of him being such a man-whore....

"And you're only too happy to show them around town, I suppose," she said.

"Sometimes," he allowed, then added, that glint back in his brown eyes, "although probably not as often as you're imagining, judging by the expression on your face."

Relief pulsed through her, which she told herself was just silly. It shouldn't matter to her one bit how many women Tony Castillo had slept with...and yet she knew it did.

He went on, "What, you didn't offer to give any handsome civilians a guided tour of Tubac?"

She shot him a pained look. "No. Besides, Tubac's so small, a tour like that would probably last about twenty minutes, tops."

That reply made him chuckle, although he sobered almost immediately. He said, looking down into the glass of wine he held rather than at her, "So...you didn't leave anyone behind there?"

There was no way for her to pretend to misunderstand. He wanted to know if she was attached, simple as that. Obviously, there was no wedding band on her finger—or an engagement ring—but that didn't always mean something.

And while she could have told him it was none of his business, she knew, in a strange way, it was. They didn't know each other very well yet, but they were both smart enough to realize that some kind of attraction had begun to build between them. Besides, if she was going to drag him along with her to Tijuana and anywhere else this hunt might lead them, then she needed to be truthful on this topic as well.

"No," she said. "I'm completely unattached. Anything else you want to know?"

He didn't take offense, only leaned back in his chair, looking relieved. "There's probably a million things about you I'd like to know," he replied. "But I'm okay with finding them out gradually. You can just tell me what you want to tell me. No pressure."

It had been her experience—limited, true, but still—that when a guy said "no pressure," he often meant just the opposite. With Tony, however, she thought he wasn't trying to play games. He was genuinely interested, but he also wasn't the kind of aggressive asshole who would keep pushing even after she told him to let it alone.

She reached for her own glass of wine, saying, "I'm not sure what to make of you, Tony Castillo."

"That's okay," he responded with another grin. "No one else does, either."

And to that comment, she had no ready reply.

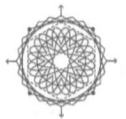

9

IT WASN'T THAT DIFFERENT FROM A LOT OF afternoons he'd spent with the civilian girls he met back home—having a drink and a snack, walking around and looking at shops and the local scenery—but somehow, the experience with Cassandra was entirely different. Tony found himself thrilling to every little thing about her, from the way the afternoon sun caught in her red hair and turned it to fire, to the sound of her laugh and those gorgeous little glints of gold in her hazel-green eyes.

Maybe this feeling was simple lust. His last hook-up had been a while back now, nearly three months ago. In a way, it would be easier if this was just a biological itch that needed to be scratched. Problem was, he had a feeling it was a lot more than that. He might have only known Cassandra Sandoval for a few days, but she seemed both as natural and as magical to him as the sun rising in the morning.

He had no idea what she might feel for him—if anything. Then again, when he'd asked her point-blank if she had anyone back in Arizona, she'd been honest with him. If she wasn't feeling just the slightest bit of attraction…if she'd wanted to give him the brush-off…then she could have lied and said there was, and that would have been the end of it. All right, maybe not all of what he was feeling, because that wasn't exactly the sort of thing you could turn off and on like a faucet, but still, he would have respected her enough to back off and try to be casual and neutral, nothing more than a partner in this crazy chase to find those stolen grimoires.

Now they were sitting outside at a folksy barbecue restaurant in downtown Temecula, where everyone was seated at long tables and benches, like they were at a picnic or something. Cassandra had chosen the place, saying she was in the mood for barbecue, but Tony had to wonder whether she'd picked it out because it was the sort of establishment that made it impossible to have a private conversation. Sure, he had no problem falling into a discussion with the retired couple sitting next to them about all the different wineries in the area, because if he had a secondary gift besides his ability to call the wind, it was being able to talk to pretty much anyone anywhere, in any kind of setting, but he couldn't help wishing that they'd gone someplace a little more intimate.

The sun had set, and the air was getting chilly, but a bunch of big gas patio heaters kept the outdoor diners comfortable. And he had to admit that the food was good, filling and hearty, so he couldn't really accuse Cassandra of bringing them someplace without caring about the quality of the cuisine offered. Even so, he knew exactly why they were here and not, say, the little Italian restaurant down the street, the one that looked like it might have offered exactly the sort of intimate experience he would have preferred.

"So you've never been to Temecula before?" the older woman next to him asked, and Tony shook his head.

"No—actually this is our first trip to California," he replied, then glanced across the table at Cassandra. "Isn't that right, hon?"

Her mouth pursed slightly at his use of the endearment, even though they'd agreed beforehand to tell anyone who asked that they were boyfriend and girlfriend. It seemed way easier than saying they were a witch and warlock on the trail of some magical books that might or might not have been stolen by a bloodthirsty clan from Central America. "First time," she agreed, then took a bite of her ribs. "Have you been to Temecula a lot?"

The husband replied, "Oh, we come all the time. But then, it's not that much of a drive for us—we live in Redlands. That's up by Riverside," the man added, as if belatedly realizing that a couple of tourists from New Mexico might not know all that much about Southern California's geography.

"Right," Cassandra said. "I think we saw the signs when we were driving in on the 10."

It was a perfectly normal response, the sort of thing someone who'd just traveled here would say, and Tony knew he wouldn't have to worry about her giving anything away to the civilian couple—or to anyone else they might encounter. Some of his Castillo relatives lived lives so cloistered, he always wondered how they managed to act like regular people when they did have to go out in public. Clearly, Cassandra didn't have that problem. But then, her mother was a civilian, and he assumed she must have a lot of civilian relatives. Or maybe not; he remembered belatedly that her uncle was married to a McAllister witch, so all her immediate cousins would be witches and warlocks as well. There could be other relations, though, people she hadn't mentioned yet. That actually made a lot of sense; he didn't know Cassandra super-well, but he got the feeling that there were a lot of things she tended to keep to herself.

After a bit of back and forth about Redlands and then Santa Fe—with him doing most of the talking because Cassandra wasn't what you could call an expert on the subject—the conversation petered out, and they all finished their meals in relative quiet. Just as she was finishing the last rib on her plate, Cassandra's phone beeped, and she quickly wiped her fingers on a napkin, pulled out the phone and read the text it displayed, then stuffed it back in her purse.

Judging by the significant glance she gave him, Tony guessed the message had probably been about the fake passport. Why they'd contacted her and not him, when he was the one who needed it and had paid for it, he didn't know, but he figured she would tell him once they got back to the hotel.

They paid the bill and left. He wanted to talk, but Cassandra walked quickly, clearly intent on getting back to their hotel room. Under other circumstances, he might have been flattered, except he knew her haste had nothing to do with wanting to be alone with him.

Sure enough, as soon as he closed the door to the modest double-queen room they were sharing, Cassandra said, "That was Olivia. The passport guy has a place he wants to meet us tomorrow morning."

"He couldn't text me himself?"

She shrugged, then slipped out of her jacket and hung it up in the closet. "Guess not. Sounds like he didn't want to leave any kind of an electronic trail with us, just in case we turn out to be cops or something. He got in touch with Olivia through her husband. I think he trusts him more because they've already done business together."

That made sense, although Tony was still a little put off by the whole cloak-and-dagger nature of the transaction. It was just a phony passport, after all—they weren't smuggling drugs here or something.

But because it had been a long day and he didn't feel like getting into an argument, he decided to go with the flow. Following Cassandra's lead, he also took off his jacket and hung it next to hers, then turned back toward her.

"What now?"

For the first time, she looked uncomfortable. "I don't know. It's kind of early to go to sleep. Some TV, I guess."

There had to be something better they could do with their time…but Tony kind of doubted she would be open to those sorts of overtures. Problem was, there was only so much you could do in a hotel room, and he knew at least half of that kind of activity was off limits right now.

"Sure," he said.

They sat down on their respective beds, and Cassandra turned on the TV and changed channels until she found a local newscast. "Do you mind?" she asked. "I figured it couldn't hurt to get an idea of what the weather's going to be like. We can switch to something more interesting later."

"It's fine," he told her. He honestly wasn't sure why she was worried about the weather, since so far Southern California seemed to be a mild seventy-two degrees all the time, but it also couldn't hurt to know if a big rainstorm or something was coming in.

While she settled back against the pillows and watched a piece about a local house fire, Tony got out his phone and checked his messages. Nothing from his father, but he'd gotten a text from his sister Ava sometime during dinner and hadn't heard the notice beep.

Mom woke up, Ava's message read. *She's a little disoriented, but she seems like she's going to be okay. Let me know you got this.*

He looked up from his phone and glanced over at Cassandra. "My mother's awake."

At once she hit the mute button on the remote. "That's great news. Did she say anything?"

"I don't know," he said. "I was just about to text my sister back."

"Well, ask if your mother said anything about the thief."

"I will."

Tony bent over his phone once again. *That's great,* he typed. *Did she say anything when she woke up?*

He hit "send," hoping that his sister was sort of hovering over her phone, waiting to hear back from him. It was still early enough in Santa Fe—a little past nine-thirty—that he hoped she was awake, nowhere close to going to bed.

His phone beeped. *Dad asked her about that,* Ava responded, *but she couldn't remember anything. She says she remembers being in the kitchen & making some snacks, and then the next thing she knew, she was waking up in bed w/Dad sitting next to her.*

Damn. It would have been very convenient to have his mother sit up in bed and rattle off a complete description of her assailant, but real life was rarely that convenient.

Another ping from his phone. Clearly, his sister wasn't patient enough to wait for a reply.

Down on the screen were the words he'd been hoping no one would ask.

Where are you, anyway?

He set his phone down on the bed next to him and looked over at Cassandra again. "My sister is asking where I am."

A flash of something passed over her features—worry? annoyance?—but then she let out a breath and said, "I figured that would happen eventually. What are you going to tell her?"

Good question. "I don't know," he said frankly. "Any lie is going to have to be plausible enough that she won't pry too much. I can't just tell her I'm at home, because she wouldn't be asking if she hadn't already checked to see if I was there."

"Don't lie," Cassandra responded. "Tell her the truth."

Tony could feel his eyebrows go shooting up. "Excuse me?"

"Well, really, what can she do? She can tell Miranda, who's sort of down for the count right now. Anyway, about all Miranda can do is get in touch with Zoe. Now, Zoe still thinks I'm in Santa Fe, so she'll know I've gone AWOL, too, but the most Zoe can do is reach out to Marisol Valdez. Since Marisol already knows we're here and knows what we're doing, it's not like she's going to try to stop us or send us home. Right?"

The slight buzz he'd had from the wine he'd drunk a few hours earlier had completely disappeared by now, and yet Tony's head still wanted to spin at all these rationalizations. Even so, he realized that Cassandra had made a very good point. Yes, their respective *primas* were probably going to be pissed as hell at them for disappearing like this, but since they had Marisol's blessing, Miranda and Zoe couldn't really do much except be angry and read them the riot act whenever they got home.

Until then...well, until then, they could pretty much do whatever they needed to do.

He picked up his phone. *I'm in SoCal. Cassandra Sandoval and I are following a lead on the books. Marisol Valdez—the Santiago prima—is cool with it. Don't know when I'll be home, but hopefully soon.*

The reply came back so fast, he guessed Ava must be using speech-to-text this time, rather than typing everything out.

Are you crazy? Do you know what's going to happen when Dad finds out—when Miranda finds out?

What can they do? he typed in response. *Like I said, the* prima *here gave us permission to be in her territory. We need to get those books back, so that's what we're doing.*

Who're you getting them back from?

Obviously, Ava hadn't been filled in on all the details, maybe because their father hadn't wanted to alarm her with the possibility that the dreaded Escobars were on the prowl again. If he gave even a hint of what they had planned, his sister would probably freak out—and so would his father when he found out…and Sophia as well, if she was lucid enough now to understand what was going on.

Not sure yet, he responded. *We're still working on it. Gotta go. Glad to hear about Mom.*

Then he muted his phone, figuring that turning it off altogether probably wasn't a good idea. This way, though, he could more easily ignore any future texts from his sister.

Cassandra remarked, "You're frowning, so I have a feeling your sister wasn't too thrilled with your answer."

"Nope, not thrilled at all." He grinned, feeling about ten pounds lighter now that the truth was out and he didn't have to keep worrying about when his family would discover that he'd skipped town. "I guess she thinks our *primas* are going to rain down fire and brimstone on us or something."

"Well, they'd probably like to, but I know Zoe isn't really capable of that sort of thing."

And Miranda might be—honestly, Tony still hadn't figured out whether she had any true limits to her power—but right now she was probably focused on making sure she didn't do anything that might interfere with her pregnancy. As far as he could tell, he and Cassandra pretty much had free rein to do what they needed.

"I'm sure all will be forgiven once we return with the books," he said, and Cassandra nodded.

"I hope so."

"It'll be fine," he told her.

For a moment, she looked as though she might reply. Then, with the faintest lift of her shoulders, she picked up the TV remote and unmuted the television.

It has to be fine, he thought as he watched a female weathercaster with improbably blonde hair and a form-fitting bright blue

204 | CHRISTINE POPE

dress talk about building high pressure and warmer temperatures.

Because he really didn't want to think about the alternative.

~

The sun beat down, bright and warmer than the day before, just as the newscast they'd watched the night before had warned them. Cassandra took off her jacket and pushed up the sleeves of her shirt, thinking she might have to buy some summer clothes while she was here. If it was this warm in Temecula, what would it be like in Tijuana...in El Salvador?

They were waiting in the parking lot of an empty office park so they could get Tony's fake passport. The guy was supposed to be here ten minutes ago, but so far there was no sign of him.

"What if he doesn't show up?" Tony asked. He, too, had pushed up his sleeves, showing off a pair of nicely browned, muscular forearms.

Cassandra tore her gaze away from his arms and pretended to be scanning the parking lot. Not that there was much to see; it seemed obvious to her that someone had over-speculated and built an office complex that wasn't needed, which was why it appeared to be completely empty. A few people had parked cars for sale in the spaces that faced out on the street, thus making her and Tony and his Fiat a bit less conspicuous. All the same, she wished they could have met in a nice dark alley somewhere, even though she guessed dark alleys were in somewhat short supply in Temecula, California.

But there was a new-looking white pickup truck coming down the street that bordered the office park on the west side, and the truck was turning in, coming toward them. She felt her heartbeat speed up a little and told herself there was no need to be so nervous. This was a simple business transaction, nothing more. If the man selling them the passport tried anything, Tony's power over the wind could blow him into the next county if necessary. Anyway, no one in their right mind would stir up that kind of trouble over a thousand dollars.

Or at least, she hoped they wouldn't. Sometimes, being part of a witch clan whose investments ensured that every person in it would at least get enough of a stipend to allow them to live comfortably, if not lavishly, tended to skew your view of the value of money.

The white pickup truck approached them, then slowed and came to a stop a few yards from where they stood. A minute later, the door opened and an innocuous-looking man in his late thirties with mid-brown hair and wearing a blue polo shirt got out of the truck.

He took off his Ray-Bans, shot Cassandra a quick glance, then turned toward Tony. "You Tony Castillo?"

"Yes," Tony replied. "Do you have it?"

"Do you have the money?"

In response, Tony got out his wallet and showed him the ten hundred-dollar bills they'd picked up at the bank on their way over here.

The guy didn't exactly crack a smile, but some of the tension went out of his lean frame. "Okay."

He approached them, then reached into his back pocket and pulled out a blue-covered passport booklet. "Check it out, make sure it's okay."

Tony nodded at her, and she took the passport and opened it. There was the photo he'd had taken yesterday—his expression was a little silly, but it was obviously him and taken recently, so there shouldn't be any problem with border agents trying to say it was a picture of someone else. As far as the passport itself went, Cassandra got her own passport out of her purse and held them up side by side, making sure everything was in the right place and that the paper and the ink used looked correct. After a long moment, she nodded.

"It looks great."

"Awesome." Tony handed the wad of hundred-dollar bills over to the guy, who counted them before he shoved them into his back pocket. "You do good work, man."

The guy just shrugged. "It's a living. Have a good one."

He got back in his truck and started up the engine, then drove off toward the exit onto the street.

"Not very social, was he?"

Cassandra couldn't help smiling. "I don't think being friendly is included in the service. Anyway, you've got your passport, so that means you're legal. Let's get going —if we head out now, we can be in Tijuana for a late lunch."

Tony's expression brightened. "That

sounds good. All this illegal activity has really worked up an appetite."

"It wasn't *that* illegal."

"Still."

There wasn't much point in arguing. She lifted her shoulders, acknowledging defeat, and walked over to the passenger side of the car. Passport still in hand, Tony opened his own door and got in, then stowed the precious document in the center console. After adjusting his sunglasses, he looked over at her. "Can you check the temperature in Tijuana?"

"It's supposed to be sunny and mild," she said, wondering why he needed that particular bit of information.

"Here, yeah. But that weather report you were watching last night didn't mention anything about Baja."

Whatever. Cassandra got out her phone, went to one of the weather apps she had installed, and added Tijuana to the list of locations. The forecast popped up immediately. "Sunny and seventy-nine degrees," she told him.

"Perfect." He reached over and pushed the button to pop the convertible top. Obligingly, it retracted, letting the bright sun cascade down on them.

She blinked and hurriedly put on her own sunglasses, then reached back into her purse to retrieve one of the elastic bands she always carried with her...just in case. After she had her hair pulled back into a ponytail, she nodded.

"Okay. Mexico, here we come."

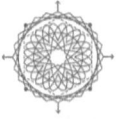

10

Tony didn't know whether it was the convertible or the burnished copper of Cassandra's hair, but they attracted plenty of attention as they traversed Tijuana's crowded streets, heading to the restaurant that Yelp said had the best tacos in town. Or at least, it was the best restaurant for Americans like them; he guessed that they could have found something even more amazing from one of the vendors on the street. But Cassandra had said it was better to go someplace that catered to tourists, that they'd be safer there. Since she'd apparently spent a good chunk of time going back and forth between her family home in Tubac and Nogales in northern Mexico, he figured she knew what she was talking about.

The restaurant had its own private lot with its own attendant, which was something of a relief. He'd noticed the stares they'd received on their way over here, and he realized that the Fiat might not have been the best choice for this particular excursion. At least it was black and not the bright red he'd first considered before deciding that was too flashy even for him, but even so, it would still probably make a tempting target for local car thieves.

They went into the restaurant, which probably had at least sixty percent U.S. tourists as its clientele. The hostess who guided them to their booth spoke perfect English, as did the waiter who came to take their drink order. Tony thought that maybe it wouldn't be so hard to get along here after all, despite his lack of Spanish skills, although he reminded himself that they were in the touristy part of town, not the slum where the convent that was their goal was located.

Although he'd wanted to order margaritas, Cassandra had overruled him, saying it was safer to stick to iced tea, especially when it was entirely possible that they might be speaking to a nun in an hour or so. Tony couldn't really argue with that, not when he remembered all too well how the nuns at the private grade school he'd attended had been quick to rap his knuckles with a ruler for the slightest transgression. Showing up even a little bit tipsy for that sort of interview probably wasn't a very good idea.

The tea was good, though, garnished with a slice of some of the freshest lemon he'd ever tasted. Sipping tea through a straw, he looked over the menu. Everything had descriptions in both Spanish and English, so he didn't have to worry about getting Cassandra to translate for him. He decided on a plate of tacos al carbon, since that was one of his favorites and he figured he might as well see how they made the dish south of the border.

Good thing he'd made a decision, because their waiter came by then and took their orders. Although Tony had been wondering whether Cassandra would place her order in Spanish, apparently she didn't see the need, and asked for her molé enchiladas in English.

With that handled, she got out her phone and went to the map application. "I figured we should take a look at how long it'll take us to get to the convent from here," she explained.

That made sense. They'd looked up the location of the convent this morning and programmed it into his car's navigation system before they left Temecula, but obviously they hadn't used those directions yet, since they hadn't known where they would be having lunch. "It's on the outskirts of town, right?"

"Looks that way," Cassandra replied. "My phone says it'll take about twenty minutes to get there, give or take."

Tijuana was obviously a lot bigger than he'd thought. The car's nav had brought them directly to the restaurant, so while he'd been looking around as they entered the city, he hadn't been paying much attention to the scale of the place. Still, he reflected that it could take a good twenty minutes to get from the Plaza in Santa Fe down to the mall at its southern end if traffic was at all thick. Maybe Tijuana was around the same size as his hometown.

"Well, even if we take our time with lunch, we'll get there before three," he said. "Plenty of time for us to talk to our nun."

"If she even exists." Cassandra drank

some of her iced tea, brow puckering slightly from worry.

It was a legitimate concern. Olivia Escobar had last visited the place when she was barely more than a toddler, and she was now in her mid-forties. A lot could have happened in that amount of time. And though they'd tried to do their due diligence by calling first, the woman on the phone hadn't seemed to understand what they were asking, even though Cassandra had repeated the request several times in her quite excellent Spanish. About all they could do at that point was come down here and see for themselves what was going on.

"I'm sure she exists, and is still there," he said in his most reassuring tones. "I mean, nuns aren't known for moving around a lot, are they?"

"No," Cassandra said. "But it's been a long time. She could be dead."

The same thought had crossed his mind, but there wasn't much they could do except go and see what they might find. If the woman they were looking for had died in the intervening years, well, they'd try to talk to the other nuns, see if she had told any of them something. Or maybe she'd kept a diary. Tony just knew they couldn't give up before they'd even started, or what was the point in coming down here in the first place?

"We'll deal with that if we have to," he told her. "In the meantime, we might as well enjoy ourselves. I mean, when you came to Santa Fe a few days ago, did you ever think you'd end up in Tijuana within the week?"

A flicker of a dimple showed next to her mouth as she gave him a rueful smile. "No, not really. I thought I'd go there, do what I needed to do, and go straight home."

"So now you've gotten a little bit of an unexpected vacation."

"This isn't a vacation," she said severely, the smile now gone.

"It can be…at least until we have to head south."

Her brows lifted. "Do you ever take anything seriously?"

"Sure," he replied. "I can be serious if I need to. But right now I'm in a fun restaurant, it's warm enough here that we can drive around with the top down, and I'm getting to see a part of the world I never thought I'd visit. I'd say that sounds like a little bit of a vacation. Besides," he added, since Cassandra was still giving him her version of the stink-eye, "my mother is doing okay, and the secret is out and we don't have to lie about our whereabouts anymore. I'd say that sounds like a very good day."

"Well, maybe," she allowed, but her tone was still grudging at best.

"Have you heard anything from your clan?" he asked. Ever since he'd told Ava what he and Cassandra were up to, he'd been expecting them to get a barrage of text messages, but so far the radio silence had been almost spooky.

She nodded but looked singularly unconcerned. "I got a text from my father this morning while you were in the shower. He asked, 'Do you know what you're doing?'"

"What did you tell him?"

"I said I wasn't sure but I was okay."

There was that honesty again. Tony admired her for being so up front with her father, but he wasn't sure he would have been as bald-faced about the whole thing if he'd been put in a similar situation. "And he said?"

"He told me to be careful and to text him if I needed any help."

For a second, Tony considered telling

her to get back in touch with her father so he could come down here and lend a hand. This was exactly the sort of situation where having a former homicide detective along for the ride might be helpful. Luckily, sanity kicked in. He was here in Mexico, alone with a beautiful girl. What kind of idiot would actually ask to have her father along as a chaperone?

"Sounds like he's being pretty mellow about everything."

"He is," Cassandra said, then sipped some more of her iced tea. "Actually, that's what's sort of freaking me out. It seems as though he should be reading me the riot act. But then, he doesn't really know what the two of us are planning. If he did, he'd probably be on the first plane down here."

Which was the last thing Tony wanted. "You're not going to tell him, though."

"Hell, no." She played with her straw, the blue stone in the silver ring she wore flashing as it caught the bright sunlight coming in through the window next to their table. "I mean, I'm not saying he wouldn't probably be a help, because his power is defensive magic and he's really, really good at it, but the more people we have working with us, the more conspicuous we are. Once we start adding people to our team, we might as well put together our own private army for a full-on assault. You know?"

He did know. They didn't have a plan yet because they didn't know where they were going, but he saw her point. Whatever they ended up doing would be done in stealth. Otherwise, they'd risk a full-on war with the Escobars, which couldn't possibly end well. Once, a long time ago, witch clans had engaged in open clashes with each other, with the result being that there were a lot fewer witches and warlocks in the world. The only way to win a witch war was to not begin one in the first place.

As he nodded, their waiter came back with their food, and they both lapsed into silence. The restaurant was noisy enough that Tony didn't think anyone sitting at any of the nearby tables could have overheard what they were saying unless they were trying really hard, but he decided it was probably better to concentrate on his meal instead of continuing the discussion.

Apparently, Cassandra was of the same mind—or maybe she was just really hungry —because she remained silent as well, attacking her huge plate of molé and rice and beans as if she hadn't eaten for days.

Well, to be fair, they hadn't had much of a breakfast, just a muffin and coffee from the breakfast bar their hotel in Temecula had offered.

His tacos were amazing, and the beans the best he'd ever had, although he knew he would never mention that particular tidbit to his Great-Aunt Rosa, who prided herself on her cooking and would be highly offended if he even dared to hint that someone else's *frijoles* might surpass hers.

They slowed down enough to comment on the food, but it seemed clear that Cassandra wanted to get on with their mission, because she went quiet again after they'd exchanged a few superlatives. Faster than he'd thought, they were done with their meal and he'd handed his credit card over to the waiter. At least Tony had remembered to inform his bank that he'd be traveling in Mexico and Central America, so he wasn't too worried about getting hit with a sudden hold on his account because of a questionable transaction.

Within a few minutes, he and Cassandra were back in the car, and he engaged the nav so it would take them to the convent Olivia had visited so many years before. They didn't have to travel very far before the streets around them grew narrower and dirtier, very unlike the touristy area they'd left behind. Despite the warm sun beating down on their heads, Tony wondered if he shouldn't have put the convertible top back up. They were getting a lot of stares, and not all of them were friendly. In fact, some of them were downright hostile, as if those shabbily dressed men and women were wondering at the temerity of the two *gringos* in the sports car for daring to come into this part of town.

He sent a quick glance over at Cassandra, wondering if she'd noticed. Being Cassandra, of course she had. However, she didn't look worried. If anything, her expression was sad.

"There's still a lot of poverty here," she said quietly. "Things have been getting better lately, but change doesn't happen overnight. But I don't think we have anything we need to worry about."

"If you say so," he responded, knowing how dubious he sounded.

"I do. I've never been to Tijuana before, of course, but I've spent a lot of time in Mexico."

She'd told him that before, and he figured he needed to take her words at face value. Even so, he found himself hoping the convent had a private parking lot the way the restaurant had. Otherwise, he'd be worrying the whole time they were inside talking to the nun they'd been looking for… if she was even there. This still could be a very short trip.

Unfortunately, when they reached their destination, Tony saw immediately that his hopes of a private parking lot had been more than slightly optimistic. The convent itself had a high wall around it, but the only place to park was on the street. Immediately next to the convent was a long, low building that had a steady stream of people coming and going.

"*La casa de los pobres,*" Cassandra murmured as he took the closest parking spot he could find, about half a block away. "That's probably where Olivia and her family stayed when they were here. The convent gives people a place to sleep, has a kitchen staff. Or at least, that's what their website said."

Of course the convent had a website. He looked around at the beat-up vehicles parked on the street and sighed. "I might as well put up a 'please steal me' sign on this thing."

To his surprise, Cassandra grinned. "Have you already forgotten what my talent is? I'll put a shield around the car— no one will be able to see the shield, but if anyone tries to get close, they're going to get the mother of all electric shocks. No one's going to take your car."

Actually, he had forgotten all about her gift. He wanted to shake his head at himself, but he decided that would be a waste of energy. "Oh, well, in that case…."

He put up the top, and then they both got out. Cassandra paused for a moment, hand outstretched. Tony couldn't be sure, but he thought he saw just the briefest shimmer of a pale orange light emerge from her fingertips and travel toward the Fiat. When he blinked, though, the light had disappeared.

"It's safe," she said. "Let's go."

They had to wait for a rusty aqua-colored pickup truck loaded with beat-up furniture to pass them. Then they crossed the street and paused in front of the convent.

"Do we go in here, or over to the soup kitchen?" Tony asked.

"Let's start with the convent," Cassandra replied after pausing for a second or two to consider his question. "It's a lot less hectic here. If our nun's still around and working at the facility next door, they can send us over there if they need to."

He nodded, then lifted the heavy knocker on the arched front door and tapped a few times. Belatedly, he wondered if the nuns would even let him in. Were men allowed in these sorts of places?

The door opened, and a young woman —well, not much more than a girl, probably younger than Cassandra—peered out at them with wide, dark eyes. She wore a short veil and a plain dress, and Tony guessed that she was probably a novice, not yet a full-fledged nun.

"¿Puedo ayudarlos?" she asked.

Tony shot a helpless look at Cassandra, who smiled slightly and responded, "Por favor—estamos buscando a alguien que trabajó aquí hace mucho tiempo." In an undertone, she added, "I told her we're looking for someone who used to work here a long time ago."

The novice frowned then said, "Puedo llevarlos a ver a la Madre Superiora. Venir de esta manera, por favor."

She opened the door a little further and

gestured for the two of them to come inside. Cassandra hadn't offered a translation, but Tony thought the girl was saying she would take them to talk to the Mother Superior. Good. She would probably know who they were talking about...or at least, he hoped she would.

They went down a hallway with white-plastered walls and shiny red tile on the floor. Crucifixes and religious art hung everywhere, and overhead was a large wrought-iron light fixture. Even though it was a warm day outside, in here the air was quite cool, although he didn't see any air conditioning vents anywhere. Maybe the building itself was comfortable because of its thick adobe walls.

The novice paused at a closed door, then knocked and said, "*¿Madre Superiora? Hay algunas personas a quienes les gustaría hablar con usted.*"

After a brief pause, the door opened, and an older woman with a kindly lined face looked out at them. Seeing her, Tony felt hopeful. She certainly looked as if she could have been here for forty years or more.

"*Gracías, María,*" the Mother Superior said to the girl. Then her gaze traveled to

Cassandra and Tony. "Come in," the woman went on, her English heavily accented but certainly intelligible.

The two of them followed her into what had to be her office. A computer that looked at least ten years old sat on the big wooden desk, and an old-fashioned metal tray held a stack of paperwork.

"Please, sit down," the Mother Superior said, indicating a pair of banged-up wooden chairs that faced the desk. "What is it I can do for you?"

Tony tilted his head slightly, indicating that he wanted Cassandra to reply. He didn't know why, but he got the feeling that the elderly nun in front of them might respond better to a request coming from another woman.

Cassandra cleared her throat. "We're looking for a nun who used to work in the Casa de los Pobres."

"Do you know her name?"

"Unfortunately, no." Cassandra paused. Trying to figure out how much of the story was safe to tell? After that brief hesitation, she continued. "This would have been a long time ago—around forty years. She helped a woman who was fleeing a bad marriage. The woman would have had a small girl with her, a toddler, and a baby who was probably less than a year old."

The Mother Superior gave her a sad smile. "That is a familiar story around here, I am afraid. I have only been at the convent for twenty-two years, so I would not have been here when this family arrived."

"Oh," Cassandra said, disappointment clear in her voice.

"But," the elderly nun went on, "Sister María Consilio has been with us that long, and has worked at the Casa de los Pobres for most of that time. It's possible she would know who you're speaking of."

"Can we talk to her?" Tony broke in, unable to contain his eagerness. "It's really important."

The Mother Superior shook her head. "I am afraid she is not here today. She and another of the sisters have traveled further south to a sister convent to take some donations to them."

Damn it. Disappointment rippled through him, but Cassandra seemed to take this setback in stride.

"When will she be back?"

"Tomorrow," the Mother Superior said. "Sometime early in the morning, most likely, but it is probably better if you come back to speak with her no earlier than eleven, in case she is delayed for some reason."

"Tomorrow morning would be wonderful," Cassandra said. "Thank you, Mother Superior."

"It is no problem." The older woman's gaze moved to Tony for a second or two before traveling back to Cassandra, as if trying to read something of their reason for coming all this way. "It is very important that you see her, isn't it?"

"Yes," Cassandra replied. "She might be the only person in the world who has the information we need."

"In that case, I am glad you found us," the Mother Superior said. "By the grace of God, Sister María Consilio will be able to provide it."

"I guess we'll find out tomorrow," Tony told her. This small delay was nothing. Actually, he was glad of it in a way, since it would give him another evening to hang out with Cassandra—and would keep them from having to travel to El Salvador for at least another day.

"Yes, I suppose you shall." The Mother Superior added, "We will see you then.

Come around eleven, I think. That should be safe enough."

The request seemed to be her way of getting rid of them, but Tony didn't mind. They'd gotten the valuable intel that their nun was still alive, and they could wait a few more hours to hear her story.

"Thank you, Mother Superior," Cassandra said.

They said their goodbyes, and a moment later, were back out on the street. As they approached the Fiat where it was parked, a skinny guy, not much more than a teenager, hurried past them, muttering under his breath and rubbing his hand. Tony looked at him as he went, then shot a mystified glance at Cassandra. "What was that about?"

"He was complaining about the *pinche gringos* and their fancy car security systems," she answered with a grin. "Sounds like someone tried to get into your car and got zapped by my shield. I told you it would work."

Apparently. Tony couldn't keep himself from smiling, too, although he kind of wished he'd been outside to see the guy get shocked by the shield Cassandra had put in place. His initial reaction probably had been priceless.

Once they were almost at the car, she lifted a hand, waving her fingers. For just a second, a shimmer of orange light surrounded the Fiat before disappearing. "Okay, it's gone. Let's go."

That sounded like a great idea to him, except…. "Where exactly are we going?"

"Back to Temecula, I guess," she replied.

He pressed the fob to unlock the doors. Once they were inside and putting on their seat belts, he shook his head. "Why not stay here? We'd have to find a new place to stay in Temecula anyway, since we've already checked out."

"Stay in Tijuana?" Judging by her expression, Cassandra didn't look too excited by his suggestion.

"Sure," he replied. "I know I've got my passport and everything, but I can't help thinking that the fewer times we go back and forth over the border, the better. If we stay in Tijuana, there are probably fewer things that could go wrong and keep us from meeting from Sister María Whatsis tomorrow morning."

"Consilio," Cassandra said absently. Now she was frowning slightly, as if wrestling inwardly with all the possible upsides and downsides of staying here in Baja for the night.

"Whatever. There have to be a few decent hotels here, right?"

"Probably. I mean, Tijuana gets a lot of tourists. Let me check and see if there are any rooms, though."

She dug her phone out of her purse. A few more suspicious characters wandered past the car, and Tony wondered if he should just send the vehicle back to the restaurant where they'd eaten lunch, since that was the only destination here that was currently programmed into it. However, since those passersby kept going once they realized the Fiat had a couple of people sitting in it, he figured it was probably safe enough to sit here…as long as it wasn't for *too* long.

"Found something," Cassandra said. "But the only room they have available is their presidential suite."

Ouch. He had money, but there was no need to go crazy. "How much?" he asked.

She chuckled. "Relax. It's Baja. A presidential suite in a four-star hotel isn't much more than we were paying for our room in Temecula."

Well, then. That put a different spin on things. A night here with Cassandra, in one of the city's fanciest hotels? Who knew what might happen?

"Go for it," he said.

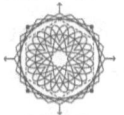

11

SHE COULD HAVE BEEN AT A LUXURY HOTEL IN downtown Phoenix, or maybe even Los Angeles, although they hadn't made it that far during their whirlwind trip to Southern California. The room was large and clean and modern, with a television embedded in a wall that separated the sleeping area from the sitting area, a huge bathroom with marble countertops, and elegant shutters opening on a balcony that offered an absolutely breathtaking view of downtown Tijuana.

Just one catch…there was only one bed. An oversized king with a pristine white duvet, the kind of bed that invited you to sink down onto it, sure, but….

"I can sleep on the couch," Tony said quickly, apparently noting her dismay.

The couch was an enormous velvet Chesterfield affair, certainly long enough to accommodate Tony's tall form, but Cassandra didn't like the idea of making him sleep on a couch, no matter how luxurious it might look.

"Oh, that's okay," she replied, trying to keep her tone as light as possible. "That's a really big bed. I'm pretty sure we can both fit on it without kicking each other in the middle of the night."

He grinned, offering a flash of white teeth she'd come to appreciate more and more. While he was handsome at any time, there was something about that smile….

"Are you saying you're a kicker?" he asked.

"No," she said at once, trying not to sound offended. "I actually don't move around very much. So I really don't think there'll be a problem."

"If you say so." He went to one of the closets—the suite was equipped with two—and set his single piece of luggage on the rack inside. "What now?"

There was a question. It wasn't quite three, way too early to even think about eating. She really wasn't used to having a lot of time on her hands that she needed to kill, but here they were. They had to figure out something to do to keep them occupied until the next afternoon.

Well, she supposed they could simply go exploring, just like regular tourists. A little shopping wouldn't hurt, either, since the replacement clothes she'd purchased in Santa Fe were too heavy for Tijuana, let alone El Salvador...if that was where they actually ended up.

"We can wander," she said. "It should be safe enough as long as we stick to the touristy parts of town. Is that okay?"

"Sure," he responded. "And then we can come back for drinks. There's a rooftop bar here." He waved a hand at the hotel brochure that sat on the table in the sitting area.

As much as she would have liked to shoot that idea down, Cassandra knew her chances of dissuading Tony from having rooftop margaritas at sunset was roughly the same as having their book thief show up on the doorstep of their hotel room and offer to hand over the stolen grimoires. "Sounds like fun," she said, although she guessed she didn't sound nearly as enthusiastic as Tony would have liked.

His grin widened, but he didn't comment. "Then let's get going."

They decided to walk because it was a nice day, and the hotel was located on a wide, tree-lined street that seemed to invite strolling. It was hard to believe this upscale area was in the same city as the ghetto where the convent was located, but then, she supposed almost every city had its rich and poor neighborhoods.

And she had to admit that Tony seemed up for just about anything. He was just as content to wait while she went into a boutique and picked up a couple of embroidered, boho-looking sleeveless tops as he'd been when she stopped into a jewelry store and made a purchase of a pair of earrings that would have made Frida Kahlo proud, intricate drops with silver birds and little pieces of polished pale pink coral.

Cassandra knew she didn't really need the earrings, but they went with the embroidery on one of the tops she'd just bought, and she knew for a fact that the price was better than anything she would have paid in the U.S. Besides, it felt good to do something so frivolous, to act as though she had nothing better to do than spend an afternoon shopping. Once they'd met with Sister María Consilio, there was a very good chance she and Tony would have very little opportunity to do something so silly and fun.

Their wanderings had slowly taken them out of the touristy district where the hotel was located, and into what seemed to be a neighborhood more for locals, with *panaderias* whose fresh-baked goods smelled sweet and succulent even as you walked past their open doorways. After her huge lunch, Cassandra wasn't hungry yet, but she had to fight the urge to go in and fill up on all sorts of unnecessary carbs.

Tony obviously noticed as well, because he sniffed the air appreciatively and said, "Maybe we should go in and get a few things for breakfast."

"The hotel provides breakfast," she pointed out, and he looked a little crestfallen.

"Right. I'd forgotten about that."

However, they'd only taken a few more steps before he perked up and pointed at a small stucco building across the street. In the window was a neon sign depicting an outstretched hand.

"Let's get our palms read," he said. "It'll be fun."

She had more than a few misgivings about that. "Oh, come on—you know most 'psychics' are just civilians looking to make a quick buck. Anyone who's a real witch doesn't advertise her services like that."

"So?" He stood there, hands in his pockets, rocked back slightly on his heels, as if he didn't have a care in the world. "We'll know that going in, so it's not like she can upsell us on something, right?"

Cassandra wanted to ask how he was so sure the palm reader in question was a woman, but in general, it was usually women who owned those sorts of psychic-based businesses. "I don't see what the point is if we know in advance that she's not going to tell us anything useful."

"Because it's something to do," he said. "That's all. I'll pay."

"Like I care about that."

"Still. It was my idea, so I should pay for it." He reached over and took her free hand, the one that wasn't holding her packages, and tugged on it. "Come on."

Maybe it was the sensation of his fingers twined with hers. Or maybe it was the devilish grin he sent her, movie-star incandescent as he stood there with the sunlight shining on his near-black hair and his laughing eyes nearly hidden by his sunglasses. Whatever the reason, Cassandra decided it wasn't worth protesting.

Besides, she had realized just then that she really liked him holding her hand.

Uh-oh.

They waited for an opening in traffic, then hurried across the street. Once they were safely on the other side, Tony let go of her hand, casually, not making a big deal of it. She gave him an uncertain smile because she wasn't really sure what else she should do. For all she knew, he'd only reached out to her to offer a little extra encouragement, and then had kept holding on because he'd realized the street was busy enough that it was safer for them to hold hands until they'd crossed.

Either way, she thought she could still feel the pressure of his fingers on hers, which was really silly. She was an adult woman, not some kid with a sixth-grade crush.

Adjusting the strap of her purse on her shoulder helped a little. Now that they stood in front of the palm reader's storefront, Cassandra could see the bead curtain that obscured the building's one window overlooking the street, and the little sign in the window that said, in both English and Spanish, that the shop was open every day except Sunday, 11 a.m. to 6 p.m., with other hours available by appointment.

"Great, she's open," Tony said, and leaned forward to press the buzzer next to the door.

So much for going about this logically. It might have been nice to mentally prepare herself, to think of something innocuous to ask the palm reader that didn't involve anything having to do with witches, warlocks, or stolen grimoires, but she wasn't given that chance, because the door opened almost at once.

The woman gazing out at them didn't look much like a civilian's idea of a fortune teller. She was probably in her late thirties or early forties, elegant rather than beautiful, with her long nose and sharp cheekbones. Her black hair was pulled back into a low chignon at the back of her neck, and she wore dangling earrings not unlike the ones Cassandra had just purchased, except set with garnet beads rather than coral. No gypsy shawls or wild colors, either, but a plain black dress with a low, rounded collar and full mid-calf skirt.

However, the most striking thing about her was the immediate zing Cassandra felt somewhere on the back of her neck, the little tingle she always got whenever she first met another witch or warlock. Tony obviously felt it, too, because his eyes widened.

"You're—" he began, but the strange witch immediately shook her head.

"Don't," was all she said—in English—but it was enough to silence him. Opening the door wider, she stood aside, an obvious invitation for them to enter.

Well, they'd gone this far. Besides, Cassandra wanted to know why a witch was working so openly as a fortune-teller. Usually, her kind did everything they could to conceal their powers.

Once she'd shut the door behind them, the woman said, in perfect English, "I am Consuelo Vega, of the Navarro clan. I had not heard that any American witches or warlocks had been given permission to visit Tijuana."

Of course she hadn't, because neither of them had bothered to ask. Inwardly, Cassandra had been hoping that she and

Tony would be in and out so quickly that no one would have time to take note of their presence. She hadn't counted on staying here overnight.

Not that she would have even known who to contact. She supposed that Marisol Valdez, *prima* of the Santiagos, probably would have had the information for the Navarro clan's leader, just because their two territories were contiguous.

Well, done was done, so about all Cassandra could do was pray that she and Tony hadn't made too serious a gaffe. "We're sorry about that," she said. "Honestly, we'd planned to come to Tijuana for a quick day trip and then leave, but our plans changed."

For a moment, Consuelo was silent, appearing to take their measure. Then she nodded, and a faint smile touched her red-lacquered lips. "Yes, I can see there is no harm in you. But...I fear you may bring harm to yourselves, if you continue on your current course."

"What do you mean?" Tony asked. His expression was still open, friendly, but Cassandra had noticed the way his eyes narrowed slightly before he spoke. "Are you a seer?"

"That is my gift," she replied. "And I see some kind of darkness following you, even though that darkness is not within you."

Although a chill inched its way down her spine, Cassandra couldn't help thinking that the seer's words seemed like a fairly accurate assessment of the situation. "We have something we're handling," she said carefully. "That's about all I can say about it."

Consuelo smiled. "You may keep your secrets. Although I have to wonder why you would come to visit a teller of fortunes if you did not want to know what the future held for you."

"Well, we didn't know you were a witch," Tony put in, smiling his most charming smile. "We thought you were a civilian and it was just something we could do for fun."

That smile didn't seem to have much effect on the Navarro witch. She crossed her arms, lifting an elegant eyebrow at the same time. "Even civilians sometimes have more insight than you might imagine," she told him. "In general, it is not a good idea to ask questions of anyone unless you are prepared to hear the answer."

Cassandra couldn't argue with that

statement. Trying to look contrite, she said, "I'd be happy to speak to your *prima* if that would help."

"It is no matter," Consuelo replied with an elegant lift of her shoulders. "The *prima* is my sister, and so I can guess what she would say to you. Which is...you have a pass this time, but do not let it happen again."

These words were somewhat reassuring, although they still held a vague threat. Right then, Cassandra understood that she and Tony needed to conclude their business here the next day and then get out, no matter what else happened. "We understand," she said. "Right, Tony?"

"Absolutely," he said. "Really, we would have come and gone already, except the person we needed to speak to is out of town until tomorrow. After that, we'll be out of your hair."

This comment made Consuelo frown slightly, but then she nodded. "Interesting idiom," she said. "But appropriate, I suppose. Now," she went on, her tone becoming more brisk, "which one of you would like your palm read?"

Cassandra and Tony exchanged a glance. "I don't think that's necessary

—" she began, but Tony stepped forward, hand outstretched.

"I want to."

That small, secret smile touched the seer's lips again. "Excellent," she said. "This way."

She led the two of them through a beaded curtain and into a smaller room toward the back of the building. In here, the walls had been painted a deep reddish-brown, and very old-looking religious icons and crosses hung everywhere. A single bookcase of pale oak was placed against the far wall, and on top of it were a series of carved soapstone candleholders, each of them containing a single lit votive.

"You can sit over there," Consuelo told Cassandra, pointing toward a bench that occupied the spot along the wall next to the door. "Please do not speak during the reading."

This command vaguely irritated her, because even though she'd never had any reason to visit a palm reader, she knew enough to watch silently and not interfere. She gave the seer a brief nod and sat down on the bench, setting her purse and shopping bags next to her.

Consuelo led Tony over to a small table

covered in an embroidered shawl. A pair of armless chairs had been placed on either side of it, and she went around the table and sat down behind it, leaving the other chair for Tony. He seated himself as well, looking vaguely uneasy now that he'd committed to this course of action.

Well, this was all your idea, Cassandra thought sourly. *Maybe next time you'll listen to me.*

"Your hand, please," Consuelo said, and Tony extended his right hand to her. For a moment, Cassandra recalled how good it had felt to have those strong fingers holding hers, and wondered if the Navarro witch might be thinking the same thing. But no, that was foolish. Consuelo had to have held hundreds of hands during her career.

For a long moment, the seer didn't say anything, only peered down at Tony's upraised palm, her brows drawing together slightly. At last she spoke, her voice quiet, musing. "You have a long lifeline," she said as she traced along the line in question with the tip of one finger.

"Well, that's good, isn't it?" he asked, obviously doing his best to sound cheerful.

"Yes, but you see this bifurcation here?" She stopped, finger resting on a spot that

Cassandra couldn't see from her current vantage point. "This means you will face a great upheaval, something that will change your life forever. I think this will happen in the very near future."

Despite herself, Cassandra couldn't quite hold back the little shiver that slid down her spine. All right, one could probably argue that Consuelo had simply put two and two together and had deduced it wasn't mere sightseeing that had brought the two of them here to Tijuana, but still….

"Sounds good to me," Tony said, sounding supremely unconcerned. "My life was due for some upheaval, frankly. What else?"

"You've walked a solitary path," Consuelo went on, staring down at his palm again. "Or rather, although one could say you've never allowed yourself to be truly alone, at the same time that is all you have been."

The easy smile Tony had been wearing seemed to slip a little. "I didn't know we were going to be playing riddles."

"This is not a riddle. It is only the truth as your palm tells it to me." The seer paused there, her gaze moving past him to rest on Cassandra for a moment. "It also tells me that you can have no chance of success if you do not allow yourself to be open to another."

"Got it," he said, as casual as though Consuelo had just given him directions to the corner store.

But Cassandra knew better, and she wasn't sure whether Tony truly "got it" after all. She'd only known him for a few days and so didn't pretend to be aware of every nuance, every shift in his tone and expression, but something about the brittle note in his voice seemed to indicate that he really didn't want to acknowledge what Consuelo was telling him, that she was only uncovering truths he'd spent a long time trying to ignore.

She also realized that she was hearing some deeply personal stuff, and that it probably would have been better for her to wait out in the reception area on one of the chairs there. However, getting up and leaving now would only create a distraction, and Consuelo had already warned her to remain quiet.

"You will not live the future you thought would be yours," she said. Now her tone was almost singsong, her eyes half closed, as if she wasn't really looking at the lines on Tony's palm anymore, but instead listening to voices only she could hear.

"What's that supposed to mean?" he asked, the question delivered far more brusquely than Cassandra would have expected from him. If asked, she would have said there didn't seem to be anything that could ruffle Tony, but right now it looked as if the Navarro seer was doing a pretty good job of getting under his skin.

"Only what I just told you…that the image of what your future will be is not what this world has in store for you." Consuelo's eyes opened then, piercing and dark under the black liner she wore. "And if you try to ignore this warning—if you try to ignore the plans fate has for you—then you will bring harm not just on yourself, but on those around you."

Once again, a cold finger seemed to trace its way down Cassandra's spine. This was not the sort of thing either one of them really needed to be hearing right now. Unfortunately, she had a feeling that Consuelo wouldn't much appreciate being interrupted. About all they could do was sit tight and hope this interview would be over soon.

Tony's jaw tightened, but he only nodded and didn't speak.

The seer looked past him, right at Cassandra. "The thing that has drawn you here…it has already set you on a dark path you cannot escape."

"I didn't have any plans to escape it," she replied, forgetting that she was supposed to remain silent. Then again, Consuelo had addressed her directly. Was she supposed to just sit there and say nothing when the seer was talking about her future?

"No," Consuelo said, and she sounded almost amused. "You have never been one to shy away from the difficulties fate has set in your way. That is good…you will need your strength."

"Anything else?" Tony asked, sounding downright testy.

Now the seer sat upright in her chair and her eyes opened all the way. They snapped with dark fire, all the dreaminess she'd displayed a moment earlier gone as if it had never been there in the first place. "There is always more," she said crisply. "However, it doesn't sound as though you want to hear it. The session is over."

"Seriously?" he began, but Cassandra

got up from her chair and went over to him, laid her hand on his arm.

"We've probably taken up enough of Consuelo's time already," she said. Glancing over at the Navarro witch, she added, "How much do we owe you?"

"Oh, the reading is free," Consuelo replied. "I have no need of your money."

No, she probably didn't. There were always differences in how the clans operated, but the one constant seemed to be that all witch families had a healthy cash reserve, probably from using their talents to subtly influence their investments as necessary. Cassandra saw no reason why things would be any different for the Navarros.

"Then thank you," she said. "We'll just be on our way."

A tug on Tony's arm, and he stood up. His smile reasserted itself, although she got the feeling he used the expression as a mask to hide what he was really feeling. "Yeah, thanks," he said. "That was…educational."

"Only if you take the time to try to truly understand what I was telling you," Consuelo responded.

Before he could make a reply that might start an inter-clan incident, Cassandra pulled him away from the inner room, then on through the beaded curtains and out the door. The street outside felt horribly bright after the dim interior of Consuelo's shop, and Cassandra quickly stuck her free hand in her purse so she could pull out her sunglasses.

"Do you want to call a cab?" she asked in an undertone as they began to walk away from the storefront.

"No," Tony replied at once. "We can walk. It's probably better."

What exactly he meant by that cryptic comment, Cassandra wasn't sure. However, she was happy to walk next to him as they headed back to the hotel, although he was moving quickly and she had to exert a little extra effort to keep up with his long strides.

Because of their speed, they got back to the hotel in less than ten minutes. By that time, it was a little after five; more time had passed than she'd thought.

When they got in the elevator, Tony leaned forward and pushed the button for the roof, rather than the floor where their suite was located. She raised an eyebrow at him, and he sent her another of his devilish smiles.

"What?" he said. "It's past five. Perfect time for drinks on the rooftop."

"Sure," Cassandra replied, guessing that there probably wasn't much use in arguing with him. He seemed easygoing enough, but a stubborn streak lurked under the ready grins and devil-may-care attitude. Besides, she had said earlier that she'd be fine with getting drinks after they'd conducted their business for the day. Well, that business was concluded, so there wasn't any real reason to delay.

No reason except getting plowed in Tijuana probably isn't the smartest thing to do, she thought. Not that she had any intention of getting plowed, or anywhere close to it. She couldn't control Tony, but she could do her best to keep watch over her own actions.

As she followed him out of the elevator, however, she couldn't help wondering whether that would be enough.

12

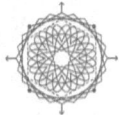

His margarita was excellent, and yet even the healthy amount of alcohol it contained wasn't quite enough to prevent Consuelo Navarro's words from swirling around in his brain.

Although one could say you've never allowed yourself to be truly alone, at the same time that is all you have been.

Words he wanted to laugh at. Alone? Tony Castillo, party animal? The guy who never passed up an excuse to hang out and have fun, drink, dance…that Tony?

Right.

Except…the seer had been correct on one level. He made sure he was always busy, always occupied, but somewhere lurking in the back of all that frenetic energy had been the realization that he really had nothing in his life of any importance. Oh, sure, there was his family, but he was one of them; they sort of had to love him. His magical gift seemed impressive on the surface, but it wasn't all that useful. He'd never been touched by any deep emotion, never felt a strong attachment to anything, except maybe making sure that he kept his life as busy as possible so he would never have any reason to stop and examine it.

Across the table, Cassandra was watching him, green-gilt eyes speculative, but she remained quiet, only sat there and sipped her mango margarita while the setting sun glinted in her red hair and turned it to pure copper.

She really was beautiful. And more than just beautiful—strong and smart and resourceful. Consuelo Navarro had said as much. Cassandra was definitely not the sort of person to back down from a challenge.

Too bad he couldn't say the same thing for himself. All right, he'd gone with Rafe and Miranda and Louisa's husband Oscar to face down Simon Escobar, but he hadn't been given much of an opportunity to say no. Besides, he'd known that Miranda, by far the strongest of all of them, would take the brunt of the dark warlock's magic. Pretty much all he had to do was stay out of the way and duck when necessary. All right, he'd used his control of the wind to incapacitate a few minor demons, but it wasn't as though he'd been the one whose magic had decided that particular battle.

"How's your margarita?" he asked, knowing how stupid that sounded. Still, the two of them couldn't sit there and not say *anything* to each other.

"Really good," Cassandra said. For a moment, she was silent, swirling the straw around in the oversized glass. Then she looked at him, gaze direct. "Do you want to talk about it?"

"Not really."

More silence. He could almost sense her disappointment coming toward him in palpable waves, and he hated that. He didn't want to disappoint her. He wanted her to think he was tough and brave and capable...all the things he was pretty sure he wasn't.

"I think she was annoyed with us for coming into her clan's territory without permission," Cassandra commented, apparently deciding to ignore his remark that he didn't want to talk about what had happened earlier that afternoon. "I have a feeling that's why she was so rough on you."

"Hmm."

She released a huff of a breath and almost but didn't quite roll her eyes. "Aren't you a little old to be pouting?"

Tony shot her a narrow-eyed look. "I am not pouting."

"Sure looks like it from over here."

"I'm thinking."

"Mmm-hmm."

"Where did you want to have dinner?" he asked, feeling desperate. The question was a total red herring, but he really needed to get her off his back for a while.

Her mouth opened and he worried that she was going to sling another sideways comment in his direction, but then he saw her shoulders lift the tiniest fraction, as if she was telling herself that she needed to cut him some slack. "I don't know. There are a ton of places to choose from, obviously. You like seafood?"

"Sometimes," he said cautiously. While he loved some fresh-caught trout, he didn't make a habit of seeking out seafood.

"It's super-popular here," she said.

"Probably because Baja is all about the ocean. Lobster tacos? Crab enchiladas?"

That actually did sound really good. "Let's do that. You can pick the restaurant."

"I already have a few lined up. Just say the word."

It was kind of early to have dinner, but they still needed to finish their drinks here and get wherever they were going. At least if they were eating, Cassandra probably wouldn't have as many opportunities to give him the third degree.

"When we're done with our margaritas."

She nodded, then swiveled her chair so she could look past the rooftop pool and into downtown Tijuana, now all hazy and golden with the last of the afternoon light. Everywhere around them, people were laughing and chatting and drinking—or eating; the bar also offered a variety of appetizers—and Tony wished he could be as lighthearted as everyone else seemed to be. He'd been that way once, or at least pretended to be.

Maybe all these laughing civilians were hiding their own secrets.

Probably, but at least none of them had to contend with stolen grimoires and evil witch clans hidden somewhere in the jungles of El Salvador.

He and Cassandra finished their drinks and left, since their order was being charged to their room. When they got in the elevator, she said, "Can we stop at the room? I want to change into something else to go out to dinner."

"Sure," he replied. If nothing else, the brief detour would let them use up a little more time.

When they got to the room, she took one of the bags from her shopping trip with her and disappeared into the bathroom. Since Tony had no idea how long she was going to take, he walked over to the window and watched as the lights of the city began to come on, glowing in the dusk. It was beautiful here, he thought, in a way that felt very different from Santa Fe, even though they'd both been settled by the Spanish and had their cultures mix with those of the indigenous people who were the first inhabitants of the area. He liked the energy of the town, and he liked the way it had been a balmy seventy-nine degrees today rather than the chilly low fifties they'd left behind in northern New Mexico.

Cassandra emerged from the bathroom,

and Tony had to keep himself from staring. While they were shopping, he hadn't paid much attention to what she was buying, since he figured that was her business. Now, though, he could tell she must have put on one of her new purchases, a pale green sleeveless top that clung to her curves without being too revealing, the low V-neckline accented with embroidery in shades of cream and peach and soft brown. Dangling earrings of silver and coral now hung from her ears, and he thought she'd deepened her makeup somehow, although he couldn't have pointed out the precise changes she'd made.

Altogether, she looked even more beautiful than she had earlier that day, more sultry and alluring. He honestly didn't know whether she'd done that on purpose to make herself more attractive to him, or whether she'd decided she needed more of a nighttime look and his increased lust was only a byproduct of her efforts.

"I like your earrings," he said, hoping the compliment sounded harmless enough.

Cassandra touched her fingers to one of the intricate silver and coral drops. "Thanks. I'd been wanting some for a long time, and I knew I was never going to find a deal like this one again." She went to the closet and got out her brown leather jacket, then slung it over one arm. "Ready?"

"Are we walking?"

"No. We'll need to get a cab. But it's not too far."

Right then, he really didn't care how far it was. A long cab ride would only take up more time, something they had plenty of.

She already had her phone out, was using one of her apps to call a self-driving cab to come pick them up at the hotel's entrance. Apparently, they weren't the only people heading out for an early dinner, because there was another couple standing near the curb, phones out, doing basically the same thing he and Cassandra were.

The other couple's cab came first, but a second one followed within a minute or so. Once the two of them had gotten in the back seat and closed the door, Cassandra said, "Misión San Javier 10643," and the cab immediately sped off.

Tony hadn't been in Tijuana long enough to get much of a sense of the city and its layout, so he had no idea where they were going. Not that it mattered; the cab would get them there without any fuss. However, when they pulled up in front of what looked like an office building, he turned and sent an inquiring glance in Cassandra's direction.

"You're sure we're in the right place?"

"Yes," she replied. "The restaurant's on the second floor. Don't ask me why it's in an office building. I'll bet the views are awesome, though."

Which they were. By that point, the sunset had mellowed to the faintest of pink glows, outlining the downtown area's tall buildings. The restaurant itself was as sleek and modern as their hotel, and obviously popular. However, they were still whisked away to a secluded table with a few minutes of their arrival, handed menus, and promised that their waiter would be along shortly.

"You do know how to find them," Tony said approvingly as he allowed himself another glance at their surroundings. On top of all her other sterling qualities, it was pretty obvious that Cassandra had very good taste.

She shrugged. "I can read the online listings, same as anyone else. It's not too hard to filter out the noise."

"I don't think you give yourself enough credit."

That comment earned him a smile. "Maybe."

For a few minutes, they were silent, poring over their menus. There was a lot of seafood offered, but plenty of other fare if you wanted a steak or pork tacos or something along those lines. However, he decided to go with the fresh local tuna, and asked Cassandra if she wanted to share a plate of oysters as an appetizer…not really expecting her to say yes.

To his surprise, she nodded and said, "Sure. I've always wanted to try some."

"And a glass of white wine to go with that course, before we get a bottle for the rest of it."

That suggestion made her raise her eyebrows, but she didn't demur, only said, "Okay. It's early enough that we'll have plenty of time to burn it off before we go to sleep, right?"

He supposed so, although he'd gone to bed slightly intoxicated more than once and had never suffered for it. Besides, he was starting to feel more relaxed, a feeling that only increased after they placed their orders and the waiter brought over the wine they'd requested.

He lifted his glass. "Let's drink to continued success."

"Sounds good." Cassandra clinked her wine glass against his, then took a sip. "I think it's all going to be fine."

"You do?" Tony asked, a little surprised by this show of sunny optimism.

"I do. Just a feeling."

His personal suspicion was that she just might be acting falsely cheerful in order to make him feel better, but he wasn't about to argue. A little misplaced optimism now and then never hurt anyone.

At least, he hoped it wouldn't.

The oysters came, and she was fairly game about eating them, although afterward she confessed that she probably wouldn't repeat the experience any time soon.

"But at least now I know," she told him. "Better to have tried and not liked them than always wonder what they're like."

Tony supposed she had a point there. "You don't like mysteries?"

"Not really." She drank some of her Chenin blanc. "Or that is, mysteries are fun if you can figure them out. I'm not a big fan of unanswered questions."

"You sound like a cop's daughter."

She grinned. "I am a cop's daughter."

True, but she was also so much more. He could only hope that she found him even a quarter as interesting as he found her.

Dinner was excellent, as was the bottle of local wine they drank with it. By the time they were done, even he was feeling just the slightest bit elevated, which he liked. The tipsiness washed away some of the sting the Navarro seer's words had inflicted on him, and he was starting to feel more like himself, bolder, ready for the next distraction, the next party.

They called a cab after dinner, but before Cassandra could pull out her phone and tell the vehicle's AI their destination, Tony leaned forward, knowing he needed to take the lead here.

"Take us to the nearest dance club, please."

"Yes, sir," came the car's programmed voice, which sounded like an actor doing a voice-over for a high-end tequila commercial.

Cassandra stared at him, an unwelcome, nervous flutter starting in her stomach. "What are you doing, Tony?"

"What does it look like?" he responded.

"It's not even nine o'clock yet. We need to work off some of that dinner."

"I don't dance," she said, her tone flat.

"That's okay," he told her, and grinned. This was going to be fun.

"I do."

13

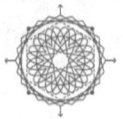

SHE REALLY COULDN'T BELIEVE THAT TONY had talked her into this. All right, there hadn't actually been that much discussion involved—he'd basically spirited her away without any discussion at all.

The club the cab had brought them to was only a few blocks away from the restaurant where they'd eaten dinner, so technically they could have walked. However, Tony clearly hadn't known where they were going, had relied on the cab's A.I. to choose an appropriate venue.

Right now, though, Cassandra was wondering exactly what the cab's idea of "appropriate" was.

Oh, the club was popular, all right. The only reason she and Tony had been able to snag a table was because a group got up from it and left just as the two of them were walking in. They'd sort of pushed the empty shot glasses and beer bottles to one side and used a paper napkin to wipe down the damp surface, since it didn't seem as if anyone was going to come by to clean up any time soon.

He went up to the bar to get them drinks, even though Cassandra protested that she'd had plenty of wine with dinner and only wanted some bottled water or something.

"A shot of tequila isn't going to kill you," he informed her as he got up from the table.

She wasn't so sure about that. Luckily, she'd seen enough of her cousins get messed up on the stuff that she'd always avoided it herself, but even so, there was a reason why the liquor's nickname was "ta kill ya."

Tony came back to the table and set down two shot glasses filled nearly to the brim with amber liquid. He pushed one glass toward her, then lifted the other in a toast. "*Salut,*" he said.

"*Salut,*" she echoed, clinking her shot glass against his, but carefully. They were so full that it wouldn't take much to spill tequila everywhere. Although, come to think of it, maybe that would be a good thing.

As she watched in amazement, Tony knocked back the entire contents of his shot glass in one quick swallow. "What?" he said in tones of injured innocence when he was done, obviously noticing the way she stared at him.

Cassandra was still holding her glass, hadn't taken a single sip yet. "Don't you think you should slow down?"

"Nah," he replied, the old smile back in place. Whatever Consuelo Navarro had done to knock him off track earlier that day, he seemed to have recovered. "You've never partied with me. This is nothing."

Why did Cassandra have a feeling he was only telling her the truth?

"Well, I'm not as much of a party animal," she said. "You'll have to bear with me."

"It's okay," he responded, dark eyes twinkling. "You can go at your own pace."

Which meant taking small sips from her shot glass, even as Tony got up to fetch himself another drink. Inwardly, she shook her head and wondered how much it would cost to pay to clean up the vomit in the back of a cab if he got himself drunk enough.

However, despite the amount of alcohol he'd already consumed, he seemed steady enough on his feet as he threaded his way back to their table. By that point, Cassandra had barely drunk a third of her tequila... and that was fine by her. She really didn't like the taste of the stuff, but it wasn't worth protesting. If she went slowly, sooner or later she'd be done with the drink—and hopefully by then Tony would be ready to call it a night.

He didn't pound the second shot like he had the first, but the mouthful he swallowed was still a lot larger than the tiny sips she'd been allowing herself. Casting about for something harmless to ask, she inquired, "Do all the Castillos party as hard as you?"

"Nope," he replied, then swallowed some more tequila. "I mean, there are a few who can keep up with me, but most of them settle down way too soon. Can't really go out and party hearty if you have to get up and go to work in the morning, or always worry about getting a babysitter."

Well, that was true enough. Once again,

she wondered what it was that drove him to avoid settling down, from behaving the way most warlocks were supposed to behave.

Maybe he just never found anyone to settle down with, she thought then. *Maybe he'd be different if he met the right person.*

Maybe *she* was the right person.

A flush touched her cheeks, and Cassandra found herself glad the nightclub was so dimly lit. She really shouldn't be entertaining thoughts along those lines, not when they were here on clan business and not a simple pleasure trip. Anyway, he might be good-looking, but Tony was so not her type. Up until that point, she hadn't really articulated what her type was, exactly, but she knew the party-animal playboy type was definitely not it. She'd always known that she wanted someone smart and tough and dependable, just like she was.

"...dance?" Tony was saying, and she blinked at him.

"What?"

"I asked if you wanted to dance."

She glanced over at the crowded dance floor. While she didn't know that much about it, she thought the people over there were salsa dancing, almost all of them fluid and expert, as if they'd been doing this sort of thing their whole lives. For all she knew, they had.

"I don't really know how—" she began, but that was as far as he allowed her to get.

"Not a problem," he told her. "Like I said before, I do. All you have to do is follow."

Easy for him to say. As crowded as that dance floor looked, she'd be lucky if she didn't get stomped on before she'd taken her first step.

But even as these new protests bubbled up to Cassandra's lips, Tony reached for her hand and pulled her out of her seat. She knew that if she pulled her fingers from his grasp, he probably wouldn't push things, but she also didn't want to make a scene. No doubt after he'd had to put up with her unschooled stumbling for a minute or two, he'd give up on the whole thing and let her sit down again.

She wasn't quite sure how he did it, but he somehow managed to slip through the moving masses of people on the dance floor and find a relatively open spot. Before she knew it, his hand was on the small of her back.

"Put your left hand on my shoulder," he told her, and Cassandra did as he asked, feeling the taut muscles beneath the cotton of his shirt.

The weight of his hand on her back wasn't unwelcome at all. In fact, a little tingle went through her at his touch, although she told herself to focus on what he was saying so she wouldn't end up looking like a complete fool out here.

"Just follow," he said. "Three steps for every four beats. If I want to spin you or turn, I'll take my hand off your back."

Spin? Turn? She'd be lucky if she didn't trip over her own feet.

No time to talk, though, because they were already moving, the gentle pressure of his hand on her back telling her where to go. And really, once she let herself relax a little and listen to the music, she could feel how her body was supposed to move to it, how if she let the wild, infectious beat move through her, it was almost instinctual where she was supposed to step.

"Awesome," Tony said, dark eyes shining down at her. "You sure you've never done this before?"

She shook her head. "Never. I haven't had the chance."

"Well, I'm glad I could correct that lack."

Before she could reply, he'd raised his hand from her back, spun her around. A startled laugh escaped her lips. It was okay, though, because almost as quickly he held her again, was guiding her through the next sequence of steps. An unexpected thought passed through her mind.

This is fun.

They weren't supposed to be having fun, though. This trip was supposed to be about locating the stolen grimoires. Then again, they couldn't do anything about that until tomorrow. Was it okay to give herself permission to enjoy this evening…to enjoy being held by Tony Castillo, even though she had no idea how this was all going to end up?

She decided it was okay. If nothing else, the dancing would help burn off some of the alcohol they'd consumed tonight. It would probably be a good thing for them to be a little more sober when they got to the hotel.

After a few more minutes, the song ended, and everyone clapped. Cassandra tried to let go of Tony's hand, thinking they should go back to their table and catch their breath, but he shook his head.

"Another song'll be starting in a minute," he said. "Do you really want to sit down this soon?"

She was surprised to realize that she didn't. It felt good to be standing here next to him, to have his fingers entwined with hers. A lot of other people had remained on the dance floor as well, so it wasn't as if they were being terribly conspicuous by hanging out there.

"Not really," she confessed.

His fingers tightened on hers, gave them a gentle squeeze. "I'm glad to hear it."

And then the music started up again, and she was moving with him once more, letting the music sink into her, into a part of her soul she'd never recognized before, letting her be wild and free and—yes, damn it— sexy. She liked the way Tony looked down at her, liked the heat that rose in her when their eyes met. Maybe it was the wine and the tequila, maybe it was the pounding beat of the music…or maybe, just maybe, it was merely her recognizing the need deep within her soul, an attraction she certainly hadn't expected but would be stupid to ignore.

They danced and danced, and then, several hours later, they both decided they'd danced enough and it was time to go. A cab came to get them and took them away to their hotel, and as they sat in the back seat, Tony held her hand again, even though they'd been in physical contact on the dance floor for hours and hours. He continued to hold on as they went inside the hotel and rode up in the elevator. During that ride, his eyes sought hers, as if trying to determine whether she was okay with him holding on for so long.

Oh, yes, she was okay. By that point, most of the alcohol had burned off, but she still felt lightheaded, not quite herself. When she shut the door to their room behind her, they stood in the little entry area for a long moment, not speaking, just staring at each other.

When Tony spoke, his voice was wondering, sounding not at all like his usual casual self. "I think I might be in love with you," he said.

Heat washed through Cassandra again. Although she'd finally allowed herself to recognize the attraction between them, she really hadn't expected him to be that blunt. Not sure what to say, she blurted, "You only think you are?"

For a long moment, he didn't reply, only stood there as his eyes scanned her face. "No," he replied at length. "I know I am."

"Tony, I—"

"Sorry," he said, and now his tone was brusque, as if he was trying to steel himself for inevitable disappointment. "I guess I shouldn't have said that."

"I'm glad you said it," she told him, and his eyes widened slightly.

"You are?"

"Yes." It was the simple truth. This was going to cause all sorts of complications, and yet Cassandra didn't want to let herself worry about any of that. Something in her soul was singing now, happy and relieved. If it had turned out that he didn't care about her except as someone to work with, possibly be friendly with, she thought she could have stood the disappointment, but that didn't matter now. He cared, just as she cared, and from here on out, they could figure out what to do as a team.

No more words then, as he bent and kissed her, gently to start, but with increasing passion as her mouth opened to his and she tasted the smokiness of tequila on his tongue. It wasn't her first kiss, but she knew she'd never reacted to a kiss like this before, never felt her body aflame with honey and fire and the sort of need she hadn't before thought was possible.

They stumbled from where they stood in the entry, moving by instinct toward the bed. When they got there, however, Tony stopped, his fingers once more wrapping themselves around hers. "We don't have to do this now," he said, his voice quiet but urgent. "I don't—I don't want it to be something we did just because we were drunk."

"I'm not drunk now," she said, gazing up into his face. He was slightly flushed, but, she thought, more from the kiss they'd just shared, or possibly all the dancing, than because he was still feeling the effects of the alcohol he'd drunk earlier that evening. "Are you?"

For a moment, he didn't reply. His hands were still holding hers tightly, but he glanced away. "I don't think so," he said. "But...."

"But what?"

To her disappointment—he moved her away from the bed, went over to the sliding glass door that opened on the balcony.

After letting go of her hands, he opened the door and stepped outside.

Wondering what in the world he was thinking, Cassandra went with him and stood there, feeling the cool, slightly salt-scented breeze tug at her hair. And since he didn't seem inclined to speak, she put a hand on his arm. "Tony, what's the matter?"

His face was mostly in shadow, outlined by the faint glow of the lamps they'd left on in the room, but she thought she could see confusion in his expression, coupled with something else she couldn't quite identify. If this wasn't Tony she was dealing with—freewheeling, always casual Tony Castillo—she might have said the emotion she saw there was a strange sort of self-loathing.

"You can do better than me," he said at last.

Did the things that the Navarro seer had said to him still rankle? At once, Cassandra shook her head. "Why don't you let me be the judge of that?"

"I'm serious, Cassandra." Again, he paused, then shifted to put his hands on the balcony's railing, forcing her to release her grip on his arm. "You can do better than a guy who drifts from party to party because he doesn't have anything else to do with his time. There's never been any need for me to have a purpose in life, so I don't. And I've never...."

"Never what?" she prompted, her tone very soft. He couldn't be trying to tell her that he'd never been with a girl before, could he? She found that very hard to believe. Yes, there were plenty of warlocks who began a marriage just as inexperienced as their new wives, but Tony was older than witch-kind tended to be when they got married.

"I've never loved anyone," he said. "I mean, a woman. Dated lots of them, sure. Civilians," he added. "I never had any interest in all those fifth cousins once removed or whoever else it was supposed to be safe for me to be with. Civilian girls were easier to deal with. We'd both hook up and move on. Now, though...."

"Now?" Although in a way it hurt to hear him talk about those civilian girls— even as she recognized the foolishness of thinking that he could have remained a virgin this long—Cassandra was glad he'd found the courage to tell her the truth. She'd much rather know that, no matter how bad it might be, rather than have him lie to her about his past.

"Now…you came along." He let out a huff of a breath. "There I was, thinking we'd go after those goddamn books and get it over with, no muss, no fuss. I really didn't think I was going to fall for you."

Happiness was a warm flush moving through her, making every single nerve ending come alive. However, she tried to sound at least halfway calm and collected as she replied, "That's all right. It wasn't exactly the first thing on my mind, either. I mean, I kind of thought you were a jerk when I first met you."

For the first time, he grinned, his teeth flashing white in the darkness. "Thanks."

"Hey, we're being honest here, right?'

"True."

"Anyway," Cassandra went on, "I tended to think all that 'love at first sight' crap that's supposed to happen with our kind must be bullshit, because I sure never felt that way about any of the warlocks I met…and I had the chance to meet McAllister and Wilcox guys when I was hanging out in Jerome with my cousins, so it's not like this was all about avoiding a hook-up with that fifth cousin you mentioned earlier."

He nodded. "Maybe our stars aligned because we're both kind of freaks that way."

"Maybe." She didn't mind Tony using that word, mostly because she'd started to think the same thing about herself. All around her, she'd seen cousins her own age already getting engaged or even married, and there she was, knowing for a fact that she'd never felt passionate about anyone. She'd gone out with a few civilian guys in high school and college, but there hadn't been any real spark. Luckily, her parents hadn't seemed too worried, her mother probably because she was a civilian and therefore had a completely different mindset when it came to getting married, and her father because he'd stayed single until he was almost forty.

But obviously, she wasn't a freak, and neither was Tony. They just hadn't met the right person yet. That her "right person" apparently had turned out to be a Castillo was a surprising development, one that wasn't without its own complications, but Cassandra knew they'd figure out the logistics once they were done with all this mess of tracking down the stolen grimoires.

She reached out and took both his hands in hers. They were still warm, apparently unaffected by the cool evening sea breeze. "If we're both freaks, then that means we should be together. And that means I don't want to hear you talking about how I deserve someone better. I can figure out what I deserve on my own, thank you very much. And that's you, so shut up about it."

Another smile touched his lips. "I kind of like it when you're being forceful."

It might have been dark out here on the patio, but she could still see the sudden warmth in his expression. "You do, huh?"

"Mm-hmm."

He bent and kissed her again, his arms going around her this time. Yes, that felt good, to be held close enough to feel the warmth of his body, the casual strength of his embrace.

"I want to go inside," she whispered as soon as the kiss ended.

This time, he didn't argue, only drew her into the sitting area of their suite and shut the sliding glass door behind them, then closed the shutters. Now that she was back in the relative warmth of the hotel room, Cassandra realized how downright cool it had been outside.

It was going to feel good to get into bed, to feel the warmth of the covers over her... the warmth of Tony's body next to hers.

And as much as she knew she wanted that, she knew she was taking a big step. Her past wasn't like his. In fact....

She blurted, "I'm a virgin."

His eyes flared with shock. "Oh."

An awkward silence fell. She said hurriedly, "I just—I wanted to tell you so it wouldn't come as a surprise. It doesn't change anything. I still want to...."

The words trailed off, mostly because she found she couldn't quite come out and say she wanted to have sex with him. Of course she did, but to say it out loud sounded so...well, so naked.

His hand touched her hair, so gentle. "I'm glad you told me."

Something in his gentleness worried her. She didn't want him to treat her like a soap bubble that would break. If telling him that one little fact had changed everything....

But then he was kissing her again, kissing her with a fierce passion that surprised her with its intensity. She opened her mouth to him, pressed her body against his, and before she knew it, they'd stumbled their way back over to the bed again. This time, they didn't stop, but fell on top of the spotless white duvet, Tony reaching out with one arm to sweep the accent pillows to the floor, then pull the covers back.

His hands were on her blouse, pulling it over her head. At the same time, she was working the buttons of his shirt, had to hold back a gasp when she saw his bare torso, the flat stomach, the muscular expanse of his chest. If asked, she supposed she would have said he had a good body, judging by the way he looked in his clothes, but she really hadn't expected quite this…perfection.

Yes, he was definitely perfect.

She didn't have very long to admire the view, though, because he'd unhooked her bra, had bent so he could kiss her breasts, mouth warm against her flesh. Heat rushed through her again, and she could feel the way she'd started to throb with need, her body feeling hot and alive and not entirely her own.

Somehow, she was then flat on her back, and he was tugging down her jeans, then her panties. His fingers caressed her, and she gasped aloud.

"Oh, God, Tony."

He was moving deeper, fingers entering her, but carefully, as if he wanted to make sure he wouldn't hurt her. Not much chance of that, simply because she'd been active her whole life, hiking and off-road biking and even horseback riding, and so she knew the physical component of her virginity was probably already a thing of the past. He seemed to realize that as well, because his touch became stronger, surer, and she closed her eyes and gasped again, realizing she was going to come, was going to come hard.

Thank God he'd shut the sliding glass door. She hadn't really expected to be that loud, but she supposed she shouldn't have underestimated the power of repressed sexual tension. Holding on to him, she rode the orgasm, breaths coming hard and fast, until she fell back against the pillows.

"Good?" he asked.

"Oh, yes," she replied. "Better than good."

He bent and kissed her again, and almost by instinct her hand moved lower, felt the heavy hardness of his cock through the dark gray boxer briefs he wore. At her touch, he released a harsh breath, and she pulled away from the kiss so she could slide down his underwear, brush her fingers against him.

"Yes," he whispered, and she began to slip her hand up and down, feeling the softness of his skin against her fingertips. As soft as that skin was, the flesh underneath it was rock-hard, eager. She didn't want to push him over the edge, so when she bent down to suckle him, it was only for a minute or two, just enough to show him she wanted to do this, wanted to know every part of him.

When she lifted her mouth from him, he seemed to take that as the signal he needed. He shifted positions, pushing against her, then stopped.

"What is it?" she whispered.

"No condoms. I didn't think this was going to be that sort of trip."

The chagrin in his voice almost made her want to chuckle. "It's okay," she told him.

"I don't want to risk—"

"It's okay," she told him again, voice a little firmer this time. "Did you use a condom all those other times?" ...*with those civilian girls,* she thought, although she didn't say the words out loud.

"Always," he replied…and she believed him.

"Then it'll be okay," she said. "My McAllister cousins taught me a charm. It's better than being on the pill."

"Seriously?"

She nodded.

He bent and kissed her. Now she could feel him against her entrance, hard, ready. "I want to, Tony," she whispered. "Please."

No more hesitations. She felt him slip into her, bigger than she'd thought. Maybe there was a faint twinge of discomfort, but it was gone almost as soon as she noticed it, and then she couldn't think about anything except the sensation of him inside her, their bodies moving together, her legs wrapped around him, pulling him closer.

Close. That's what this felt like…the sensation of being closer to him than she'd ever been with anyone else in her life. The wonder of his body, all muscles and heat and strength, so different from her own. His flesh was damp with sweat, and she could smell his perspiration, too, musky and masculine and strangely erotic.

He began to move faster, and although

this was the first time she'd ever done this, somehow Cassandra knew he was about to come, was about to orgasm as spectacularly as she had just a while earlier. She wasn't sure whether she was going to climax this time but wasn't too worried; she knew they'd have plenty more opportunity later on. Besides, she'd heard so many horror stories about how the first time could really hurt that she was just glad this felt as good as it did.

His body tensed, and then he let out a low moan, hips driving into her as he came. She held on to him tightly, let him ride it until she could feel him relax, feel his lips brush against her neck.

His voice was a hoarse whisper. "I love you, Cassandra."

"I love you, too," she said. And she knew she did, wanted nothing more than him, someone who was probably the opposite of everything she thought she'd wanted in a man, and yet somehow was the perfect person for her.

As relaxed and sated as she felt, she didn't forget the words of the charm that her cousin had taught her.

Blessed Brigid, now is not the time. Bestow your blessings elsewhere.

Cassandra wasn't even sure whether she believed in Brigid, but Summer had told her that didn't matter so much—Brigid believed in all women, and would allow a witch this one special freedom. All you had to do was ask.

Because while she knew she loved Tony and wanted to make a life with him when this was all over, she knew this definitely wasn't the time. They would worry about a family and children and all that later on, once they were safely back home.

The word "if" didn't enter her mind. They would be successful, she just knew it. Surely the universe wouldn't have allowed them to find love like this, only to take it away.

At least, she hoped the universe would be that kind….

14

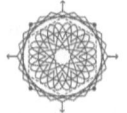

THEY ORDERED ROOM SERVICE THAT MORNING, and then showered afterward together in the huge marble enclosure the suite provided. Tony already knew that Cassandra's body was beautiful, but this experience just proved it beyond a shadow of a doubt, the bright light in the bathroom showing off what he hadn't been able to see as clearly in the shadowy bedroom where they'd made love.

She was so perfect...too perfect for the likes of him.

As best he could, he tried to shut down that thought. She'd told him the night before that she loved him. More, she'd told him he would be her first. No one else had ever suckled her beautiful breasts, or touched the hot, sweet center of her womanhood. He knew better than to think of someone so strong and bright and fierce as his own, and yet she'd given something to him that she hadn't offered to any other man. No matter what he might think of his own failings, clearly, Cassandra didn't think of him that way.

Now he'd just have to try his damnedest to make sure he was worthy of her.

He noticed that she dressed soberly this morning, ignoring the pretty embroidered blouses she'd bought in favor of a plain dark green long-sleeved T-shirt, jeans, and boots. The outfit would probably be way too warm for Tijuana's mild weather, but he thought he could guess at her motivations for wearing it. After all, they would be going to meet with a nun this morning. Probably better not to look too sexy.

And hope that they wouldn't show any evidence of the passionate lovemaking they'd shared the night before. Tony had soaped Cassandra's back and used the flexible shower head to rinse off the suds, so he'd gotten a good look at her. There was a faint reddish mark on the side of her neck, but with any luck, her hair would cover that. Otherwise, he couldn't see any sign of their activities of the previous evening.

"What do you want to do about the room?" he asked her as she stood in front of the mirror and brushed out her lustrous autumn-colored hair.

Her mouth pursed. "Good question. I suppose we might as well check out. If Sister María Consilio has the information we need, we're going to head on to El Salvador anyway. And if she doesn't, then we'll have to go back to Santa Fe. It's not as if there's anyone else here in Tijuana who could help us."

No, probably not. Tony could hope there might another nun the sister had confided in, but he somehow doubted that was the case. For one thing, María Consilio was a witch; she wouldn't betray the trust of someone who was witch-kind, not even to a civilian who had taken vows. And, judging by what Olivia had said about her mother's flight from El Salvador, she definitely hadn't revealed her secrets to anyone else. If the sister couldn't remember where the Escobar family had come from, then their mission here would definitely be at an end.

They packed their things and made sure the room was tidy, then used the electronic checkout on the television to close out their account. Afterward, all they had to do was take their bags down to the Fiat, which looked none the worse for wear after its night in the hotel's parking lot, pay the parking attendant, and be on their way.

It was another sunny day, bright and beautiful and mild. Tony looked over at the woman who occupied the passenger seat and couldn't quite believe that she'd slept in his arms the night before. Now she looked no less beautiful, but there was a sort of ferocity to her this morning, to the lift of her chin as she watched the streets outside pass by. That was the expression of a woman on a mission.

He hoped it wouldn't be a vain one.

Since they'd been leisurely about their breakfast and their shower, it was now almost eleven o'clock, well within the time frame the Mother Superior had suggested as the optimal time for their visit. As they pulled up and parked, this time in a more convenient spot almost in front of the convent door, he noticed the same skinny guy who'd been skulking around the car the day before.

"Great," he muttered under his breath.

"Not a problem," Cassandra said, obviously noting the object of his disapproval. "I honestly doubt he'll come close again, but if he does...."

By that point, they'd exited the vehicle, so all she had to do was stretch out her hand as she'd done previously, letting that flash of warm light move over the car before it disappeared.

"He'll get zapped," Tony finished for her, feeling pleased. In a perverse way, he almost hoped the guy would try something again. Maybe another painful lesson was just what he needed to decide boosting cars wasn't exactly his best choice of profession.

They went up to the door and knocked, and the same wide-eyed young novice peered out. Clearly, she was expecting them, because she said, *"Ven conmigo. La hermana Maria Consilio te espera."*

Tony assumed she was saying that the sister was ready to see them, or something along those lines, because Cassandra nodded and smiled, saying, *"Gracias,"* and then they all went down the hall, past the door to the Mother Superior's office, and on to another set of doors, one that opened onto a lush courtyard. Even in November, flowers bloomed brightly here, roses and lilies and something bright pink that climbed the fence encircling the property.

A woman in a nun's black habit was sitting on one of the stone benches there. She rose as soon as she heard them approach—or maybe she didn't need to hear them, had felt the tingle of their witchy presence, just as he and Cassandra sensed hers. Or at least, he assumed she'd felt something, since as soon as they were within ten feet, he'd gotten the familiar tingle at the base of his neck that told him he was with someone of witch-kind.

"¿Eres sor María Consilio?" Cassandra asked.

The woman nodded. She was quite elderly—probably in her seventies some-where—and yet Tony could still see that she had probably been very pretty when she was younger, with large dark eyes and a small, straight nose. "You are Cassandra and Anthony," she said.

Well, of course she must know who they were. And thank God she could speak good English; Cassandra was a great translator, but this would be a lot easier now that he knew he wouldn't have to wait for her to pause and translate everything for him.

"Yes," Cassandra replied, even though it

was clear the sister hadn't been asking a question. "Do you mind if we speak with you?"

"Not at all," María Consilio said. "Please, take a seat."

There was another stone bench facing the one where she'd been sitting, so Tony and Cassandra settled themselves on it as requested. The sister sat down as well, then folded her hands in her lap. A gold band shone on the ring finger of her left hand, the symbol of her marriage to Christ.

"You wish to ask about the witch who sought sanctuary here so many years ago," the nun said.

They both nodded, and Cassandra added, "Yes, it's very important for us to find out where she came from."

María Consilio frowned. "Unless things have changed greatly, it is not the sort of place I would recommend that you go."

Tony and Cassandra exchanged a glance. He could see the way her lips tightened, as if holding back a quick reply. He smiled at the sister and said, "We know it could be dangerous. But unfortunately, it's not something we can avoid, either. We need to do this to keep our clans safe."

As he'd hoped, this angle seemed to

work, because María Consilio nodded. "I understand. I suppose that I can tell you, since the woman who begged me to keep her confidences is long dead."

"You knew that?" Tony asked. "How?"

"I kept in contact with Señor Santiago for a time. I wanted to see how Isabella and her family were faring."

You probably didn't like a lot of what you heard, Tony thought, and noticed the way the nun frowned slightly, as if she was thinking nearly the same thing.

"Well, then," Cassandra said. "What can you tell us about where she came from?"

"It was a place in El Salvador," María Consilio replied. "A small village called Pico Negro outside the town of San Matías."

San Matías. Tony wondered if Joaquin Escobar had named his son after the town, or the saint who was its namesake. Maybe a little of both.

"Pico Negro is very difficult to get to," the nun went on. "You will not find this place on any map—it is merely what the local residents called the place. From what Isabella said, it sounded as if the village was deep in the rainforest, shaded by the peaks of one of the local volcanoes. Hence its name."

Cassandra nodded knowingly, but of course Tony didn't know what the nun was talking about. He'd have to ask later on.

"But if we can get to San Matías, then we should be able to ask one of the locals how to find Pico Negro, right?" Cassandra asked.

"If they are willing to tell you," María Consilio said. "Pico Negro is a town only inhabited by Escobars, and the nonmagical people who live in nearby San Matías know better than to give up its secrets. Isabella made it sound as though her husband reigned over the whole area, and the regular folk in the region feared his wrath too much to speak of what they knew."

Well, considering what Tony had heard about Joaquin Escobar, he figured that was only prudent. But....

"Escobar's been dead for decades," he pointed out, and although the sister nodded, she still wore a sad little smile.

"True, but does anyone know who he left behind to watch over his lands, his people, while he was gone? I am sure he would not have abandoned them without making some kind of arrangement."

"Maybe," Cassandra allowed, "but how do we even know he left voluntarily? Some of us have speculated that he was somehow driven out."

The nun's smile never wavered. "If you had heard how Isabella spoke of her husband, you would not think such a thing. He was immensely, frighteningly powerful. She said there was no one in the clan whose powers came close to his, although the clan boasted quite a few very strong witches and warlocks. There is no one who could have 'driven him out.' When he came to seek vengeance for what had happened to his son, he did so secure in the knowledge that there would be no one to challenge him when he returned."

For once, a piece of good news. Because if Joaquin Escobar had left El Salvador of his own will, that meant there wasn't anyone he'd left behind who was stronger than he. It sounded as though the reason no one had heard from the Escobars was simply that none of them had the necessary powers to come to the United States and make trouble. And if that was the case, then he and Cassandra just might be able to slip in and get the grimoires without too much trouble.

...except for the minor detail that someone in the clan had been strong enough to slip into Castillo territory with no one noticing...strong enough to somehow get past Miranda's wards and take the books they wanted. Maybe the person in question wasn't as strong as Joaquin Escobar had been, but that didn't mean they might not still be a very formidable adversary.

"But he never returned," Cassandra said, sounding satisfied. "And no one came looking for him, either. It sounds to me like we don't have too much to worry about."

"I suppose that is possible," María Consilio said, her overly polite tone seeming to indicate that she didn't agree with Cassandra's view of the situation but wasn't going to argue with her.

"Is there anything else?" Tony inquired. "Anything Isabella told you that might help us to get to Pico Negro?"

"Not that I can remember," the nun replied. "She was worried for her children, worried that Joaquin would somehow be able to find them, even though she had traveled thousands of miles to escape him. She only told me of where she'd come from because she wanted me and the other sisters working in the shelter to keep an eye out for anyone with a Salvadoran accent. But no one like that ever came."

Lucky for Isabella, Tony thought. He sort of doubted that a bunch of nuns would have been able to do much against a powerful warlock like Joaquin Escobar.

"Thank you very much, sister," Cassandra said. She got up from the bench, and Tony rose as well, guessing that she wanted to get back across the border to San Diego as quickly as possible so they could book a flight to El Salvador. "We really appreciate your time."

"It is no problem," she responded. "My life is one of service. Only…."

Tony almost didn't ask, because he didn't much like the worried expression the nun now wore. But he found himself saying, "Only what?"

Her smile was sad. "I only hope I have not done the both of you a disservice by telling you where to find the Escobars."

There were no non-stops from San Diego—the closest international airport—to San Salvador. Cassandra realized she should have guessed that would be the case, since San Diego wasn't exactly what you could call a hub. "I can book two separate flights —one from here to Mexico City, and one from there to San Salvador—or I can get a flight on United with a three-hour layover in Houston."

Tony wrinkled his nose. "Neither one of those options sounds all that great."

They hadn't sounded great to her, either, but she supposed beggars couldn't be choosers. "I know, but I also don't want to drive all the way to L.A. just to catch a direct flight. So those are our choices."

"Stopping in Mexico City could be fun," he said after a pause to evaluate their two options.

Tony mentioning "fun" was enough to set off alarms in Cassandra's mind. While she might privately admit that it would be interesting to spend some time in Mexico City, that wasn't what this trip was about. They'd already wasted enough time in Tijuana.

All right, she probably shouldn't say "wasted," since they'd gotten some valuable information from Sister María Consilio. Also, Cassandra knew that without their forced stay in Tijuana, her relationship with

Tony might not have progressed to where it currently was now. But enough was enough. They needed to get to El Salvador, find Pico Negro, get the books, and get the hell out of there.

"We should probably take the flight with the layover in Houston," she said, and Tony grinned at her from where he sat on the bed in their hotel room near Lindbergh Field in San Diego.

"Why did I know you were going to say that?"

She shook her head and made her selection on the travel website. At least there were still tickets available. "I need your credit card."

"Expensive tickets?" he asked.

That was an understatement. Round-trip for the two of them would cost almost three thousand dollars. "Um, kind of," she replied.

Looking resigned, he got up from the bed, dug his wallet out of his pocket and extracted the credit card, then came over and handed it to her. "Just don't tell me," he said. "I'll see it on my statement at the end of the month."

"What if it's close to your limit?"

He grinned at her. "It won't be."

Right, because he's an independently wealthy warlock, Cassandra reminded herself. Although her family was definitely comfortable enough, she had a feeling that their net worth was probably considerably lower than Tony's.

Might as well go for broke. "And I'll need to book a hotel room, or get us an Airbnb." She opened the tab with the map of El Salvador on it and squinted to estimate the distance between the country's capital city and the small town that was their destination. "It looks like it's only about twenty-five miles or so from San Salvador to San Matías, so I think we'll be okay staying in San Salvador and driving from there."

Tony frowned. "I would have thought the Escobars would be hiding someplace more remote than that."

"Well, remember that San Matías is just the jumping-off point. I don't know how far Pico Negro will be from there." Cassandra paused, trying to remember all the details of Olivia's narrative about her family's escape from the Escobar village. "It must be walkable, though, because that's how Olivia's mother got out. But even so, we're probably talking about some pretty thick rainforest. I have a feeling you probably don't have to go very far before it's really hard to tell where you're going."

He sat down on the bed next to her, his expression less than thrilled. "Then how are we supposed to find it?"

"Ask around, I guess. The locals sound like they're pretty scared of the Escobars, but I'll bet that we can find someone who's willing to tell us where to find them if we offer enough cash."

To her surprise, he grinned. "That's a pretty cynical assessment. You're starting to sound like me."

About all Cassandra could do was shake her head at him. "I don't know about that. Anyway, the flight leaves at 9:50 a.m., so we'll need to be up early. Hopefully, we'll have enough time to get some local currency, since I kind of doubt we can use a Visa for that sort of thing."

She turned back to her phone, did a quick search, and sent Tony a relieved smile. "Thank God for AirBnb. I just got us an awesome condo." Turning her phone's screen toward him, she scrolled through a couple of the listing's photos. The place was bright and clean and modern, with an absolutely amazing view of San Salvador's skyline and the volcanic mountains that encircled the city.

He let out a whistle. "Damn, that's nice. Any chance we can hang out for a few days before we go book-hunting?"

"I doubt it. Since we're not like Simon and don't know how to hide our witchy natures, about all we can do is get in and get out as fast as we can. I'll book for two nights, since we're going to be arriving so late, but I'm hoping we won't even need that second night."

"What about the plane tickets?"

"I bought us one-way for now. It looks like there are usually some seats available on those flights last-minute, so we'll buy them when we need them."

Tony was quiet for a moment, apparently absorbing all this. "What if there isn't a flight?"

That possibility had already crossed her mind. They didn't have a lot of options, but.... "Then I guess we'll take our rental car and drive like hell. It's about three hundred miles to the Mexican border."

"Wouldn't Guatemala be closer?"

"Yes, but do you know anyone in Guatemala?"

He shook his head. "Nope."

"Whereas I've got those distant relations up in Sonora. That's a long way from the southern part of Mexico, but I'm sure if I called, I could get someone to help us out in a pinch." She let out a breath. "That's just contingencies, though. If we're lucky, we'll be able to grab the books, high-tail it back to San Salvador, and be on the earliest plane out of there."

"And if we're not lucky?"

Somehow, she'd known he was going to ask that question. "Then we'll have to hope that that silver tongue of yours can get us out of trouble."

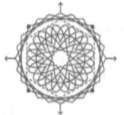

15

TONY COULD TELL CASSANDRA WAS WORRIED, but that didn't stop her from letting him persuade her to spend their evening together in San Diego's Gaslamp District. They wandered the streets, looked in the various shops and galleries, had dinner at an Indian restaurant whose food was as delicious as the decor was elegant. Afterward, they went back to their hotel room and made love, only this time slower, more measured, the two of them exploring each other's bodies, getting used to their rhythms.

As he'd thought, Cassandra tasted delicious.

The next morning, they got to the airport two hours ahead of time. No one seemed to look twice at his passport, and Tony let out a relieved breath once he and Cassandra were safely inside the United lounge. As it turned out, El Salvador had been using American dollars as its currency for decades, so there was no need to exchange their money, although he still went to an ATM and got as much cash out as possible, figuring that would make things go more smoothly once they were on the ground in Central America.

Their flight was delayed by about twenty minutes, which he could tell annoyed Cassandra. Once they were on board, he put his hand on hers where it lay on the seat rest.

"It's okay," he said quietly. "Our Airbnb is reserved, so it doesn't matter what time we get there."

"I know," she replied. "I just...I just want this over with, you know? Whatever happens."

Personally, he would have liked their departure to be delayed indefinitely. There were a lot worse things he could think of than being stuck in San Diego for an extended period...like being captured by the Escobars and tortured to death. Did the Escobars even do that sort of thing? He realized he really didn't know much about them, except that Joaquin Escobar had definitely managed to produce a couple of very bad seeds, and the man himself had been ruthless, cunning, and downright evil.

They'll probably just kill you, he thought. While that wasn't exactly the world's most cheerful notion, at least if death came quickly, he wouldn't have anything more to worry about. He was far more concerned about Cassandra. It was probably better not to dwell on what the warlocks in that rogue clan might do to a young and beautiful captive witch.

Great. Now that such a horrible possibility had entered his mind, he couldn't seem to get rid of it.

"What is it?" she asked, sending him a sideways look. "You're frowning."

"Nothing," he said quickly. He sure as hell wasn't going to tell her what he'd just been thinking. Besides, this was Cassandra. She'd probably already considered the possibility and decided it was an acceptable risk.

Tony wasn't sure he could look at the situation quite that coldly, but there wasn't much he could do about it now. The jet's engines had begun to rumble, and the signs to fasten seat belts and raise trays were lit. No backing out at this point.

Since she was still staring at him, obviously seeing something in his face he hadn't been able to hide, he added, "First time flying. Guess I'm just nervous."

"Ah."

"I forgot you were an old pro."

She shrugged. "I don't think one flight to Albuquerque exactly qualifies me as a 'pro.' But I have some cousins in Tucson who have a small plane, and I've gone up in it a few times."

Well, that was still way more experience than he had. There were Castillos who owned private planes, but Tony had never had the urge to ask for a ride. He'd gone ballooning in Taos once, and that was fun, but otherwise he figured he might as well keep his feet on the ground. After all, it wasn't as though witches and warlocks had the opportunity to travel much.

Unless they were chasing after items pilfered by members of another clan, of course.

The jet began to taxi down the runway, and without thinking, he clutched the armrests of his seat.

"It's perfectly safe, you know," Cassandra said.

"Yeah, I know," he returned. "I guess I didn't think it was going to *vibrate* so much."

A smile touched her lips, but she didn't say anything, only patted his hand, then left hers lying on top of his, palm warm against his skin. Yes, that was better. It was good to feel her touch, know that she was there, so very beautiful, so very *real*.

They'd both talked to their families that morning, Cassandra to both her parents, Tony to his sister because it seemed safer than getting dragged into a discussion with his father and having it turn into the sort of grilling Henry Castillo generally saved for the courtroom. Ava sounded horrified that Tony and Cassandra were heading to El Salvador, but there wasn't much she could do about it.

"There has to be a better way," she'd argued. "Someone else in our clan should do this. Or, better yet, some of the de la Pazes. It's their books that got stolen."

"Who?" he asked. "The de la Pazes sent their best witch for the job—Cassandra Sandoval. And you know our clan isn't exactly overflowing with people who can hold their own in a magical battle."

"And you can?" his sister asked, sounding skeptical and worried at the same time.

"Come on—you know I have an awesome power. I'll blow all those Escobars into next week."

Ava had let out a huff of a breath, but she didn't directly contradict him. Maybe she'd gained a little more respect for his magical abilities after he'd survived that confrontation with Simon Escobar...or maybe she'd simply realized that it didn't matter how much she argued with him. Nothing she said was going to change anything.

"All right," she said finally. "Just...be careful. Mom's sitting up in bed and eating, and it would really suck for something to happen to you just as she was getting so much better."

"Don't worry," he told her. "I'll be home to give Mom a hug before you know it. Talk to you later."

He'd ended the call there, figuring there was no point in dragging things out any further. The news about his mother was encouraging, and he took his sister's words to heart. He'd be home to tell her all about his and Cassandra's success, no matter what happened.

It sounded as though her own conversation had run along basically the same lines. "My father thinks we're nuts," she'd said frankly while they drank coffee in the United lounge. "But he also said there isn't much he can do to stop us. He reminded me that the Escobars will have all sorts of tricks up their sleeve, so we can't let our guard down for a moment."

"We kind of already knew that," Tony pointed out.

"Yes, but he told me about Joaquin Escobar being a null—someone who blanks out all magic around him—and said there's a possibility others in the clan might have that same power."

Tony sincerely hoped not. About all he and Cassandra had going for them was their magical gifts. If those were taken away, he didn't know what they would do.

But that was just borrowing trouble. So what if Joaquin Escobar had been a null? Neither of his sons had apparently possessed that same talent, so it wasn't as if it was strictly hereditary, something to be expected of an Escobar witch or warlock.

Maybe Joaquin had been a genetic freak, a sport of some kind? That seemed to make the most sense, considering all the magical gifts he'd been able to command.

Because the flight was fairly crowded, they didn't talk much on the first leg of their journey, the two-hour flight to Houston. Their layover spanned nearly the same amount of time, but neither he nor Cassandra were much in the mood to wander around the airport. Instead, they hung out in the lounge, had a snack, and talked about mundane things, mostly because there were way too many civilians around to attempt any kind of a strategy session.

And then they were wheels up and headed southeast, the sun at their backs and disappearing as they flew. When they finally landed at El Salvador International Airport on the outskirts of San Salvador, it was nearly ten o'clock local time and far too dark to see anything of the city. They retrieved their luggage and got a cab—one driven by a real person, a thin middle-aged man in one of the loudest Hawaiian shirts Tony had ever seen—and Cassandra gave the address once they were settled in the back seat.

"*Torre 91, Colonia Escalón, por favor,*" she said, and the driver nodded.

"*Sí, senorita.*"

They sped off into the darkness, Tony hoping the entire time that the cab really was taking them to the Airbnb and that they weren't going to be driven somewhere and robbed...or worse. Not that the guy driving gave off that sort of vibe, but you never really knew, did you?

"Relax," Cassandra said in an under-tone. "Crime is bad for business."

"If you say so."

She smiled and poked him in the leg, and he couldn't help grinning back at her. Of course, she was right. He was probably just feeling a little disoriented after sleeping for a couple of hours on the flight here. And also, he reflected, he'd spent almost his entire life in Santa Fe and the area surrounding it, and now he'd been to California and Mexico and El Salvador, all in the space of a few days. No wonder he couldn't quite seem to get his bearings.

The condo was just as nice as Cassandra had said it would be, and viewing the basically brand-new furniture and neat little galley-style kitchen made him relax that much more. True, the bed was only queen size, but he figured they would make do.

"Nice bed," he said, sitting down on the foot and giving it a few experimental bounces.

That comment earned him some serious side-eye. "I think we'd better save our energy."

He raised his eyebrows. "What if this is our last night on earth?"

"Not funny, Tony."

"I mean it."

She'd been occupied with putting her luggage in the closet, but now she turned around and stared at him, hands on her hips. "Do you really think we're doomed to failure? Why'd you come along, then?"

Oops. He got up from the bed and went over to her, pulled her into his arms. She offered just the slightest resistance at first, but then relaxed into his embrace, her head against his chest.

"I don't think we're doomed to failure," he said. "And you're right—we should be getting our rest tonight, because God only knows what's going to happen tomorrow."

"Exactly." She was quiet for a moment, head still resting on him, silky strands of her hair brushing against the backs of his hands as he held her. "Don't think I don't—don't want you." The words came out quickly, as if she was embarrassed to state such a thing so baldly. "But it's been a very long day, and tomorrow could be crazy. We need to rest."

He brushed his mouth against the top of her head. "I know. Kiss me, though—that'll be a down payment for later."

A low chuckle escaped her lips, seemed to resonate in his body. "I can do that."

She pulled away a little, raised her face to his. They kissed, and he could feel blood rushing through him, could feel himself stiffen at her touch. No time for that, though...or rather, plenty of time, not enough energy. Now that they were someplace safe, he realized how tired he really was. They'd made love the previous two nights; it was okay if they skipped tonight.

After all, they would have the rest of their lives to be together...if they survived the next twenty-four hours.

Tony's regular breathing told Cassandra he slept deeply. Good. She needed him to get his rest.

She should be sleeping, too, but even though she knew the importance of a good night's sleep, she couldn't get comfortable, couldn't find the right position that would magically induce slumber.

It wasn't the bed's fault; it was just as comfortable as any of the other hotel beds she'd slept on since this whole crazy adventure began. No, her damn mind kept racing, picking at the problem of confronting the Escobars, despite her conscious realization that there was only so much preparation they could do when they were flying blind.

At least she hadn't felt the presence of any other witches or warlocks in the airport, or during their drive across the city, or here in the tall condominium building where the Airbnb was located. That didn't necessarily mean much, since generally she needed to be within ten or fifteen feet of a person before she was able to detect that they were of witch-kind, but it was something. For all she knew, the Escobars reigned supreme in El Salvador, having rid the country of any other rival clans years before. It seemed to fit their M.O., but again, she was working on very sketchy information at best.

If that was true—and the Escobar clan

remained mostly in their village of Pico Negro—then there was a good chance they might not be able to detect the two inter-lopers until she and Tony were very close by. After all, witches and warlocks tended to stay in their home territories. It was mostly unheard of for them to venture into another clan's area without permission... especially a clan as bloodthirsty as the Escobars.

All right, say that luck was finally in their favor, and they were somehow able to get the drop on the Salvadoran clan. The first order of business would be to locate where the books had been taken. Cassandra guessed they would probably be kept in the house that belonged to the *primus*. After hearing of how Joaquin Escobar had taken over the Santiagos, how his son had wanted to do the same thing to the Castillos, she was under no illusions that the Escobar witch family would be run by a *prima*.

And if the books were in the *primus's* house, then they'd have to make damn sure he was nowhere around when she and Tony went to steal them back. How that would work, she wasn't really sure, but she assumed they'd have to do their best at hiding in the area, close enough to see who was coming and going but not so close that any of the Escobar witches and warlocks could sense their presence.

Easier said than done, probably, but she couldn't think of what else they might do. Too bad neither of their powers was turning invisible.

She went quite still then, eyes widening as she stared up at the dark blur of the ceiling above her.

Maybe not invisible…but what about *invincible?*

Her power created a shield that protected anything inside it. Although she couldn't cast that shield on herself, there was no reason why she couldn't cast it on Tony. That way, even if the Escobars were able to detect his presence, there wasn't a damn thing they could do to hurt him as long as the shield was in effect. And since a shield remained in place until she consciously removed it, there didn't seem to be much chance of the magical barrier disappearing at exactly the wrong moment.

Well, unless one of the Escobars turned out to be a null like Joaquin had been. That would definitely make the situation much more difficult. No, she didn't want to think about that. The odds of the Escobar clan having another person with that peculiar talent had to be astronomically high. At least, she needed to think that was the truth, because otherwise, how would they have any hope of success? The presence of a null would stop them faster than anything else.

"Hey," Tony whispered, and she rolled over onto her side to see him staring at her.

"Sorry," she murmured. "I didn't mean to wake you up."

"It's all right." He reached over and brushed a strand of hair away from her eyes. "Can't sleep?"

"My brain won't leave me alone. It's getting annoying."

In the darkness, his teeth gleamed in a smile. "Maybe I should try to tire you out."

"Tony, I—"

She'd been about to say, *I'm not sure that's a good idea,* but she didn't get the opportunity because his mouth was on hers, still tasting of toothpaste, and his body pressed up against her as well. She could feel him hard against her leg, and a thrill of desire went through her.

Maybe her body knew something her brain didn't.

Her fingers were pulling at the waistband of his boxer briefs, and he caught hold of the T-shirt she'd worn to bed and pulled it up and over her head. Then his hands were on her bare breasts, caressing, before he bent and ran his tongue over her nipple. She gasped and buried her fingers in his thick hair, holding on to him as he suckled her...another moan escaping her lips when his hand slid inside her panties and began to stroke her.

"Damn it, Tony," she moaned.

For a second, he paused so he could look up into her face. "Do you want me to stop?"

"Don't you dare."

He chuckled. "That's what I thought."

In the next second, he'd slid down her panties and tossed them over the side of the bed, then kissed his way down her stomach, his tongue touching her. She grabbed one of the pillows to cover her mouth because if she cried out as loudly as she wanted to, she feared they might be able to hear it in the condo next door. God *damn*, he was good.

She came hard, all but screaming into the pillow, her body arching as the orgasm rippled its way through her. Then she felt Tony pull the pillow away, toss it over to one side. He caught hold of her, picked her up so she was straddling him, his cock buried deep within her.

Oh, yes, that was good, too. More than good. She rode him, let him fill her, deeper and deeper, as if every thrust, every movement, only cemented the bond between them. Now she understood how important it was for them to do this, how vital it was that she and Tony reaffirmed their connection, made certain it was as strong and as sure as it could be so they'd be ready to face whatever happened the next day. Her fingers twined in his and held on as they both built toward the inevitable climax, this time hitting them almost simultaneously, her moans and his groans blending together until she couldn't quite tell who was giving a voice to their ecstasy.

At last she fell over onto her side of the bed, breath coming quickly as she recited the McAllister charm in her mind. Her right hand was still clenched in Tony's left, and they lay there like that for a long moment, their breath coming in gasps.

"I hope you didn't mind that," he said at last.

"'Mind'?" she repeated incredulously. "Did I sound like I minded?"

He propped himself up on one elbow and looked down at her, eyes glinting in the semidarkness. "Well, no, but after everything you said about getting some rest—"

She swatted half-heartedly at his arm. "So I was wrong. Sue me."

"Nah, I can think of better things to do than that."

Before she could reply, he bent down and kissed her, not to invite another round of lovemaking, but with a sort of amused gentleness, as if he'd known damn well how this evening was going to end up. She kissed him back, then got out of bed and went to the bathroom to get herself cleaned up. When she got back to the bed, he was already half asleep, the gentlest of snores emerging from his parted lips. Since she didn't want to wake him up, she settled for blowing a kiss at him in the darkness, then sank down next to him, pillow in exactly the right position under her cheek.

In the next minute, she was asleep.

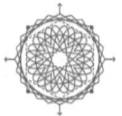

16

THEY ENDED UP RENTING A FOUR-WHEEL-drive Toyota truck, mostly because the man at the rental agency had shaken his head and told Cassandra in rapid-fire Spanish, "Where you're going, you'll need four-wheel-drive."

Which was why she was driving now—El Salvador obviously didn't have any regulations about self-piloting cars, unlike the United States, which mandated their use on the highway—with Tony doing his best to navigate with his phone from the passenger seat. At least their carrier had a signal here, which was a minor miracle neither one of them wanted to investigate too closely.

She'd grown up with four-wheel-drive,

had been off-roading since before she even had a learner's permit. Tony had just sort of shrugged helplessly when she asked him if he wanted to get behind the wheel, then said, "I've always been more of a sports car kind of guy."

In town, the roads were in very good repair, better than some parts of Tucson she could mention. Now, though, barely five miles outside San Salvador, the asphalt had already deteriorated into a mass of potholes, although at least the road was still paved.

Sort of.

There hadn't been a direct route from San Salvador to San Matías, mostly because there was a volcano in the way. They'd decided to head north out of the capital city rather than take the more well-traveled highway that went west first before jogging back toward their destination, since it seemed like the most direct route. Based on the condition of the road, Cassandra was starting to question that decision. But since they were already going this way, there wasn't much they could do except continue grimly forward.

"At least it's a nice day," Tony said, wiping the sweat from his forehead.

Because on top of everything else, the truck's A/C was only working intermittently. It was still better to have it on than not; opening a window wasn't really an option, thanks to all the mosquitoes and other flying insects she really didn't want to identify.

"Define 'nice,'" she muttered, swerving the truck around yet another pothole. Even inside the truck with partial air conditioning, the humidity felt like an oppressive force all on its own. She supposed you would get used to it after all, but of course, they didn't intend to stay here long enough for that to be an issue.

A bus was coming down the highway from the other direction, an ancient, rusty piece of machinery that looked like it was probably older than both she and Tony combined. It was massive, leaning partly into her lane because there wasn't enough room for it on its side of the road.

"Shit," she muttered, and pulled over to the shoulder, feeling the truck bounce and shudder as it went over a truly impressive series of ruts.

But then they had passed the monstrosity, and the road was theirs again. Tony glanced back at the bus as it disappeared around a curve and shook his head. "Guess they don't have the NTSB here, huh?"

"Doubtful."

Cassandra realized she was clutching the steering wheel much harder than she needed to, and released her grip slightly. Yes, she'd driven on terrain that would make your teeth rattle, but that had just been her and her father's Jeep versus the washboard, rock-strewn Forest Service roads near the house where she'd grown up. It wasn't quite the same as having a bus the size of a whale barreling down at you at fifty miles an hour.

That encounter was the only incident of note on their route, however, and about forty minutes later, they came to the outskirts of San Matías, a pretty little village that, Cassandra realized with some shame, looked far more civilized than she'd been expecting, with its neat whitewashed houses and streets that were far better paved than the highway they'd just traversed.

"What now?" Tony asked, looking around with interest.

"I guess we park somewhere and see if we can find a place to ask a few questions. Maybe a restaurant."

"We ate breakfast only an hour and a half ago," he pointed out.

"I know," she replied. "We'll order coffee or something."

This answer seemed to mollify him, because he shrugged and resumed his inspection of the streets outside. "What about there?" he asked, jerking a thumb toward a smallish building on a corner, its walls painted a warm ochre tone, vines climbing everywhere.

The sign over the door said, *"Restaurante,"* followed by *"Antojitos y Comidas Mexicana,"* so it seemed like they were in the right spot. There were even a couple of cars parked next to it on the street, seeming to indicate that the place served some kind of breakfast.

"Works for me," Cassandra said, driving past the restaurant until she found an open place next to the curb for their rented truck.

As she climbed out, though, she found her heart beating a little more quickly. San Matías might not be a stronghold of the Escobars, but it was close enough that she knew she and Tony were now in what you could call enemy territory. The mere thought made a chill move through her, despite the warm, humid air that surrounded them, and she took a deep breath. No way could she allow herself to lose it now, not when they were this close.

There was no need to tell Tony that she would do all the talking, since his Spanish was about restaurant menu–level and nothing more than that. In silence, they went inside the building. It was small but clean, with six rectangular wooden tables arranged in the space and the same warm-toned paint as the exterior on the walls. A wooden counter stood at the far end, with several stools arranged along its length. Behind the counter was a woman in her late thirties probably, rounded and pretty, her sleek black hair pulled back into a leather clasp.

"*¿Puedo ayudarte?*" she asked politely.

"*Dos cafés, por favor,*" Cassandra replied.

"Sit anywhere," the woman said in Spanish. "It will be a few minutes."

Cassandra smiled and thanked her, and went with Tony to sit down at one of the empty tables. Despite the cars parked outside, there didn't seem to be anyone else in the restaurant; maybe the cars belonged to the people who worked there.

He glanced around, one eyebrow

cocked at an inquisitive angle. "It looks innocuous enough."

"Well, this isn't where our friends actually live," Cassandra said. "They just come into the village from time to time. Or at least, that's the story."

"Still."

The woman who'd been working behind the counter—Cassandra couldn't tell for sure whether she was the owner or just the person who happened to be on duty this morning—came over to them, a heavy white stoneware mug in either hand. Even though they'd had excellent coffee earlier that morning in their Airbnb, this smelled even better.

Cassandra took her mug from the woman and said, "*Muchas gracías.*"

Across the table, Tony waggled his eyebrows at her, apparently his signal for her to start asking questions.

All right. She still didn't know exactly what she should say, since coming right out and asking about a witch clan in the area probably wasn't going to earn her any points. Maybe it was better to be blunt, or at least not try to dance around the name of the place they were looking for.

"Do you know of a place called Pico

Negro?" she inquired in Spanish. "A friend of mine is a nature photographer, and he said there was some spectacular scenery out that way."

Almost as soon as the words "Pico Negro" left Cassandra's lips, the woman's eyes widened.

"*No lo sé*," she said, then shot a frightened glance over one shoulder.

On instinct, Cassandra looked in the same direction the woman had been looking, but she couldn't see anything. They were alone in the restaurant.

"You're sure?" she asked. "My friend made it sound as if it wasn't very far from here."

The woman pressed her lips together. "I know nothing about that." Voice lowering, she went on, "You should go. They don't like people asking about them."

"Who doesn't like it?" Cassandra pressed, even though she was fairly certain of the answer.

"No one. I should not have spoken. Just go. The coffee is free."

"But—"

"*¡Vayanse!*"

Even Tony seemed to understand the meaning of that word…or maybe the vehemence in the woman's voice was enough to provide the necessary context. He shot a questioning look at Cassandra, and she said, "She wants us to go. Guess I asked the wrong question."

Although she knew the woman wasn't capable of throwing them bodily out of the restaurant, it also didn't seem like a very good idea to insist on staying, not when she appeared so agitated. Besides, it appeared pretty obvious that she wasn't going to provide the information they needed. The best thing to do would be to keep looking for someone who might be a little more open to communication.

They got up from the table and went out to the truck, then climbed in. Cassandra pushed the starter button.

And nothing.

"What the hell?" she demanded.

"Does it have a full charge?" Tony asked, leaning over to peer at the instrument panel.

"Of course it does," she snapped. At the same time, a niggle of doubt went through her. Could someone have sabotaged the vehicle? No, that was impossible—they'd been inside the restaurant for a couple of minutes at the most, and there hadn't been any sounds from the street outside except a couple of very noisy birds. Trying not to sound impatient, she added, "I double-checked everything before we left this morning. We had a range of more than four hundred miles, and we've only gone about thirty-five."

"Maybe there's a mechanic here some-where," he suggested.

Cassandra thought that sounded like a long shot, but they didn't have a lot of alter-natives. The truck was a rental vehicle, true, but it wasn't as though the agency where they'd gotten it offered twenty-four-hour roadside assistance. They had a number they could call, but then they'd be sitting around and waiting for a tow truck to show up. She knew how to change a tire and test a battery for charge, but this wasn't like the good old days before electric vehicles when you could whack at a carburetor with a wrench and get things running again.

"All right," she said after a long pause during which she weighed their options and realized they didn't have many. "Let's see if we can find something on your phone."

He got it out of his pocket, then did a quick search for mechanics. "There's an

ATV repair shop," he said after a moment. "I don't see anything about an actual mechanic, though."

"Well, that's better than nothing. Even if they can't work on the truck themselves, maybe they can point us in the direction of someone who can."

Tony didn't appear terribly hopeful about this suggestion, but at least he didn't try to shoot it down. "Okay. Looks like it's on the other side of town, toward the north end."

"Lead on," Cassandra replied, although her instincts were already telling her that they should be heading in the opposite direction, the one that led back to the highway. Something about this place gave her the creeps, despite its picture-postcard appearance.

They started walking in the direction he'd indicated, Tony still holding the phone out so he could follow the map's murmured prompts to get them where they needed to go. An older-model Ford truck drove by, and the young boy in the passenger seat gave them a curious glance as he passed them. That was the only traffic they saw; clearly, San Matías was either a very sleepy place, or word had gone out that the two

Americanos who'd gone into the café were asking the wrong questions and should be avoided at all costs.

A fitful breeze tugged at Cassandra's hair, but even it wasn't quite enough to mitigate the oppressive humidity, so different from the desert environment where she'd grown up. Nearer to the coast, it hadn't been so bad, but now they were inland, the countryside all around the village lush and green, thick with unfamiliar flowers and plants. A strange, sweet scent hung on the heavy air, one she couldn't identify.

"This way," Tony said, and they turned a corner onto a street that looked much like the other ones they'd traversed, with houses of various sizes built nearly right next to each other, some painted bright white, others the ruddy hue of dark brick, some a brilliant turquoise. Flowers bloomed in planters and terra-cotta pots, adding their various perfumes to the air as well.

As she'd noted almost as soon as they arrived in the village, there didn't seem to be much separation between businesses and houses. A shop might be set right between two people's homes, or a restaurant in the middle of what appeared to be a residential block. Because of that, she wasn't too surprised when they came upon the ATV repair place, which consisted of a shabby-looking open garage with several bays attached to a modest little white-washed house.

But at least it had a sign out front, and there actually was a man working on an old Polaris ATV in one of the bays. Tools were strewn everywhere, and he apparently hadn't noticed their approach, since Cassandra had to call out to get his attention.

"Discúlpeme, señor," she said. *"¿Usted repara vehículos regulares?"*

The man straightened up and raised a single thick eyebrow at her. He looked like he was somewhere in his fifties, short and stocky, with grease-stained hands and broken fingernails. "What is wrong with it?" he asked, in passably decent English.

"It won't start," Tony said, his expression one of relief. Cassandra guessed that he was getting tired of having to keep figuring out what she was saying in Spanish. "We left it parked on the street around the corner from the café."

"Hmm," the man said. "I promise this ATV to a customer already. Can you wait?"

After all the effort they'd made to get here, having to wait to continue with their mission felt excruciating, but she knew they didn't have much choice. She sent a helpless glance at Tony, who only shrugged, looking resigned to yet another delay.

"Sure," she said. "How long?"

"Not long," he replied. He tilted his head toward the little house attached to the garage. "You can wait inside. The first room is waiting room, *sí*?"

That made her feel a little better. It would have been very strange to go into this man's house and sit there and wait for him to look at their truck, but if he'd already set up part of it as a waiting area for his clients, then that didn't seem quite so bad.

"Okay," Cassandra said, after Tony gave her the faintest of nods, letting her know that he was all right with this plan as well. "*Muchas gracías, señor.*"

They went in through the door he'd indicated. Almost at once, they were hit with a welcome rush of cool air from the A/C unit mounted in the window. That was the room's one real amenity, since its furnishing were shabby and looked like cast-offs from his neighbors—a couch with patched brown vinyl upholstery, a banged-up coffee table, an ugly brass floor lamp.

But hey, the air conditioning worked. As for the rest...it was a mechanic's waiting room. She shouldn't have been expecting the Ritz-Carlton.

The two of them sat down on the couch. Even though the jeans she was wearing felt far too heavy in this tropical climate, right then Cassandra was grateful for them. If she'd had on shorts, she probably would have stuck to the vinyl.

"Well, this is...anticlimactic," Tony said, then ran a hand through his hair so he could push it away from his damp forehead.

"That's for sure." Unfortunately, there wasn't much they could do about the situation, except wait and see what the mechanic had to say. At least it was still early enough in the day that someone from the rental company should be able to get back out here with a tow truck before it got too late.

"Maybe we should ask him about the Escobars," Tony suggested.

"That didn't work too well the last time," Cassandra replied.

"True. But if he does know something

and is willing to tell us, then this trip won't have been a complete waste."

That was a possibility, but even if the mechanic was willing to talk and gave them some kind of actionable information, what were they supposed to do with it? With their truck out of commission, they didn't have a lot of options.

Or maybe we do, she thought then. *After all, Isabella Escobar walked from Pico Negro down here to San Matías with a baby in arms and a toddler in tow, so it can't be* that *far.*

Still, she didn't want to get too hopeful. "What if he freaks out like the woman in the restaurant did?" Cassandra asked. "Then we won't even have someone to work on the truck."

This possibility obviously hadn't occurred to Tony, because as soon as she spoke, his expression fell. "Right. We probably don't want to risk that."

"Unless he says he can't fix the truck," she said. "At that point, we won't have much to lose. We'll end up having to call the rental company and see if they can send someone out to look at the truck."

He nodded, looking a little more cheerful. "Okay, we'll wait and see what the guy has to say, but let's hope he can fix the damn thing. I'd rather not have to spend the night here...or walk back to San Salvador."

It wasn't a great plan, but better than nothing. Cassandra realized that the village had other people living in it, people who might have been able to offer information, and yet she guessed that it probably wouldn't be very smart to start roaming the streets, asking anyone they bumped into if they knew how to find Pico Negro. Doing so would probably be the easiest way to attract the Escobars' attention, and she sure as hell didn't want that.

She reached over and took Tony's hand. His fingers were warm but comforting, not damp the way she'd halfway expected them to be. The air conditioning was doing a good job of keeping the worst of the humidity at bay.

"Sorry I got you into this," she said.

"Into what?" he asked. "It's car trouble. It happens to everyone sooner or later."

"True, but most of the time it doesn't happen out in the middle of nowhere in a foreign country."

He chuckled. "I'm not worried. Worst case, the rental company bails us out. Complications like this are why we didn't book a round-trip ticket. If we end up having to stay longer than we first thought, it's no big deal."

His words cheered her slightly, as did his relaxed outlook about the situation. She knew she had a tendency to overthink things, to worry too much. Cassandra supposed she had inherited that quality from her father, but knowing where it had come from didn't do much to change how she reacted to things.

She leaned over and kissed his cheek. "Thanks, Tony."

"For what?"

"For being you."

He began to smile, but stopped as the door to the waiting room opened. However, the man standing there wasn't the mechanic, but someone much younger, probably in his mid-twenties at the most. And, unlike the mechanic, the stranger was tall and slim and almost model-handsome, with his chiseled features and piercing dark eyes.

"Hello," he said, in perfect, almost unaccented English. "I am Gabriel Escobar."

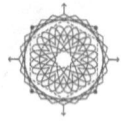

17

TONY'S FIRST INSTINCT WAS TO GRAB Cassandra and make a run for it out the room's other door—which he guessed opened into the rest of the mechanic's house—even though he knew there wasn't much chance of them getting away. Unlike Cassandra, he'd seen Simon Escobar in action. He knew what the warlocks in that clan were capable of.

But although her eyes flared wide with shock for just the barest second, she remained sitting, then looked at the newcomer and said coolly, "I think you have something that belongs to us."

Damn, what a woman. He didn't know too many people who could stand—all

348 | CHRISTINE POPE

right, sit—in Escobar territory and calmly face one of their warlocks down.

The man—Gabriel Escobar—chuckled. "Oh, is that why you have invaded our territory without asking permission?"

Without blinking, Cassandra returned, "I really don't think an Escobar has the right to comment on a witch or warlock coming into someone else's territory uninvited."

This remark only made the strange warlock smile, then glance over at Tony. "Your woman is very brave."

"I'm not sure I'd call her 'my' woman," he said, still wary, but also somewhat relieved that Escobar hadn't just blasted the two of them into the next century. "Cassandra is her own person."

"Yes," she said, then let go of his hand so she could stand up and face Gabriel Escobar straight on, her arms crossed and expression defiant. "I am. And I'm here to represent the de la Paz clan and ask that you return our stolen property immediately."

Gabriel's right eyebrow assumed an amused tilt. Right then, Tony was just glad that Cassandra had already proclaimed her love for him, because otherwise he might have felt a bit threatened by someone so ostentatiously good-looking, Escobar or not. "But we have stolen nothing."

"That's not true," Tony protested, standing up as well. Although it felt a bit surreal to be standing here and arguing with one of the fearsome Escobar warlocks, he figured he might as well at least look as though he was bargaining from a position of strength. "The evidence seems to indicate that it was an Escobar warlock who—"

And then he broke off, since he wasn't sure Cassandra wanted him to go blurting out the exact nature of the items that had been stolen from them.

"Who what?" Gabriel asked, expression all innocence. When neither of them said anything, he smiled again and went on, "All right, I suppose there is no use in playing these games. Yes, we took your books from you. In fact, I was the one who took them."

Anger flared through Tony as he recalled the way his mother had looked crumpled on the family room rug, so small, so helpless. No one should ever have to see a parent like that. And although she seemed to be fine now, that didn't erase what this handsome, arrogant son of a bitch had done to her. "So you're the bastard who struck down a defenseless woman?"

Gabriel's smile faded. For a second, he looked almost regretful, but Tony figured he just wasn't reading the guy's reactions correctly. He was pretty sure that no Escobar was even capable of remorse.

"She would have seen me," the warlock said quietly. "I had to make sure she couldn't do that. However, I did take care that she would suffer no permanent harm."

"Thank you for the humanitarian effort," Cassandra remarked caustically. "That doesn't change the fact that you stole my clan's property."

"If it was your property, what was it doing in the hands of the Castillos?"

He probably knew very well why it was there, so it was obvious she wasn't about to waste her breath pointing out that particular detail. Instead, she planted her hands on her hips and said, "It was being kept safe."

"Not safe enough, apparently."

Her eyes narrowed and her lips parted, and Tony got the impression she was about to say something they might all regret. To forestall her, he said, "All right, you've caught us. What happens now?"

For a second, Gabriel didn't reply, only glanced back and forth between the two of them, as if he was doing his best to take their measure. When he spoke, he sounded almost amused. "What happens now? I suppose I will just have to help you steal them back."

Wait...*what?* Tony looked down at Cassandra, saw the same confusion in her features that he knew he was currently experiencing.

"I don't understand," she said slowly.

"I've startled you," Gabriel said. "I suppose this is not so surprising. You see, I took the books because I am the only one in my clan with the ability to travel in such a way—"

"Teleporting," Cassandra put in, and the Escobar warlock nodded.

"Yes, teleporting. But you see, I wanted you to know who had taken the books. I could have covered up all trace of the magic I used, but I hoped there would be someone in your clan with the gift to identify magical residue, someone who would be able to tell that it was the magic of my own clan that had been used to steal the grimoires."

Tony wanted to shake his head, which currently felt as though it was spinning with the effort to understand this complete reversal. "You wanted us to track you down here."

"Exactly."

Cassandra was frowning fiercely, as if trying to figure out what the hell was going on had given her a massive headache. "But...why?"

"We should go somewhere else to talk. Hector"—Gabriel inclined his head toward the door that opened on the repair shop, clearly indicating the ATV technician—"is a good and faithful servant to the Escobar clan, just as are everyone in San Matías. However, what I am about to say is not something I want him to hear."

"All right," Tony said, his tone dubious. It wasn't as if they had much of a choice. "Where do you want to talk?"

"A safe place."

Before any of them could reply, he'd stepped forward and taken each of them by the hand, grasping it firmly. And then the shabby waiting room around them disappeared, and they were standing in a much more elegant space, the kind of room that wouldn't have looked out of place in Santa Fe, with its white plaster walls and wrought-iron chandelier overhead and heavy Spanish colonial antique furniture.

"Where are we?" Cassandra asked, looking around in confusion.

"As I said, a safe place," Gabriel replied. A wave of his hand, and a pitcher of water and three glasses appeared on the coffee table in front of the linen-covered sofa.

So much power…used so casually. Tony had known the Escobars produced some of the strongest warlocks the world had yet seen, but, aside from that final battle with Simon, he'd never personally witnessed the evidence of their magical talents. Now, though, after Gabriel had brought him and Cassandra here without batting an eye, Tony had much more of an idea about what they were up against.

Or…were they? Gabriel was acting like an ally, not an enemy.

Forehead still creased in a frown, Cassandra said, "Why are you helping us?"

"Because I fear what my brother will do with those books he has taken," Gabriel told her. "He is already powerful enough, for our father's magic came to him in almost its full strength. He does not need the assistance of those grimoires."

"Your father?" Tony asked, already guessing at the answer even though he really didn't want to believe that was what they were dealing with here.

"Yes, my father," Gabriel replied. Then he added, just in case there was any doubt, "Joaquin Escobar."

"Jesus!" Cassandra exclaimed. "How many kids did that bastard have?"

Rather than appear offended, Gabriel only smiled. "He was a man who believed in spreading his seed around. First, there were Olivia and Matías, whom he had with Isabella and who she stole from him. Then there was Renata, who came to your land to help Joaquin seek vengeance on those who had wounded his son...and to help Matías recover his powers."

"So that was her name," Cassandra murmured, frown gone, a sort of angry sorrow in its place. Gabriel made an inquiring sound, and she went on, "Renata murdered my grandfather."

"Ah," the Escobar warlock said. "I am sorry for that. Her talents were immense, but she was her father's daughter, and used those talents mainly for ill. I did not know her very well, for I was barely more than an infant when she left Pico Negro to go to Arizona and assist our father."

"And your brother?" Tony asked, hoping he could keep all these Escobars straight in his head. "The one who's running things now?"

"Vicénte." Gabriel went over to the table and poured some water for himself, then sent his two guests an inquiring look. Tony wasn't thirsty—or rather, he was more interested in hearing what the warlock had to say—so he shook his head. Cassandra also demurred, and so Gabriel went on, "He is ten years older than I, and was too young to be left in charge back then, but such a minor detail did not stop my father. Only a son of Joaquin Escobar would be in command of the clan in his absence, and his word was law."

"Is that why we didn't hear anything of your clan for so long?" Cassandra asked. "Because the person in charge was a child?"

"Yes," Gabriel replied. He drank some of his water and paused, looking thoughtful. "The clan elders ran everything until Vicénte was of age, and things were quiet for a time after that as he began a family of his own. But lately he was been brooding more and more on the loss of our father, planning and plotting. Word came to him of a cache of magical books, grimoires that would give the Escobar clan more power than they have ever had before."

It always came back to those damn books. Right then, Tony thought the world would have been a much better place if his mother had had the sense to throw a match on the goddamn things and be done with it. The Castillos could have lied and told the de la Pazes the books had disappeared. Who would have known?

"So Vicénte sent you to get them," Tony said.

The other man nodded. "Exactly. Although I did not want the books in his hands, I knew better than to go against his wishes."

"Why?" Cassandra asked frankly. Her arms were crossed, and her expression seemed to indicate that she wasn't too thrilled with their host. "Why help him, when you knew what he was planning to do with the books?"

"Because of my mother."

Tony shot a questioning look at Gabriel. His expression now was subdued, hard to read.

"What about your mother?"

Now a faint smile touched the Escobar warlock's mouth, but only for a moment before it disappeared again. "As I said, Joaquin believed in spreading his seed around. I do not share a mother with Vicénte, just as Renata was born from another woman entirely. After Isabella betrayed him, he made sure he wouldn't trust his heart to a woman ever again."

Did Gabriel blame Olivia and Matías' mother for leaving? Hard to say, although Tony tried to give him the benefit of the doubt, thinking that Gabriel certainly wouldn't be confiding in them now if he believed what his father had done was right.

"And your mother...?" Cassandra prompted him.

"My mother is not from El Salvador," Gabriel said. "She was a young girl from Portugal, traveling here with some college friends. She met my father in a bar in San Salvador."

And the rest is history, Tony thought. He'd heard stories about Joaquin Escobar's ability to control minds, to bend everyone around him to his will. Probably he'd seen

Gabriel's mother and wanted her, and the poor kid didn't have a chance.

"She wasn't a witch?" he asked, and Gabriel shook his head.

"No. He was interested in seeing whether I would be as powerful as his full-blood children, but of course he died…was killed…before he had a chance to see me grow up."

"It doesn't look like your civilian blood affected your powers," Cassandra remarked.

"'Civilian'?" Gabriel repeated, and then comprehension dawned in his face. His mouth quirked, and he added, "That is an amusing term. I will have to remember it. But no, my powers were just as strong as Joaquin's—in a way, stronger than Vicénte's, although of course you will never hear him admit to such a thing."

"So why aren't you in charge?" Tony asked, genuinely curious.

"Because I am not Joaquin's heir."

While that still didn't make a lot of sense, Tony decided to roll with it. All witch clans were bound by tradition, and he supposed the Escobars were no different in that regard from anyone else.

"I don't see why that has anything to do with your mother," he said.

A frown pulled at Gabriel's brows. "Once Joaquin had had her, and had a child by her, he saw no reason to keep her around. He cleared her memory of everything that had happened from the moment they met and sent her back to San Salvador. It was supposedly all over the newspapers, for of course everyone had suspected the worst— that she had been taken by human traffickers, or killed by drug smugglers. To have her walk back into town, alive and unharmed… it was quite a sensation, or so I'm told."

"Did she know she'd had a child?" Cassandra asked.

"Yes, because that was not something Joaquin's magic could hide. And that was why she remained in El Salvador and would not go back to Portugal—she knew she had a child here and would not abandon that child."

What a horrible story. Joaquin Escobar truly was the gift that kept on giving…just as soon as you thought you'd heard everything, along came another despicable act to prove he probably was one of the worst human beings to ever walk the planet.

"And because she's still here, Vicénte uses her as leverage over you," Cassandra said, eyes blazing with indignation. Tony didn't know whether she was even aware of it, but her hands had clenched into fists as she spoke. "He's threatened to harm her if you don't cooperate, right?"

"I am afraid so," Gabriel replied.

"Then why help us now?" Tony asked. "I mean, aren't you putting her in danger by even talking to us?"

The Escobar warlock glanced away from him, toward the tall windows on one side of the room, which showed off a courtyard lush with tropical plants. "I suppose I am, but it is a risk I have to take. Vicénte must not have those books."

He sounded weary but resolute, and Tony figured it was probably better not to push too hard. "Why now?" he asked suddenly. "Why the change of heart?"

Gabriel released a breath, brows furrowed. He glanced away from Tony, out through the window that showed the lush garden beyond. Maybe he was looking toward where Pico Negro lay, although since Tony had no idea where this villa was even located, he couldn't say for sure. "Because of your presence here," the

Escobar warlock said quietly. "You and Cassandra can take the grimoires away, and Vicénte will never have to know about my part in the scheme."

Yes, that would make things a lot easier for him, wouldn't it? Gabriel could place all the blame on the two interlopers and stay in his brother's good graces. Maybe not the most heroic thing to do, although Tony wasn't sure he wouldn't have devised a similar plan if he'd been placed in a similarly difficult position. What would he do if someone were threatening his own mother's safety...or his little sister's?

Cassandra's eyes narrowed suddenly, and she sent Gabriel a piercing look. "There really isn't anything wrong with our truck, is there?"

"No," he replied. "I needed to send you to Hector's shop so I could speak privately with you. None of my clan have any need of his services—we Escobars do not believe in tearing up the rainforest with those vehicles—and so there was little risk of running into anyone who would try to stop me."

Despite everything, Tony had to struggle to hold back a laugh. How crazy was it that this witch clan that left so much death and destruction in its wake also seemed to be a bunch of environmentalists?

His companion didn't seem similarly amused. Voice brisk, she said, "Is it going to be a problem that we were asking about Pico Negro in the café?"

"No," Gabriel replied. "María will not even remember you were there."

"Because you put the whammy on her."

"I do not know what a 'whammy' is, but if you mean that I used my magic to erase her memories of you, then yes, that is what I did."

Because that was just how the Escobars rolled. Although Tony could see why doing such a thing had been necessary, he still wondered how much truly separated Gabriel's actions from those of his half-brother if he could act so cavalier about messing with someone else's mind.

Then again, maybe he'd thought he was protecting the café's owner.

All Cassandra did was nod. Her expression was grim, though, her pretty mouth pulled down at the corners, eyes still narrow. Hands on her hips, she faced Gabriel squarely and said, "Why are we supposed to believe any of this?"

He looked as though he'd been

expecting that question, because he shrugged and said, "You will have to make the decision whether or not to trust me. However, if I'd truly meant you harm, I could have killed you back in the waiting room at Hector's shop. I would not have had to bring you here."

Tony had no doubt of that; he could tell that the Escobars had all of San Matías under their thumb, and so if Gabriel had decided to murder them in that shabby little room, Hector probably would have only gone in afterward and quietly cleaned up the mess. But even if Gabriel didn't mean to hurt them directly, it was entirely possible that he wanted to use them as patsies in case this all went south and he needed a convenient scapegoat to direct attention away from himself.

"Too bad Ava isn't here," he murmured, and Gabriel looked at him inquiringly.

"Who is Ava?"

"My sister," Tony replied. "Her talent is reading minds. She could look right inside your head and tell us whether you were lying or not."

"A useful gift," Gabriel agreed. "Yes, that would probably be helpful, but since she is not here, you will have to rely on your own judgment."

And there was the problem. Everything Gabriel said had the ring of truth, but if he really was Joaquin Escobar's son, then maybe he'd also inherited the ability to bend everyone around him to his will. If that were happening, would he and Cassandra even be able to tell whether their minds were their own?

Not exactly the sort of conundrum Tony had thought he and Cassandra would face when they came to Escobar territory, but they had to figure out somehow whether any of this was legitimate.

"Your mother lives in San Salvador?" Cassandra asked.

"Yes. She is a secretary at a law firm."

That sounded so normal, Tony wanted to shake his head. However, there wasn't anything normal about this situation.

Gabriel went on, "I've done my best to observe her from a distance, to make sure that she is safe and comfortable in her life. Unfortunately, I cannot come close without risking her safety."

That all sounded unutterably sad. Cassandra asked gently, "And she doesn't know anything about you?"

A simple shake of the head. "No. Vicénte made sure that I would have no contact with her. He said it was because he thought it would be too dangerous, but I know it was merely a way of him asserting his power as *primus*."

Well, Gabriel's reply seemed to settle that particular question. Tony knew people had wondered whether Joaquin Escobar was merely an aberration, or whether the Salvadoran clan had a tradition of male clan leaders like the Wilcoxes in northern Arizona did. Clearly, the Escobars followed that same model, or Gabriel wouldn't have spoken so casually of his brother's role as *primus*.

"So, what's your plan?" Cassandra asked. "You must have something in mind, or you wouldn't have brought us here, would've just let us try to get the books back on our own."

Gabriel shook his head. "That would have been certain death for you," he said. "Or rather, it would have been certain death for you," he added, fixing Tony with a direct stare. "Cassandra, I fear, would have met a different fate."

A fate worse than death, no doubt. From what he'd heard so far, Tony was pretty sure that Gabriel's brother Vicénte wouldn't scruple at a little casual rape, just like his father.

Cassandra gave an overly off-hand shrug. "Well, they could try."

"You are a very brave woman," Gabriel said, "but I fear you would be no match for my brother. But," he went on, "we have no need to worry about such things. I will use my powers to protect you, to give you the help you need to get close to the books. And then you will take them away with you. I can only hope that once they are in the possession of your clan, Cassandra, you will be more careful with them in the future."

"No worries," she said. If what Gabriel had just said about her clan's carelessness rankled, she didn't show any sign of it… maybe because Tony was fairly certain the same thing had already passed through her mind on more than one occasion. "Our *prima* just built a library attached to her house so all the clan's grimoires can be gathered in one place and be watched over by her—and her successors—at all times. I don't think we need to worry about any more thefts."

Gabriel said, "Good," but there was still

something troubled about his expression, as though he didn't know for sure whether Zoe's protection would be enough.

Tony had a few reservations along those lines as well, although he knew better than to bring them up with Cassandra. The important thing was to get the books out of the hands of the Escobars. After that, they could worry about beefing up the magical security around Zoe's house. From what she'd told him when she cast the shield to protect his car, Cassandra's magic apparently was the type that was "set it and forget it"—in other words, she could cast one of her magical spells and it would remain in place until she purposely removed it—which meant that might be an easy way of protecting the books in the library without having to take extraordinary measures.

"Where are the books now?" Tony asked.

"In my brother's house," Gabriel replied. "He already had his own small library of such things, although the de la Paz grimoires have made it much more extensive."

Well, that was great. Tony had been kind of hoping that the books were being stored in a neutral location, maybe the Escobars' village library, if such a thing even existed. But he probably should have realized that Vicénte would make sure to keep such valuable items close to him.

"And how are we supposed to get the books out of your brother's house?" Cassandra asked, tone dubious. "I mean, he must have the place warded up the wazoo, right?"

Gabriel stared at her for a moment, eyes narrowed, before he appeared to nod to himself, as if he'd just worked out the idiom she'd used. "Yes, he has protections in place. They were set by one of our elders, a woman who is skilled at such things. However, what she doesn't know is that I've been able to undo her warding spells for some time now, so they are not as effective a protection as she or my brother think."

That was encouraging. At the same time, though, Tony felt a stir of unease. He was used to witches and warlocks who possessed one specific talent—two at the very most—and yet it seemed as though Gabriel was able to produce new magical gifts at the drop of a hat. If nothing else, his prodigious abilities had to be proof that he was not ambitious, or scheming to take his brother's position in the clan, because he certainly should have been able to do such a thing fairly easily...as long as he wasn't lying about Vicénte's powers being lesser.

Cassandra's thoughts appeared to have run along the same lines. She crossed her arms and tilted her head, surveying Gabriel through narrowed eyes. "If you can do all that, I don't see why you need our help. Just, I don't know, teleport the damn books back to Arizona."

That suggestion made Gabriel chuckle. "I know you think my powers seem unlimited, but truly, they are not. I can only send living things in such a way. That means I need the two of you to be holding the books when I send you away from Pico Negro."

"Send us—" Tony broke off there, shaking his head in bemusement. "You held our hands when you brought us here. Did you not need to do that?"

"No," Gabriel said. "I expend less energy when I can have physical contact with the people I am teleporting, but it's not necessary. I only need to know where to send you."

"Which in this case would be Zoe's house in Scottsdale," Cassandra put in.

"That would be convenient. No explaining the books to some customs officer, no paying penalties for all the extra baggage we'd be hauling back with us."

She probably wasn't being completely serious, because those concerns were minor compared to getting the grimoires out of the Escobars' hands. However, Gabriel seemed to take her comments at face value.

"Yes, that would be easiest. It is a very great distance, but I think I can manage it."

"You 'think'?" Tony demanded. He wasn't too thrilled about the idea of Gabriel's magic coming up short and dropping him and Cassandra in the middle of the Gulf of Mexico or something. "What happens if it doesn't work?"

"Nothing happens," Gabriel replied. "That is, the spell will fail, and you would remain wherever you were standing when I made the attempt."

Which also wasn't so great. If Vicénte caught them in the middle of the heist….

However, Cassandra didn't seem too worried. "I can live with that," she said. "So you'll…what, make us invisible or something?"

"Not precisely," Gabriel said. "More that I will cast an illusion over you so you look like two of the people from my clan, probably the women who clean my brother's house, since they would have the most reason for being there."

That made sense. Someone who sounded as arrogant as Vicénte Escobar probably wouldn't even look at them twice while wearing that kind of a disguise. He definitely didn't seem like the sort of person who would pay much attention to the help.

"And we go in and grab the books, and you send us away," Cassandra said.

"Exactly."

On the surface, it all sounded pretty simple...provided Gabriel's magic really was powerful enough to do everything he said it could. So far, Tony didn't see much reason to doubt him. He didn't know of anyone—except Miranda and possibly her parents—who could teleport from place to place with such ease, not to mention displaying the vast variety of abilities Gabriel apparently possessed.

"What about the truck?" he asked.

"What about it?" Cassandra said.

"Rental companies take a dim view of vehicles not being returned," he pointed out. "The security deposit is being held against my credit card, remember."

"Someone from San Matías will drive the truck back to San Salvador," Gabriel said. "It will not be a problem."

Well, it wouldn't be a problem if everything went smoothly. If the plan backfired and Vicénte figured out his brother was behind the attempt to steal the books, then Tony kind of doubted any of the Escobar clan's lackeys in the village would be too eager to give his accomplices a helping hand.

Of course, if that happened, then the deposit on the rental truck would probably be the least of his worries....

"We have luggage at our Airbnb, too," Cassandra said. Now she was frowning slightly, as if she'd realized that there could be drawbacks to Gabriel's form of instantaneous travel.

"Which you can pay someone to pack and ship back to the U.S. for you," Gabriel countered. "Do you think any of that is more important than getting your clan's books away from my brother?"

"No," Cassandra said at once. "You're right, of course. So when do you want to do all this?"

"Now," Gabriel replied. "Or at least, in a few hours. The women go in to clean during the afternoon so that everything is tidy for his evening meal."

Vicénte sounded like one demanding s.o.b. He probably didn't pay them for their work, either…no doubt he figured that the honor of serving the Escobar *primus* should be enough.

"All right," Cassandra said. "Tell us exactly what we need to do."

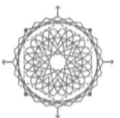

18

ON THE SURFACE, IT WAS A SIMPLE ENOUGH plan. Gabriel would send Alba and Jimena —the two women who kept his brother's house clean—on an errand to San Matías to get them out of the way for a few hours... and also to provide them with an alibi, just in case something went wrong and Vicénte suspected them of stealing his precious books. They would be seen by enough people in San Matías that it would be clear they had nothing to do with the theft.

With Alba and Jimena gone, Gabriel would cast the illusion on Cassandra and Tony to make them look like the two women, and they would enter his house through the kitchen as usual, then go to the room on the ground floor of the house that he'd turned into his library. Once there, they would fill up the nylon bags Cassandra had stashed in her purse with the stolen grimoires, and he would send the two of them away with no one the wiser.

Of course, the simpler the plan, it seemed the more things that could go wrong with it.

Unfortunately, she and Tony didn't have much of a choice. Cassandra knew there wasn't a snowball's chance in hell of them getting that close to the books without Gabriel's assistance. They needed him to get them inside the house, and safely away as well. Even going flat out in their rented pickup truck, there was too much risk of someone catching up with them on the way back to San Salvador, or even at the airport. Security here in El Salvador wasn't the same as it was in the U.S., and it was entirely possible that the Escobars could grab her and Tony somewhere in the terminal before they even boarded their plane. Gabriel could send them away in the blink of an eye. You really couldn't do much better than that.

While they were waiting for the proper time to arrive, he played the gracious host, giving them water tart with lemon, feeding them pupusas—traditional masa flour turnovers filled with cheese, or beans, or spicy shredded pork. Although Cassandra had had pupusas at Salvadoran restaurants in Arizona, these were definitely the best she'd ever had, fresh and not doughy at all, and with spices that were subtly different from the ones she'd eaten before.

He asked about their clans, and was obviously relieved to hear that Tony's mother hadn't suffered any permanent harm.

"I tried to be careful," he said, "but it's not always possible to tell how a spell will rebound on a person."

"She's fine," Tony said. His earlier anger had disappeared, although Cassandra had a feeling he wouldn't have been nearly as relaxed if he hadn't heard from his sister Ava that Sophia was almost back to her old self. "My sister says she's up and walking and doing well."

"The mind-reading sister," Gabriel remarked, and Tony grinned.

"Yes, Ava. She wasn't too happy about Cassandra and me coming to El Salvador."

"I imagine she was only being protective."

"Maybe," Tony allowed, although he

didn't seem convinced. "Honestly, I think she was kind of ticked I was getting to see a part of the world that she'd never be able to visit."

"Yes, it is difficult sometimes, knowing we must all be constrained by the territories we were born in." Gabriel reached for his water glass, looking contemplative.

"Is all of El Salvador the Escobars' territory?" Cassandra asked. She'd been wondering this ever since they'd landed in San Salvador, since she hadn't felt even the slightest twinge of another witch or warlock's presence in the capital city.

"Yes," Gabriel replied. "Actually, our territory extends slightly over the border into Honduras as well."

"But you all live in Pico Negro," Tony said.

"Mostly. Some of us have holdings in other parts of the country—like my house here—but in general, the Escobars like to keep to themselves."

Well, except when they wander into San Salvador looking for young women to forcibly seduce, Cassandra thought. The story of Gabriel's mother haunted her. How terrible to have been used in such a way, to know that you'd lost nearly a year of your life, had a child, and yet couldn't remember anything of where you'd been, of who had done such a thing to you.

She wondered if Gabriel's brother Vicénte had done the same thing, or whether he'd taken a wife from among his own people. Then she recalled that Gabriel had said something about his brother starting a family of his own, although he hadn't mentioned anything else about them. In a way, that was probably good; while Vicénte didn't sound like a very nice guy, Cassandra still didn't want to think about being forced into a situation where she or Tony would have to hurt or kill someone who was a husband and a father.

But no, it wouldn't come to that. Gabriel would sneak them in to take the books and get them out afterward, and Vicénte would never have to know they'd been in his home.

"Let me tell you of Pico Negro, so you know what to expect," Gabriel said then, setting down his half-eaten pupusa. "There are several thousand of us, so it is actually a town larger than San Matías, although it remains hidden from the world. There are no roads, only paths through the rainforest, until you get to the town itself. That part has been paved, mostly to control the mud. We have houses and shops and cantinas, and live a self-sufficient existence."

"How do you get supplies in there?" Tony asked.

"They are brought to San Matías, and then taken by hand cart on the forest paths. It is not as difficult as you might think. Also, people have little cleared plots to grow their vegetables, and we also keep goats and chickens."

All the comforts of home. Cassandra wondered how they kept themselves from getting completely inbred, but she supposed the Escobars must have people who kept track of all the cousins, just as the stateside clans did, and they probably did bring in nonmagical people from time to time to dilute the Escobar blood a bit. Did those civilians remain silent because of their love for their witchy spouses, or did the Escobars have some kind of spell that guaranteed none of their secrets would pass beyond the borders of Pico Negro?

Gabriel went on, "Vicénte's is the grandest house in the town, of course. It lies on the northern border of the settlement, and has several garden plots and a shed for his herd of goats. We will enter that way, for

Alma and Jimena usually stop to check on the animals before they come into the house."

"You're not worried about your brother being there?" Tony asked.

"No, because in the afternoons he usually spends time at one of the cantinas, drinking *cerveza* or tequila."

Great, Cassandra thought. *So we're not just dealing with a powerful asshole of a primus here, but a possibly drunk one, too.*

However, Tony didn't seem too troubled by this particular revelation. "Good. That means he probably won't be paying too close attention to anything."

"I would not be so sure of that. He drinks, yes, but not to the point where he is impaired."

Hmm. Maybe a drunk *primus* would have been better. However, Cassandra knew they'd just have to roll with whatever happened, since they didn't have any choice at this point. Those books had to be taken away from Vicénte Escobar, no matter what.

"But he won't come home while we're there," she said, and Gabriel nodded.

"The chances of that are very small."

"Wife?" Tony asked. "Children?"

"He has none," Gabriel replied, and now he looked a little troubled. "That is, he had a wife, but she died in childbirth, and the son my brother wanted so desperately died with her."

This revelation startled Cassandra…and also revealed the reason why Gabriel hadn't said much about his brother's family. While she could understand that such things might happen under normal circumstances, and that this sort of tragedy might not be so very strange in such a remote community, they weren't dealing with normal circumstances here. "Your clan doesn't have a healer?" she asked.

"We do," Gabriel told her, "but even Lupe could not save Vicénte's wife. It happens sometimes, despite a healer's efforts. At any rate, you do not have to worry about anyone else being in the house when we arrive. It is because my brother does not have a wife that he has Alma and Jimena in to clean and cook for him."

Well, Cassandra hoped they'd be out of there before the cooking was supposed to start, because she knew there was no way in the world she could fool anyone that she was competent in a kitchen. With coaching, she could make roast chicken and rice, and that was about as far as her culinary talents extended.

But she reassured herself that they'd be long gone before Vicénte sat down to his evening pupusas, or whatever might be on that night's bill of fare. She had to confess she didn't know much about Salvadoran cuisine; the meal she and Tony had eaten that morning had been very similar to the food they'd had in Baja. From what she could tell, a lot of the dishes seemed to cross over.

And she realized she was distracting herself with ruminating on the differences between Mexican and Salvadoran cuisine because that was better than worrying about their upcoming raid on Vicénte Escobar's house. Even though she knew he wouldn't be around, and apparently didn't have the magical ability to tell when interlopers entered his village, she could feel her stomach beginning to knot up from anxiety.

That anxiety only worsened when Gabriel glanced out the window, as if to confirm the time of day, then said, "I must leave you for a few moments. I will go to Pico Negro and send the two women down to San Matías."

"They won't think that's strange?"

Cassandra asked. "I mean, you sending them on a random errand like that?"

"No, because Vicénte often has me act as his intermediary. That is also why no one should think anything strange about me walking with them over to the house."

Too good to talk to the help, she thought, but didn't say anything. She'd never before encountered a warlock who treated members of his own clan like servants rather than family members. It was strange, because although people in a witch family might barter services—gardening for house painting, or tax preparation, or whatever—if they were going to hire people for ongoing domestic help, then it was always civilians.

But obviously the Escobars were in a world of their own, one that she'd be glad to get away from as soon as possible. Maybe they'd taken up the practice of having their own people act as servants because they kept themselves so isolated. Whatever the reason, it really didn't matter in the long run.

"Okay," Tony said. "Cassandra and I will hang tight here until you come back."

Obviously, because neither of them even knew where they were. She was pretty sure this house wasn't in Pico Negro, but otherwise, they could be any place within the borders of El Salvador...or even in Honduras, since Gabriel had said the Escobar clan holdings extended that far.

At least the house was beautiful. She could think of worse places to have to hang out and wait.

"It won't be long," Gabriel promised them.

And then he disappeared.

Cassandra blinked. Of course she knew intellectually that the Escobar warlock was able to teleport, since he'd brought them here using that means of travel in the first place, but it was one thing to have it happen to you and quite another to sit there and watch a human being disappear into thin air.

"Kind of freaky, isn't it?" Tony remarked. He got up from where he was sitting and came over to her, then put his hands on her shoulders and began to rub them gently.

Ah, that felt good. She hadn't even realized she was that tense until she felt his fingers massaging the tight muscles of her shoulders and neck. "A little," she said.

"Yeah, imagine it happening when

you're standing in a cathedral watching your cousin get married, and his fiancée goes poof into thin air."

She turned slightly so she could look up at him. "Is that what happened with Rafe and Miranda? I heard there was some weirdness going on, but I never got the whole story."

"Yep, she disappeared in front of everyone. Really crazy, because at the time we'd all heard that she didn't even have any magic. But they got it all worked out in the end."

Despite Simon Escobar's best efforts. That thought cheered Cassandra up a little; it reminded her that, for all their formidable powers, the Escobars weren't invincible. They could be beaten.

She stood up and went to Tony. At once, his arms went around her, as if he knew she needed to feel his touch right then, needed to be reassured that he was going to be at her side through all of this.

"Do you really think we have a chance?" she asked.

He bent and kissed her on the top of her head, then brushed a strand of hair away from her face. "Of course we do. I mean, I think we have a much better chance now that we have Gabriel on our side. That guy's powers are intense."

Cassandra couldn't argue with that assessment. On the other hand…. "I hope he's really on our side, that this isn't all just some kind of act to torture us. What if he's gone to get Vicénte, or other people from his clan? He could have been lying to us this whole time."

"But he wasn't," came Gabriel's voice, and both she and Tony startled.

"I'm sorry," she said hastily, hoping she hadn't offended him too much. "I just—that is, I—"

"It's all right," the Escobar warlock said. Luckily, he didn't look offended, the expression on his handsome features almost amused, as if he thought it was funny that he'd popped back in on them while they were discussing his possible motivations. "I suppose I would be suspicious, too, if I were in your place. But we are ready—I told Alma and Jimena that Vicénte decided at the last minute he wanted *dulce de tres leches* cake for his dessert tonight, and that they needed to get fresh cow's milk down in San Matías. We only have goats in the village, not cows, and so it was not a request that raised their suspicions. And once we are done with this and are successful, I will make sure to erase that part of their memories so they cannot tell Vicénte that I was the one who sent them down to San Matías."

"Going to get milk doesn't sound like the sort of errand that requires two people," Cassandra remarked, hoping she didn't sound too dubious. But come on—two grown women to go fetch some milk?

Gabriel only smiled. "Normally, I would say yes. But although it is safe enough here, the women of Pico Negro do not leave our little town unaccompanied, which is why the two of them were necessary for this errand. We should have several hours, but it is best if we do this now and get it over with."

"Right," Cassandra said. The knots in her stomach were back, as well as the tension Tony had begun to massage away from her neck.

"We're ready," Tony added.

He did look ready—chin up, a determined light in his dark eyes. Gazing at him, she thought she'd never loved him as much as she did in that moment...loved him for his unexpected strength, for his dedication to seeing this thing through despite the risks involved.

"Excellent." Gabriel was silent for a moment, studying them both. Then he went on, "Tony, you will be Jimena, as she is the taller of the two, and illusions are easier when you don't have to work quite so hard to make an illusion hide something that is utterly different from its true appearance. So Cassandra, you will be Alba."

She nodded. Honestly, she didn't really care if Gabriel made her look like Mickey Mouse, as long as all this worked.

And although she didn't know quite what to expect, since her clan currently didn't have any illusion-workers, it felt a bit anticlimactic for Gabriel to merely stand there and inhale deeply, then close his eyes. When he opened them, he smiled at her, then Tony.

"Yes, that should work."

There weren't any mirrors in the room, so Cassandra had no idea what she looked like. However, when she glanced over at Tony, she let out an audible gasp. Standing where he'd been was a tall, thin woman in a plain black skirt and embroidered blouse, her gray-streaked dark hair pulled back into a severe bun.

"Wow, you're—"

"Totally not me," Tony said. The contrast between his obviously male voice and his appearance was so jarring, Cassandra put a hand up to her mouth to hold back a laugh.

Only that hand wasn't hers. The skin was darker and the nails short, unpainted. It was also much chubbier.

So was the rest of her. She looked down and saw a round body with ample breasts, so large she had to bend slightly to see her feet. It was utterly strange, because although she still felt like herself, she knew she sure as hell didn't look it.

"Wow, Cassandra, you've really let yourself go," Tony said, appearing as if he wanted to burst out laughing as well.

"Great—now I know you only love me for my body," she retorted.

Gabriel shook his head. "They are only illusions, you know."

"Oh, we know," Tony said, the laughing lilt in his voice horribly at odds with the severe face of the woman whose appearance he currently wore. "That's why it's so funny."

Judging by the way Gabriel's brows drew together, he didn't find anything particularly amusing about their current situation. But then his shoulders lifted, and he said, "Let us go. Remember, we will be appearing near the goat pens, so I do not think there is much risk of us being observed."

"Except by the goats," Tony cracked, and now it was Cassandra's turn to shake her head. She knew this was just his way of whistling in the dark, but she thought it was probably time to sober up and focus on the difficult task ahead.

Whether any of that got through to him, she wasn't sure, but at least he was silent as she slid her purse satchel-fashion across her body—luckily, Gabriel's illusion hid it as well—then pulled out two of the nylon bags she'd brought with her and handed them to Tony. He folded them as small as possible and tucked them in a pocket of his jeans—which she knew were still jeans and still there beneath the illusion, despite what her eyes were telling her.

Then the Escobar warlock took their hands again, and just like before, the room where they were standing promptly disappeared, this time replaced by an outdoor scene. As Gabriel had said, they were standing by the goat pens, each of which contained a half dozen of the animals. They all looked up and swiveled their heads to stare at the newcomers who'd arrived so precipitously in their vicinity, but he paid them no attention.

"This way," he said, leading them across the open area that had been cleared between the house and the goat pens. The air here didn't seem as humid as it had been down in San Matías, even though the rainforest crowded in on every side, the vegetation lush and almost virulently green.

The house itself was an impressive two-story building, done in the Spanish style with white-plastered walls and a red tile roof. Birds of paradise bloomed in the beds that surrounded it, and everything looked well-tended and clean.

Well, of course it is, Cassandra thought as she followed Gabriel along the path that led to the back door. *Vicénte Escobar probably has clan members gardening for him, too.* As frustrated as she could sometimes get with all the restrictions involved in being part of a witch family, at least she didn't have to worry about a high-handed *prima* lording it over everyone. Zoe was probably one of the world's most laid-back clan leaders, maybe sometimes too laid-back.

But even as relaxed as Zoe tended to be about clan business, this mess with the books certainly wasn't her fault. It had been a tradition going back generations for individuals to store and maintain the grimoires they collected, and some people had been more careful with their property than others. Then again, how were you supposed to guard against someone like Simon Escobar, a warlock who could mask his very nature and come and go like the wind?

Gabriel put his hand on the knob for the back door and turned it. "Come inside," he said.

Cassandra wasn't sure what she'd been expecting—probably a kitchen as rustic as the scene outside—but the room she and a disguised Tony entered was surprisingly modern, with scrubbed butcher-block counters and appliances newer than the ones in her own condo. Her astonishment must have registered even through the illusion she wore, because the Escobar warlock smiled.

"We have solar here, and propane for

cooking. And of course Vicénte must have the best of everything."

Of course. Since she really didn't have an answer for Gabriel's comment, she only shrugged.

Now brisk, he went on, "This way. The library is on the other side of the main room."

He took them through the kitchen and out into a large, open space in the center of the house, with high ceilings and dark beams overhead. To one side was a staircase that led to the upstairs rooms, and on the other side of the living area were several doorways. Gabriel headed toward the one on the right, Cassandra and Tony only a few paces behind him. She still wasn't entirely sure about her companion's motivations, but she knew she didn't want to get too far away from their guide, just in case…well, just in case.

The room they entered was small, not much more than ten feet square. Each wall had a bookcase made of dark wood placed against it, although she saw right away that the bookcases weren't yet full.

And the one directly across from them held the stolen grimoires, those twenty-odd volumes that had caused so much mischief.

Sitting on top of the bookcase where they now rested was a metal dish, and in that dish was a black pillar candle, its flame moving sullenly in the still air.

The scent it released was something she couldn't quite identify, but it felt cloying and heavy and slightly off, sort of like musk that had gone bad. Tony obviously noticed it, too, because the thin nose of the illusion he wore wrinkled slightly.

"What is that?" he asked.

Gabriel shook his head. "Something one of the elders made. She said it would help to enhance the power of the books, allow it to be more focused."

That sounded like a bunch of mumbo-jumbo to Cassandra. However, she'd be the first to admit she didn't know anything about the dark magic those books contained, how to use it, how to make it even more powerful than it already was. She supposed it was possible the Escobar elder had been speaking the truth. It was also entirely possible that she'd made the whole thing up to enhance her own influence with her clan's *primus*.

"Go ahead," Gabriel went on, glancing over his shoulder as if to make sure they were the only ones in the house. "Take the books."

Delay would only cost them, and Cassandra wanted this over with as quickly as possible. She hurried forward and pulled the first nylon bag out of her pocket, unfolded it, and then filled it with as many books as would fit. Tony did much the same thing, stuffing books into his own bag with an alacrity that surprised her a little, considering how relaxed he seemed most of the time.

Two bags down, and two more to go. Still, it only took less than a moment to shove the remaining volumes into her bag. Tony finished at nearly the same time, and he straightened and turned back toward Gabriel, wearing a triumphant expression.

"Well, that's that," he said. "Guess it's time for you to send us on our way."

"Thank you for this," Gabriel replied. As he spoke, the illusion that had shielded Tony disappeared—as did the one that had concealed Cassandra's identity as well. Or at least she guessed it had, since the hands clutching the two bags of books were now hers again, slender and pale, the nails coated in iridescent polish.

"No, thank *you*," she said. "We could never have done this without your help."

"Do not be so quick to congratulate yourselves," came a new voice, one that sounded almost like Gabriel's, only somehow sharper-edged, laced with cruel amusement. This newcomer had spoken in English, as if he'd overheard part of their conversation earlier and wanted to make sure that the intruders in his house could understand everything he was saying.

A man stood at the doorway, arms crossed. He appeared to be a few years older than Gabriel, handsome in his own way, but not nearly as model-pretty. Standing on either side of him were a man and a woman, both much older than the man they flanked.

Oh, shit, Cassandra thought, even as Gabriel said evenly,

"Hello, Vicénte."

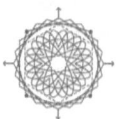

19

ALL THREE OF THE ESCOBAR NEWCOMERS fairly vibrated with power, so Cassandra guessed the older man and woman must be clan elders. How they'd known she and Tony were here, she had no idea, but at this point, it probably didn't matter.

"Put the books down," Vicénte said. There was almost something frightening about how calm he seemed, as if he knew he had the upper hand here and so had no need to lose his temper.

"Or what?" Tony asked, trying to sound cocky. His voice didn't shake, and he met Vicente's gaze stare for stare, but the impression was marred a little by the sweat beading on his forehead.

"Or this," the *primus* replied, and raised

his hands. There was no flash of magic, nothing to indicate that he'd done anything at all, but at once Tony let out a shocked cry and doubled over, clutching his stomach in pain. The bags of books he'd been holding fell to the floor, and the volumes inside slid out, making a messy pile on the terra-cotta tiles.

Worry overriding her fear, Cassandra went to him. Before she could speak, ask him how he was doing, a wave of agony went through her, feeling like the lightning sharp stab of her appendix failing when she was fifteen. It had been fine, because the local healer took care of her, but the memory of the pain remained, the sensation that something was horribly, terribly wrong inside her body. Her hands unclenched, and the bags she'd gripped with all her might slipped from her fingers, the books within joining the ones Tony had already dropped.

"Enough," Gabriel said.

The pain lingered for a moment longer, as if Vicénte needed to prove that he had no need to obey his brother's commands, and then was gone. Cassandra let out a gasp of relief and straightened, her hand reaching over to take Tony's. His fingers pressed down on hers, strong and warm, and so she knew that whatever Vicénte had done to them, its effects weren't permanent.

"No, what *you* have done is enough," the *primus* said. He was watching his brother through narrowed dark eyes, and yet Cassandra couldn't help but note a certain air of satisfaction about him, as if he was almost happy about Gabriel's betrayal. She had a feeling there was no love lost between the two; maybe Vicénte had been hoping for the opportunity to remove someone he saw as a rival, and Gabriel had handed it to him on a silver platter. "To try to take these things away, when we Escobars worked so hard to claim them as our own?"

Gabriel's chin went up. "What work did you do, brother? For I was the one who went to retrieve them, since your own gifts were not sufficient to the task."

That remark earned him a fearsome scowl. "It is not the *primus's* place to do such dirty work. But yes, they were dearly bought...or have you forgotten about our own brother's death at the hands of this one's clan?" Vicénte flickered an angry glance in Tony's direction before returning his attention to his brother.

"A half-brother neither of us had ever

met," Gabriel observed dryly. "But I do commend you for your family loyalty."

Still frowning, Vicénte said, "You know nothing of loyalty. Your actions here only prove that." He looked at the older man who stood next to him and asked, "What should we do with them, Raúl?"

"Kill the one interloper," the man replied in Spanish. He was much shorter than either of the Escobar brothers, almost gnome-like with his fringe of white hair and broad nose and close-set eyes. Cassandra couldn't tell for sure whether he'd spoken in Spanish because his English wasn't that strong, or because he hadn't realized that she spoke Spanish as well as he did. "But it would be a shame to get rid of the witch. She is strong, and would be a valuable addition. Perhaps to warm your bed for a time, *primus*?"

She immediately recoiled in disgust and anger, and Vicénte's mouth lifted in an ugly smile as he stared at her. Although Tony couldn't have understood the exchange in detail, he obviously had caught enough of the gist to know they were discussing something horribly wrong. He began to step forward, hands knotting at his sides, but Cassandra shook her head at him.

Turning back to Vicénte, she said clearly, *"Tócame, y te arrancaré las bolas!"*

The elder drew himself up, a shocked expression on his face, but the *primus* only smirked at her. "Oh, if you are touching my balls, beautiful witch, it will not be to tear them off."

"Enough of this," the other elder, the older woman, said. She was tall and thin, and, if not the actual sister of the woman whose face Tony had worn as his disguise, then obviously a close relation. "Do whatever you will with them, but it is your brother who is the biggest problem here."

Gabriel, who'd watched the previous exchange without comment, as if waiting to see what sentence the elders would deliver, spoke then. "Yes, I am, Elisa. More than you can ever know."

His hands raised, and although Cassandra couldn't see exactly what he'd done, at once the trio in the doorway staggered and stumbled backward a few paces, as if they'd been simultaneously punched by a series of invisible fists. The woman made no sound, although Raúl, the male elder, and Vicénte both grunted.

Unfortunately, they both recovered soon enough, Vicénte lifting his right hand to send his own invisible attack toward his brother. Gabriel's eyes closed for a moment, and Cassandra could see the way his jaw clenched in pain, but he still stood his ground and even took a step toward the *primus*. Another invisible blow hit the younger Escobar, and he ground his teeth so hard the sound was audible from a few feet away.

"Get the null," Vicénte spat out. "It is the only way."

Cassandra exchanged a frightened glance with Tony. This was the situation she'd feared the most—that there would be one of those terrifying, magic-quelling people in the Escobar clan, and that the clan's leader would use that individual as a weapon. Clearly, Vicénte now understood he was no match for his younger brother, and so had sent for the one person in the clan who would be able to render all Gabriel's formidable talents useless.

Elisa hurried out, although the squatty elder Raúl remained. Black eyes flashing, he snapped his fingers, and it was if unseen hands had grabbed Cassandra's ankles, holding her and Tony in place so they couldn't take a single step.

Tony swore, and the elder gave them an

evil smile. "No chance of escape now, I think."

Gabriel seemed to be similarly immobilized, although Cassandra thought she saw one foot move the slightest bit, as if the spell didn't have as strong a hold on him as it did on his two companions. "Release them," he demanded.

"I think not," Raúl said. He looked up at his *primus*, a toadying smile touching his thin lips. "Much better to have them this way, don't you think?"

"Yes," Vicénte replied, that gloating expression returning to his features. If he'd been a few feet closer, Cassandra would have loved to reach out and punch it right off his face.

As it was...she was useless. Tony as well, and even if Gabriel was able to free himself eventually, she had a feeling he wouldn't be able to overcome the elder's horrible magic before the null got here and made this whole exercise basically a pointless one. It seemed the fears that had surfaced the night before they'd come here to Pico Negro were going to come true; if she hadn't been immobilized so completely, she would have been shaking with fear.

Gabriel seemed to understand the depth

of their predicament as well, because his angry, frustrated gaze moved to her...then, for some reason, *past* her. For a few seconds, Cassandra couldn't quite figure out what he was looking at, until she realized he was staring at the flickering candle on top of the bookcase.

Was he really thinking...?

It seemed he was, because in the next moment, he apparently reached out with another of those invisible salvos. This time, however, he wasn't directing it toward his brother or the clan elder who stood next to the *primus*, but toward the candle.

Before she could even blink, it had sailed through the air and landed on the pile of books, wax splattering, the flame flickering for a few seconds before it regained its strength.

It touched the edge of one of the books, and the ancient binding began to smolder.

"No!" Vicénte shouted, moving forward.

Next to her, Tony nodded grimly. His feet might have been held rooted to the floor, but he still had his power...and obviously knew what to do with it.

A small breeze came out of nowhere, touched the flame. The smoldering binding caught fire for real this time, blazing up, running along the edge of the book and touching the one next to it as well. Then the breeze became a wind, tugging at her hair, encouraging the fire to grow and spread to more and more of the books in the pile. Now she could feel the heat coming from them, could smell the acrid scent of the old paper and leather burning in the confined space. If left unchecked, the fire would probably burn the whole house down, but right then, she couldn't feel too bad about that.

Frantic, Vicénte called out, "Fetch me some water!"

"Oh, that won't do you any good," Cassandra said. Time to use her power now, to make sure neither the *primus* nor his ugly little elder could stop what Gabriel and Tony had started.

She reached out with her gift and created a shield to protect the pile of burning books. Yes, the fire needed oxygen to keep burning, but she knew that wouldn't be a problem. The shield let air in just fine; she'd honed her power by casting these magical shields to prevent rabbits and deer from destroying her parents' vegetable garden, and so she knew the shield didn't block the atmosphere itself, only anything solid. The water Raúl had bolted to the kitchen to get wouldn't help at all, because it would only splash over the shield and run down the sides. Back in the day, she'd had to take down the shields every few days or so to let her mother water the plants, and that was why she knew there was no danger of anyone putting this fire out.

Well, at least until the null arrived. After that, all bets were off.

Now the pile of books was fully engulfed. Looking at them, Cassandra couldn't even be sad over the knowledge within them that was being destroyed. It was terrible knowledge, something that no human being should be able to control.

And with the grimoires gone, there would be no reason to fight over them, no worries about the next dark witch or warlock trying to capture the books for their own nefarious purposes.

She glanced over at Tony and saw that he was grinning, as if he, too, had realized this was the best possible end for those horrible volumes.

Raúl arrived, a pitcher of water in either hand. He ran into the library and attempted to douse the flames, but of course the water only ran over the shield, exposing it for moment, like a strange, fiery soap bubble before the water was gone and the shield had returned to its usual invisible state.

"A very good talent, indeed," Gabriel said. While the elder was gawking in dismay at the utter futility of his effort, the Escobar warlock moved quickly, the magical hold on his feet now apparently gone.

"Not so fast," Vicénte snarled, then hurled himself at his brother, knocking him to the ground.

And while Gabriel might have been a stronger warlock than the *primus,* he wasn't quite as heavy, and obviously hadn't been expecting a physical assault. He let out a grunt of pain, but then seemed to gather himself and swung with the arm that wasn't pinned down under him, catching his brother in the jaw.

Now it was time for Vicénte to groan, but the blow didn't stop him. He lashed out with his right hand, hitting Gabriel in the temple. The watching toad-like elder chuckled, as if glad to see the upstart get what was coming to him.

"You know," Tony remarked in oddly

conversational tones, "I'm really getting tired of you."

Before the elder could react, Tony raised his hands and a blast of wind came from nowhere, wailing with hurricane force as it struck the man with its fury and blew him all the way across the living area until he hit the back wall with an audible crack and fell to the floor, unmoving.

Even though she had no liking for the man, either, Cassandra couldn't help wincing. However, she noticed right away that, with the elder knocked out, the force holding her to the floor was now gone. Tony also seemed to realize he was no longer constrained, and at once ran over to where Vicénte and Gabriel were wrestling and made an enthusiastic swing that connected with the *primus's* nose, which exploded with blood.

He howled and slumped over, clearly down for the count, and Tony stepped away, shaking his hand. "Ouch."

"First time clocking someone?" Cassandra asked with a grin.

"Yep. Now I know why boxers wear gloves." After giving his abused fingers another flex, he reached down to help Gabriel to his feet.

The Escobar warlock was looking slightly bruised, but he flashed a smile at them as he stood up, a smile that broadened as he looked at the pile of books in their protective shield, now fully engulfed. The shield kept the flames from spreading farther into the room, and so the rest of the house seemed safe.

For now, at least.

The front door opened with a bang. Gabriel's smile disappeared, and he said, his tone urgent, "You must go."

"What about you?" Cassandra asked. Surely he couldn't be considering staying here—his clan would eat him alive, after what he'd done.

"The distance is too great for me to travel with you. I can only send you two, no more." He glanced over his shoulder, and Cassandra followed his gaze to see the female elder hurrying toward them, a much younger, intense-looking man who must have been the null at her side.

She didn't know how close a null had to get to destroy a person's ability to use their magic, but she really didn't want to find out, either.

"Tell me where you must go!" Gabriel said, his voice tight with worry.

"My house in Santa Fe," Tony replied at once. "Hillside Avenue—322. It's a gray Victorian house with green trim and a big oak tree in front."

How that was supposed to help, Cassandra didn't know, but she guessed that Gabriel's power must allow him to triangulate on a place even if he'd never been there before. He nodded, eyes closed tight as if visualizing their destination, and then she felt an odd tingling in her fingers and toes. The room began to dissolve around them—the fire roared, hungry and angry now that it had been released from the shield she'd cast—and the female elder and the null ran into the library, clearly thinking they might be able to rescue the books, even though they were already fully engulfed and beyond salvaging.

And then, right before the room disappeared altogether, Gabriel's despairing eyes met hers as his brother rose from his faint and swung his fist.

Cassandra never saw whether the blow connected.

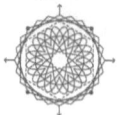

20

It was if someone had been holding them approximately three or four feet above the floor and then abruptly dropped them. He and Cassandra fell onto the Persian rug in the living room, both of them letting out a shocked "oof!" as the air was knocked out of their lungs.

"Jesus Christ," Tony muttered, then rolled over so he could look over at his companion. She'd pushed herself up to a sitting position and had a hand held to her temple, as if trying to determine whether the fall had done any actual damage. "You okay?"

She gave him a cautious nod. "I think so." After sending a quick glance around the room, she asked, "We're back at your house, right?"

"Yes. He did it." Tony got to his feet and extended a hand, then pulled Cassandra up from the floor. She still looked kind of dazed, but not so dazed that she didn't immediately go to him and put her arms around his waist.

"I honestly didn't think he'd be able to send us this far," she murmured. Then she pulled in a hitching sort of breath and said, her tone urgent, "Tony, we have to help him."

"How?" he asked gently. While he could understand why she'd be fearing the worst for their benefactor, the sad truth was that there really wasn't much they could do for Gabriel.

"I don't know!" she burst out, then let go of him and stepped back a pace. The pain and worry in her eyes was clear, and he wished he could say something to make it all better. However, there really wasn't anything to say.

He had to try, though.

"Our clan isn't going to invade the Escobars' territory," he said, trying to sound calm and matter-of-fact. "Yours isn't, either. It would take a lot of us to make a difference, and that simply isn't going to happen. We both know that."

Cassandra was silent for a moment, face pale. At last, she gave a reluctant nod. "You're right, of course. It's just—he helped us, and we just *left* him there!"

"I know. It sucks. It really, really sucks."

"What do you think they'll do to him?"

Her hazel-green eyes were enormous, imploring. And while he could try to tell her some pleasant lie, say that Vicénte wouldn't do anything too terrible to Gabriel because he was his brother, Tony wouldn't do that to Cassandra. She was tough and smart and brave, and she knew just as well as he did that the Escobar *primus* was utterly without mercy.

"I honestly have no idea," he said at last. "They brought the null in, so Gabriel wouldn't have been able to use his powers. And although the guy has a mean right hook, there's no way he could fight the whole damn clan. I guess it really depends on what they do to traitors."

Cassandra winced at the word, but she didn't try to contradict him. She had to know that the Escobars would look at Gabriel as the very worst of traitors. You weren't supposed to go against your clan, especially when such a betrayal meant destroying something that could have granted your family a considerable magical advantage.

"But at least they don't have the books anymore," Tony added, and she nodded, looking a little less troubled.

"Thank God for that," she said.

"So you're relieved?"

"Of course I'm relieved," she shot back. "Why wouldn't I be?"

He shrugged, not sure what to say. "Well…they were your clan's property."

"Yes, and now they're no one's, which is how it always should have been."

Tony went to her and took her in his arms again, and she snuggled her head against his shoulder. "I feel the same way," he said. "Someone should've taken a match to those damn things years ago."

"I know. That kind of power is too tempting." She released a breath, and he felt some of the tension in her slender body begin to melt away. "Still, we're going to have a heck of a time explaining all this…."

∾

His parents took the news calmly enough,

especially after Cassandra said she'd talked to her *prima* and that Zoe had informed her it was probably all for the best. Tony's sister Ava, however, didn't appear nearly as satisfied with the story.

"Seriously, you just left him there?" she demanded as she sat on the couch across from him, echoing Cassandra's words from a few hours earlier.

"What were we supposed to do?" Tony countered, wishing he didn't feel so guilty. After all, it had been Gabriel's wish that they leave without him. He'd known the extent of his powers, had known he couldn't get out and still ensure that his compatriots made it safely home. And, Tony realized, Gabriel had probably guessed that such an outcome was a definite possibility...and had taken the risk anyway. "Neither Cass nor I can teleport, Ava, and there was no way we could have fought the whole goddamn village."

Ava opened her mouth as if to protest, then subsided, apparently realizing that her brother was only a warlock and not some super-powered action hero. To tell the truth, Tony had halfway been expecting this reaction from her, just because his little sister had always been the kind to rescue stray dogs and kittens and the occasional wounded bird. Their mother hadn't been very happy about any of those strays and the messes they brought with them, given how picky she was about keeping the house clean. She'd allowed Ava to keep one dog, a lively little chihuahua/terrier mix, who'd lived to the ripe age of sixteen before finally passing away just as Ava was about to go off to college.

The rest of the animals had either found homes within the clan or had been sent off to the shelter, which luckily was a no-kill facility and worked very hard to adopt out all the various dogs and cats. But anyway, Tony could see why Ava would immediately fear for the man they'd had to leave behind, even though she'd never met him.

"I guess so," she said, then went quiet, her big brown eyes sad. Maybe she was inwardly mourning Gabriel, although of course none of them really had any way of knowing what had happened to him.

Still, Tony could guess…and what he was speculating wasn't very pretty.

Eventually, he and Cassandra were able to escape the questions, slip away and get her a few items to replace the things she'd left behind in their Airbnb in San Salvador, then go out to dinner. He noticed that she didn't have much appetite but guessed it was probably better not to call attention to her apparent disinterest in the excellent meal they'd ordered.

And that night, they made love, fiercely, furiously, as if they both needed to confirm that they had survived the ordeal, were alive and well, if not completely whole.

While Cassandra showered the next morning, Victoria the ghost appeared in the kitchen as Tony was making coffee, her translucent brow furrowed in annoyance.

"Am I to expect more of those goings-on?" she demanded.

"'Goings-on'?" he repeated.

She jabbed an accusing finger upward, as if indicating the second floor of the house that had once been hers. "Your nocturnal activities."

Trying not to smile, he poured the coffee he'd just ground into the coffeemaker. "Um, Victoria…wasn't it those sorts of 'activities' that got you in trouble in the first place?"

Arms crossed, she retorted, "A lady doesn't confess such things."

"Of course not." He turned back to her. Now she was floating in the middle of the kitchen, the toes of her buttoned boots a few inches above the tile floor. "Not to get snotty, Victoria, but this is my house. I think I'm allowed to be with my girlfriend if I want to." As he spoke, however, he could see why the ghost might be a little miffed with him; he'd never brought any of the civilian girls he'd slept with back to the house, had always shared those encounters in their hotel rooms. For all he knew, his home's resident ghost thought he was celibate.

Ha.

"Your girlfriend," Victoria repeated, looking pained. Except for being partially see-through, she was still very pretty, and Tony could understand why her husband had been so inflamed with jealousy that he'd shot both her and her lover. "So I am to expect more of this?"

"'Fraid so," Tony replied calmly, even as he wondered exactly how this was all going to shake out. It was early days yet, and he and Cassandra certainly hadn't made any promises to one another. Still, he knew he wanted to be with her, didn't want to say goodbye and send her back to her clan and call it a day.

But did she feel the same?"

"Hmph," said Victoria with a sniff before disappearing.

"Typical," he remarked, just as Cassandra entered the kitchen, looking slightly confused.

"Was someone in here? I thought I heard voices."

"Oh, that was just Victoria, my friendly neighborhood ghost. She was registering her displeasure over our 'nocturnal activities,' as she put it."

Cassandra's lips quirked. "Oops. I forgot we weren't alone in the house."

"Well, Victoria kind of made herself scarce the last time you were here, so it's not as if you'd even seen her yet. Coffee?"

"Love some."

Tony got out a mug and filled it with Italian roast, then handed it over to her. Cassandra looked more like herself this morning, face bare of makeup except some mascara and lip gloss, the shadows of sadness and fear gone from her face. But even as she sipped at the coffee, he thought he could see a trace of worry in her hazel eyes. Had she, too, been wondering exactly where the two of them were supposed to go next?

"You can stay here as long as you like," he blurted, and she smiled at him.

"Thanks. It's going to be weird to slip back into normal life."

"Is life ever normal for us witches and warlocks?"

Her mouth pursed, and she shrugged. "Good question." She was silent for a moment, drinking coffee in a contemplative sort of way, as though she had so many thoughts running through her head, she wasn't quite sure which one to articulate first. When she spoke, though, it was to make a comment he hadn't been expecting. "You know, you're going to need to get your car out of hock. It's still sitting in the long-term parking at the airport in San Diego."

Tony wanted to clap a hand to his head. In all the insanity, he'd completely forgotten about the Fiat sitting there in a corner of the fourth level of the parking structure. It was a "pay when you leave" kind of setup, so he knew he didn't have to worry about the car getting towed or anything, but obviously, he couldn't leave it there. And then there was the truck they'd rented and left behind in San Matías, not to mention all the stuff presumably still sitting in their

Airbnb. They hadn't been due to leave until today, so they still had something of a buffer before anyone started asking questions. Even so, he was going to have to get on the phone and handle some logistics this morning, no matter what else happened.

"I can go with you, if you want," Cassandra offered, and he sent her a relieved smile.

"You can?"

"Sure. I'm on kind of indefinite leave from my job—business of the *prima* and all that." She swirled the coffee in her mug for a moment and stared down into it, as if trying to decipher some meaning from the patterns of dark and light in the doctored Italian roast. "We can fly to San Diego, and then you can drop me in Tucson on the way back."

"Oh," Tony said, not sure he liked the sound of that. While he knew Cassandra would have to go home eventually, he really didn't want to think about the moment when he'd have to say goodbye to her.

That sort of attitude really wasn't like him. Usually, he was all too happy to bid farewell to the girls he'd hooked up with, their company growing staler by the minute. Cassandra wasn't like that, though. Every day she surprised him, and he wanted her to go on surprising him.

But since he didn't know if he could or should articulate all that to her right now, he only said, "Another road trip? Sounds great."

She looked slightly relieved by his response, although he didn't know for sure whether that was because they'd still have some time before they had to say good-bye...or because he hadn't tried to argue with her about going back to Tucson.

Maybe a little of both.

As expected, he spent a chunk of the morning on the phone or on his computer, trying to tie up all the loose ends they'd left behind them. The guy at the car rental agency in San Salvador, who luckily spoke decent English, told him that the truck had been dropped off late the day before, after they'd closed. The keys had been left in the night dropbox, so no one had seen who'd brought the vehicle back. It was a mystery that probably would never be solved, although Tony knew that Gabriel couldn't have been the person who'd driven the truck back to the capital. One of the Esco-bars? Maybe. Or, more likely, Hector at the

ATV repair shop or one of the other residents of San Matías doing their master's bidding. While Tony figured that Vicénte Escobar had no reason to do him any favors, he most likely would have wanted to avoid any interference from the outside world. The truck, like all vehicles these days, had a built-in location tracker; sooner or later, someone would have come to retrieve it.

Their belongings didn't fare as well, since the owner of the Airbnb was highly annoyed that they'd left their luggage behind. When Tony offered to pay him to ship everything back, he said he didn't have time to deal with it, and that his cleaning crew would take anything they'd left and consider it a tip.

"Darn," Cassandra said, looking a little dejected. "I really liked those earrings I bought in Tijuana."

"I'm sorry," Tony replied, but she only shook her head.

"It's all right. It's not your fault. I'm sure I can find something like them."

Right then, Tony vowed to track down a similar pair if it was the last thing he did. He remembered how those silver and coral earrings had danced as he held her at that salsa club in Tijuana, gleaming beneath the lush waves of her burnished copper hair. That was the night they'd made love for the first time, and she shouldn't have to suffer such a loss just because the owner of the Airbnb was a jackass.

He didn't say anything, though, because he guessed Cassandra would only protest that he didn't need to buy her anything. It would be a surprise.

After that, it was a simple enough procedure to book them a pair of airline tickets to San Diego, and to let his parents know he was leaving to retrieve his car and would be back in a couple of days. They took this information in stride, because of course he had to get the Fiat back, and it made sense for Cassandra to go with him so he could take her home on the return trip. Whether either of his parents picked up on his connection to her, Tony wasn't sure; while his mother seemed much better, he could tell she still would need a little more time to get completely back to normal, and his father of course was preoccupied with his wife's health and probably didn't have a thought to spare for his son's love life.

The flight to San Diego was completely

uneventful, and because they got to the airport a little before three in the afternoon, they decided to get in the car and go ahead and drive to Tucson.

"It's only a little over five hours, after all," she pointed out. "We'll get there after dark, but we can have a late dinner and crash at my condo afterward."

"Sounds like a plan," he said, although he wondered if she was eager to keep their momentum going so she could get him on the road early the next day and go back to her life. Ever since they'd left Santa Fe, she'd been brisk and friendly and businesslike, and he couldn't tell if she was still processing everything that had happened, or whether she'd decided that she'd really made a mistake with him and wanted to get this over with as quickly as possible.

The weather was mild enough that they drove with the top down for part of the way. Tony enjoyed being able to indulge himself in such a fashion, even though it was early November—and especially because a cold, dreary rain had started to fall just as they left the airport in Albuquerque. The thought of returning to Santa Fe wasn't all that appealing, but what the hell else was he supposed to do?

They cruised into Tucson around eight-fifteen, with Cassandra giving him directions to her condo on the southwest edge of town. He had to park in one of the visitor spaces, since of course she didn't have the remote for her garage with her, but they didn't have a lot of luggage to carry.

The "condo" was really a two-story townhouse in a complex of other townhouses, done in a sort of mishmash of Southwestern and Tuscan styles that really shouldn't have worked but somehow did. It was spotlessly clean and a lot more professionally decorated than he'd expected the home of a barely twenty-one-year-old to be, but when he made a careful remark along those lines, Cassandra just laughed.

"I bought it furnished. Total turn-key. So I shouldn't get credit for any of that."

He reflected that that was one way to go. Since he didn't exactly know how to respond, he just said, "Well, that sounds like an easy, low-stress way to handle it."

"It was." She'd just set her purse down on the round oak table in the dining area, and now tilted her head at him. "Speaking of easy, would you rather just order in? There's a really good Mexican place that'll deliver up to nine o'clock."

"Sounds perfect," he replied. And it did. He was tired after the drive, even though it had felt good to be behind the wheel of his beloved convertible again. Also, maybe it was a good sign that Cassandra didn't want to go out. Usually, confidences were more easily shared in a private space like this, rather than out at a noisy restaurant.

She pulled up the menu on her phone, and they made their choices and called in the order. After that was done, she went to the pantry and came back out with a bottle of Tempranillo. "The one and only bottle in the house," she told him as she set it down on the table. "It got left here during my housewarming party, and since I wasn't that much of a wine drinker, it's been sitting in there ever since."

Wine sounded even better than the Mexican food they'd just ordered. "Do you have an opener?"

"Of course I do," she said, her tone mock-severe. Then she seemed to relent and added, "But only because someone gave me one at the party."

She fetched it from one of the drawers and handed it to him. Tony could see why it had been a present—the opener was really nice one, with wood and turquoise inlays.

He opened the bottle while she got a pair of glasses—also a housewarming present, he guessed—and brought them over to the table. After he filled the glasses, he gave one to her.

"To journey's end," he said, raising his drink.

To his surprise, she didn't respond right away, but only stood there in silence for a moment, watching him. "Is it, though?" she asked quietly. "I mean, you still have a ways to go."

Disappointment stabbed through him, but he made himself say, tone casual, "Well, true, but not until tomorrow."

Cassandra pulled in a breath. Still cradling her glass of wine in both hands... and not really looking at him...she said, "What if you didn't go?"

He blinked. "Excuse me?"

Her eyes were like shimmering green glass, but he couldn't quite read what was in them. "What if you...stayed?" she said. "Here with me?"

Was she asking what he thought she was asking? He put down his glass of wine without tasting it and stared at her.

Apparently misreading his silence, she

went on quickly, "Never mind. I just thought…."

Well, he needed to clear that up right away. He went to her and took the glass of wine from her hands, then pulled her close and kissed her, kissed her long and hard so she'd know exactly how he felt. "Cassandra Sandoval, I would love to move in with you…if that's what you were asking."

She let out a breathy laugh and held on to his hands tight, gazing up into his face. "I think it was. I mean, I know it's kind of crazy. You have that big beautiful house in Santa Fe—"

"Which is haunted," he cut in.

"Still…."

Tony thought of how the desert air had felt as they walked to her condo from the car. Yes, it had cooled with the coming of night, but it still had been mild and gentle, not harsh and cold the way it would have been back in Santa Fe at this time of year. He remembered walking down the bright streets of Tijuana with her at his side, her arms bare and beautiful in the sunshine. That was what he wanted, he realized—Cassandra, and warm, sunny days that weren't just a memory, but a life he was living every single day.

"I'll give my sister Ava the house," he said. "She'll be graduating from UNM in less than six months anyway, and I know she'd love to have her own place rather than go back to live with our parents."

"You'd just...give her the house?" Cassandra responded, looking a little stunned.

Tony couldn't really blame her. He was feeling a little surprised himself, startled at how quickly he'd made a decision about something that had been a major part of his life for the last five years. But he knew it was the right decision. Already he felt lighter, as if his body and spirit recognized that he'd come to the place where he was supposed to be.

To the woman he was supposed to be with.

"Yes," he said. "The whole way over here, I kept thinking about how I didn't want to go back to Santa Fe. Now I know why. Because some part of me knew that my home was with you."

She still didn't look entirely convinced, or maybe she just wanted to make sure she presented all her arguments up front so they wouldn't be an issue later. "Here in Tucson. A town you hardly know."

"True," he replied, and couldn't quite help grinning down at her. "But that's okay. You'll show it to me, won't you?"

"Of course." Cassandra went up on her tiptoes and kissed him again before adding, "That's not the only thing I'd like to show you."

"Oh, really?"

She opened her mouth to reply, but the doorbell rang. Looking crestfallen, she said, "Oops…I forgot about the food we ordered."

"It's all right," he told her.

Cassandra lifted an eyebrow at him, her gaze questioning.

He added, "We have the rest of our lives, after all."

The Witches of Canyon Road will continue with Ava's story in *Higher Ground*, releasing in August 2019.

THE WITCHES OF CLEOPATRA HILL*

(Paranormal Romance)

Darkangel

Darknight

Darkmoon

Sympathetic Magic

Protector

Spellbound

A Cleopatra Hill Christmas

Impractical Magic

Strange Magic

The Arrangement

Defender

Bad Blood

Deep Magic

Darktide

Books 1-3 and Books 4-6 of this series are also available in two separate omnibus editions at special boxed set prices. Chronicles of Cleopatra Hill includes the series' two "back in time" novellas, *Bad Blood* and *The Arrangement*.

Or get the entire series in one enormous, specially priced boxed set! (Not available on Amazon.)

THE DJINN WARS

(Paranormal Romance)

Chosen

Taken

Fallen

Broken

Forsaken

Forbidden

Awoken

Illuminated

Stolen

Forgotten

Driven

Unspoken (June 2019)

Books 1-3 and Books 4-6 of this series are also available in two separate omnibus editions at special boxed set prices!

THE WATCHERS TRILOGY*

(Paranormal Romance)

Falling Dark

Dead of Night

Rising Dawn

The Watchers Trilogy is also available in a specially priced boxed set!

THE SEDONA FILES*

(Paranormal Romance)

Bad Vibrations

Desert Hearts

Angel Fire

Star Crossed

Falling Angels

Enemy Mine

Get the first three books of this series in an omnibus edition, or read the complete six-book series in one super-low-priced boxed set!

TALES OF THE LATTER KINGDOMS

(Fantasy Romance)

All Fall Down

Dragon Rose

Binding Spell

Ashes of Roses

One Thousand Nights

Threads of Gold

The Wolf of Harrow Hall

Moon Dance

The Song of the Thrush

Books 1-3 and Books 4-6 of this series are also available in two separate omnibus editions at special boxed set prices.

THE GAIAN CONSORTIUM SERIES*

(Science Fiction Romance)

Beast (free prequel novella)

Blood Will Tell

Breath of Life

The Gaia Gambit

The Mandala Maneuver

The Titan Trap

The Zhore Deception

The Refugee Ruse

Books 1-3 of this series are also available in an omnibus edition at a special boxed set price!

~

STANDALONE TITLES

Hearts on Fire

Sympathy for the Devil

Taking Dictation

Night Music

Golden Heart

* Indicates a completed series

ABOUT THE AUTHOR

USA Today bestselling author Christine Pope has been writing stories ever since she commandeered her family's Smith-Corona typewriter back in grade school. Her work includes paranormal romance, fantasy romance, and science fiction/space opera romance. She makes her home in Sedona, Arizona.

Don't miss out on any of Christine's new releases—sign up for her newsletter today!

Christine Pope on the Web:
www.christinepope.com

www.ingramcontent.com/pod-product-compliance
Lightning Source LLC
Chambersburg PA
CBHW021121260626
47169CB00005B/1395